To

Ma[...]

Your Country Needs You!

Best wishes

Mark Harland.

Your Country Needs You!

M.V. Harland

© M.V. Harland, 2009

Published by Shaffron March 2009

ISBN 978-0-9556155-4-2

M.V. Harland has asserted the right under the Copyright, Designs and Patents Act 1988 to be identified as the author of the book.

Cover designed by Clare Brayshaw

Set in Lucida Bright 9/13

Prepared and printed by:
York Publishing Services Ltd
64 Hallfield Road
Layerthorpe
York YO31 7ZQ
Tel: 01904 431213
Website: www.yps-publishing.co.uk

In memory of
Donald Lindsay Macdougall
'A man of Jura'
R.I.P.

'I know I have the body of a weak and feeble woman,
but I have the heart and stomach of a King,
and a King of England too:
and think foul scorn that Parma or Spain
or any Prince of Europe,
should dare to invade the borders of my Realm.'

Queen Elizabeth 1st, Tilbury, Essex. 1588

Author's Note

I first self-published this book in Spring 2008. My website was bombarded with readers asking 'why *don't* they have MPs picked like jury servers?' or 'why *doesn't* the Queen do something about our rotten MPs?' A gentleman in Queensland even suggested that Australian politicians were hated even more than ours – 'Can the author come up with a suitable plot for Down Under?'

To everyone who gave me feedback I thank you. The recent disclosures by a respected national newspaper that over six hundred avaricious MPs have had their noses in the tax-payer funded trough for years, if not decades, has sickened the entire nation. How dare they call each other Honourable Members!

As for a sequel and even Australia – watch this space.

Mark Harland

Acknowledgements

The author gratefully acknowledges the assistance of the following friends and acquaintances who have given their time to read and comment on the manuscript and without whose help and encouragement the task would have been so much harder.

Alanoosh Aghanian, Cher Atkinson, Ann Aveyard, Jackie Bailey, Liz Birch, Susan Blackmore, Geraldine Cook, Christine Copland, Steven Garry, Maureen Horton, Lynne Kirk, Margaret Jenkins, Carol "Nylon Brain" Ledger, Marlene Lister, Barbara Ralph, Connie Scott, Pauline "P" Slater, Mike Stead, Jane Stockdale, Sandra Taylor, Joy Wooley and John Wilkinson – my fellow diner at the *Cat's Whiskers Cafe* in Scarborough – who is never short of a tale or anecdote to add to my scripts. And of course, Terry Ralph, who inspired me with the idea over a few ales one evening!

Mark Harland

Prologues

Greenwich
England
7th September 1533

The only child, a girl, from the Union of Anne Boleyn and King Henry the Eighth was born on September 7th 1533. She inherited her mother's beauty and her father's ambition. Elizabeth the First, Queen of England and Defender of the Faith, ruled her country for forty-five years. The nation had never experienced such success as during her monarchy. It expanded culturally and militarily throughout her entire reign. How fitting that she was born at Greenwich, the location chosen two centuries later to mark the meridian of zero degrees longitude – the very centre of the then known world and from where the whole planet's clock would tick.

When she succeeded to the throne in 1568 she did so without any open opposition. Diplomacy and compromise were the keystones of her reign. She was responsible for the establishment of the Church of England on a basis which, she fervently hoped, would be acceptable to all, Catholics and Protestants alike. The Thirty Nine Articles and the Book of Common Prayer as we read them now were also products of her reign. Despite her Catholic education however, she became a Protestant - not from religious convictions but because it was necessary for the salvation of England and the increase of English power that she should be recognised as the Protestant champion of Europe.

As Good Queen Bess she and her Ministers steered the ship of state through difficult times. She kept England at peace until it was absolutely essential to fight, and when she struck, she struck with the whole force of a united England behind her. She played off her opponents skilfully one against the other and in this way saved England from disaster.

She expanded her navy in size and reach and her ensigns fluttered on every sea and ocean. When the Armada came it cannot be said that England was prepared, save that every Englishman was prepared, united, to face the efforts of Spain and the speech she made at Tilbury when England was faced with the greatest of her dangers, mirrored exactly the opinion of all England.

As a Queen, Elizabeth could only be described as popular, brave, courageous and diplomatic but perhaps her true greatness lay essentially in the fact that in her and through her, England found her own ideals and aspirations most amply expressed. She owed her great power and popularity also to the fact that she was able to read the mind of the nation. That was perhaps her finest attribute.

The English Renaissance came in her reign and Shakespeare and Marlowe gave due notice that this was the Golden Age of English literature and that English was to be the universal language of tomorrow.

Before she died at Richmond in 1603 she could never have foreseen that her time on the throne would become known not as a reign but as an era - the Elizabethan Era - and that all future Kings and Queens of England would try to emulate her success.

All of them would fail. All, that is, except one.

Buckingham Palace
London SW1
Today

Queen Elizabeth the Second had not been a happy lady for many, many months – if not years. Her Coronation in 1953 had brought with it the hope for a second Elizabethan Era. One to emulate that period of British history when King Henry the Eighth's daughter had launched England towards a position of global expansion and supremacy that would one day result in an Empire that ruled over half the planet's humanity and make the bailiwicks of Genghis Khan, Caesar and Alexander look like mere chattels.

She was alone on this grey afternoon in January. Looking out over the gardens from her favourite sitting room towards Green Park she could just make out the distinctive shape of Clarence House, her late mother's former residence. What a happy place it had been for over thirty years with parties, official dinners, receptions and the like. And who in the whole country did not shed a tear or two when in August every year a military band marched past her mother's home playing 'Happy Birthday' and the nation rejoiced. But since the death of her mother in 2002 it seemed as if the whole country had changed for the worse. As if the nation's spirit had died with her. Gone was the Dunkirk spirit. Gone was the attitude of 'we'll be all right mate' as the nation and its Empire pulled together as one against a common foe.

Less than three months had passed since the President of the Free World and his First Lady had been her guests at her official London residence. Only her very closest advisers, and none of her family, knew that that was to be the last State visit that she would ever host at the behest of a Prime Minister. She had made up her mind. Her resolve was absolute. Never again would a party politician use the Monarchy as a prop for 'media opportunities' and never again would a Prime Minister be able to use executive power in quite the same way again. Her Majesty had often admired the American system whereby a President had to seek re-election every four years and the Constitution forbade him more than two terms. In Britain the Prime Minister could pick the time of the next election to suit him best – usually when he was ahead in the polls and scandals were at a minimum.

It was this last bit that stuck in her Royal craw. Hardly a month had gone by during the present Government's term of office when some nasty little slug hadn't crawled out from under a stone. Corrupt Ministers. Gay Ministers. Ministers caught in bed with other Ministers' wives. Even Ministers caught in bed with other Ministers. Little wonder that in a recent national opinion poll when the question was asked who the voter would like to see run as an elected Head of State the results had stunned the nation. Not a single current politician featured in the Top Twenty. A parallel poll had even suggested that politicians were trusted even less than estate agents. But the results had not surprised Her Majesty. Far from it. Today she had had a little fillip to her normal routine. She had signed the approval papers for the naming of the two new aircraft carriers for the Royal Navy. They were to be called HMS Queen Elizabeth and HMS Prince of Wales. These two new capital ships were to have a planned hull life of fifty years – long past her expiration. She was honest enough to admit to herself that if she were able to place a bet she would not place much money on there being either a Queen or a Prince of Wales in twenty let alone fifty years. An article in yesterday's papers exposing a Government MP photographing himself almost a nude for a gay website was scandalous to say the least. But it was nothing compared to the breaktaking headlines in a respected broadsheet that morning. A whistle blower had leaked details of every single MP's expenses starting with Government Ministers. A sickened nation found it almost impossible to grasp that over six hundred avaricious, greedy MPs had been feeding at the tax-payer funded trough for years, if not decades. There seemed to be no limit to their 'claims' which ranged from X-rated movies and horse manure at one end of the scale to chandeliers and swimming pools at the other end. They all blamed the system not themselves. Not one of them hung their head in shame, let alone announced their intended resignations. How dare they call each other Honourable Members! It had to stop. To her it was justification for what she was about to do.

She finished the last of her Chelsea bun and drained the Earl Grey tea from an exquisite Noritake tea cup – a gift from the Japanese Ambassador on entering the Court of St. James – and dialled her internal telephone to speak with her Personal Equerry. She needed to speak with him urgently. Time was of the essence. He wasn't long. He never was.

She bade him sit down, the look of a thousand problems on her face. She told him of her plans. The Permanent Head of the Civil Service was to be summoned to the Palace tomorrow morning. Within days a political programme was to be instigated in the United Kingdom the like of which these islands had not witnessed since Cromwell.

Buckingham Palace
The next day

Sir Michael de la Nice, the Permanent Head of the Civil Service, was almost unknown in public circles. At sixty-four he was a career civil servant with impeccable credentials. Born in Winchester, the son of an Army general, in the first year of World War Two, he had done National Service in Egypt where he had been wounded defending an air base at Helwan near the Canal Zone. He then joined the Defence Ministry, the Foreign and Commonwealth Office and finally the Home Office without putting a finger wrong. His Knight Commander of the British Empire at the last Birthday

Honours List had been well earned. He was a tireless worker for umpteen charities, a Trustee of five charity funds and involved with everything from Aids to zebra preservation. His wife Clarissa was the same age and also a fine well-bred woman whom he had met at a charity fundraising luncheon in aid of a new children's theatre in the East End of which they were both Patrons. They had married late in life and had no children of their own. Sir Michael was punctiliously apolitical. As a civil servant he had worked with politicians of no less than eight separate administrations, conservative and socialist, and he had seen it all. If only the electorate knew him he would have made a great candidate for Head of State in that opinion poll.

Instead the leading contenders had been three English Premier League footballers (one of whom was on police bail for an alleged rape), five male pop stars, two female popstars (one was ineligible being Australian), two newspaper columnists, a Team Jaguar Grand Prix racing driver, the recent winner of the Booker Prize (also ineligible as his nationality was uncertain), a Scottish comedian, a champion jockey still trying to clear his name after a doping scandal, a well-known and respected male newsreader of Trinidadian descent, a blonde TV weather presenter with huge mammaries, a TV game show presenter and finally a twenty-year-old self-styled eco-nut called 'Okipinokee' who had dug a tunnel under the controversial new second runway at Manchester Airport. The tunnel had collapsed on him following heavy rain, killing him instantly on live TV, and the nomination was a posthumous one. He had in fact polled the most votes – over two million – but after the coroner had released his body for burial only a handful of people turned up for the funeral in Manchester's Moss Side. City were at home to United in the new City of Manchester Stadium that day.

For over an hour a transfixed Sir Michael listened attentively to his Queen. At first aghast at her ideas as she slowly and carefully formulated her reasoning and arguments, he gradually came to realise and understand her orthodoxy. His mind was spinning. Would it work? It would have to.

In little over ten weeks time Her Majesty would dissolve Parliament and all Members of the House of Commons would be out of a job. For good. There would be no more elections to the House of Commons. Instead every county in the land would send a representative to the House. Like Premium Bond winners they would be selected by computer to serve as a Member of Parliament for a period of four years. Just like an American President. Only those who were under eighteen or chronically medically unfit were exempt. Those over eighty years of age could decline if they so wished. All foreign nationals and former Members of Parliament were automatically excluded. Once selected, attendance would be compulsory – imprisonment for the four years was the only alternative. There would be no conscientious objectors strolling the streets. If the computers selected YOU! then it was your duty.

Successive Parliaments throughout her reign had let her down badly. No nation on earth had witnessed such moral, political and material decline in fifty years. Since 1953 the country that had painted half the world map pink had sunk from being top dog to underdog. John Bull's bulldog was now a mere poodle. Concorde no longer graced the skies. The R.A.F. would be hard pressed to put more than a dozen fighters into the air at the same time. Half the nation's youth was unemployable. Shell suits and baseball caps were the accepted attire. Estuary English was de rigeur. The Spithead Revue of the Fleet took half an hour instead of three days. The trains didn't run on time anymore. Even the trains themselves were built in Italy and Spain. The great locomotive sheds of York, Doncaster and Swindon were silent. Rolls Royce cars were made by Germans. And the Government was talking about disbanding the Black Watch.

For Her Majesty, that was the ultimate sin. A heinous crime. Her late Mother had said that they could do what they wanted with the Army as long as they don't touch the Black Watch. No, enough was enough!

It was time for ordinary people to prove that they, with the aid of the best Civil Service in the world, could govern the world's fourth biggest economy more morally, astutely and with less corruption than the six hundred overpaid, bloated career politicians that they would replace.

Tomorrow, at her weekly audience with the Prime Minister, she would tell him of her plans. Later that same evening she would go on live television to speak to the nation and Commonwealth, just like on Christmas Day. Except that instead of speaking to six million people snoozing after too much plum pudding she would go 'live' at twenty hundred hours Greenwich Mean Time precisely, the scheduled kick off time for the European Nations Cup match between England and France at the new Wembley Stadium. The sixty-four thousand dollar question was – would she carry the People with her like her forebear had done at Tilbury over four centuries earlier?

Chapter 1

The gleaming new seven hundred million pound stadium was already a national icon. The delays and disputes that had dogged its progress were forgotten. It was filled to capacity for the opening ceremony to be followed by the first big game to be played there. And what a fixture – England versus France! Both teams were on the pitch in two neat lines and being introduced to various footballing dignitaries – all unknown outside the sport. One by one the players shook hands with their masters who earned only five per cent of their salaries, let alone their sponsorship deals for dodgy trainers made by pittance-earning children in Far Eastern sweatshops. All the twenty-two players bar three were chewing gum.

Suddenly the band of the Royal Marines stopped marching back and forth on the manicured pitch that looked like a billiard table and stopped neatly within the centre circle, the fading bars of 'Sunset' echoing around the stadium's steel and glass superstructure. A new 'Arch of Steel' had replaced the old familiar twin towers and lent an almost military feel to the edifice even without the band. The colour sergeant barked an order that could be heard as far away as Rorke's Drift and three kettle drummers commenced a roll. The French players, six white and five black, momentarily stood almost to attention as the band gave a very creditable rendition of the Marseillaise. The French players stopped chewing their gum for the forty second duration but eighty-five thousand partisan England supporters decided to whistle 'Rule Britannia' at the same time. It was just as well Her Majesty was not present. She disliked vulgarity in all its forms and the 'Entente Cordiale' was always close to her heart. What a splendid gesture of friendship by France it had been so recently to invite the British Army to head the Bastille Day military parade down the Champs Elysee in Paris on the 100th Anniversary of the Entente. The Household Cavalry, Royal Marines and Grenadier Guards had on that day done more for cross Channel relations than a hundred Eurostars. Perhaps, in reciprocation, she could next year invite the Armé de l'Air's equivalent of the Red Arrows to perform a flypast at the next Trooping of the Colour in London. Her Majesty's French was almost perfect and when visiting France she never spoke English in public.

The band stopped followed by another drum roll and the familiar dirge of the National Anthem rattled from sixty-four trumpets, cornets and bassoons. Only one England player, the goal-keeper wearing a different coloured shirt to the other ten, was singing. Maybe the others didn't know the words. In any event they continued chewing their gum. There were no French supporters to sing 'Inky Pinky parlez-vous?' or 'Frère Jacques' as a riposte. The Anthem rituals over, the twenty-two players rapidly dispersed to different ends of the ground to warm up in the two minutes left before the official kick-off time.

High up in a new TV and radio commentary box bristling with satellite dishes the BBC 'Five Live' correspondent was giving a last minute run through the two team sheets for the benefit of listeners –'Le Blanc, Haricot and finally Zidane.' He pronounced the last name with about four zeds as if he was some kind of serial killer. The two team captains had come together with the referee in the centre of the pitch to toss up. They shook hands. The referee threw the coin into the air and it landed on the billiard table – all three men craning forward to see the result. A distinctly sharp breeze was blowing up the Thames estuary from the east and the French captain decided they would play into the wind in the first half and go for the kill in the second. This meant that both teams had to change ends.

As the players repositioned themselves the four huge plasma screens that dominated the four sides of the stadium flickered into life and for just a few seconds the players could see themselves on the monitors that would relay highlights of the match just seconds after realtime incidents. It was Japanese TV technology at its best. There were just seconds to go before the kick-off. The England inside forward placed his right foot on the ball and waited for the referee's whistle. It never came. At least not yet. All four screens momentarily went blank then came back to life. The crowd groaned. What was this? A re-run of the Queen's Christmas Broadcast? No, it wasn't. It was Her Britannic Majesty Queen Elizabeth the Second speaking on live television to her subjects. She spoke calmly and with great deliberation for fifteen minutes.

Her last words were … 'Your country needs You. May God bless you all.'

Such was the import of Her Majesty's address that the result of the match, an honourable draw, was forgotten even more quickly than usual. In just a quarter of an hour a reigning monarch had explained to her subjects that although Defender of the Faith she might be, she was putting *her faith* in the ordinary people of this country. Parliament was to be dissolved and MPs would be replaced by ordinary citizens selected at random from every county in the land. The United Kingdom of Great Britain and Northern Ireland was never the same again. Not ever.

Chapter 2

The following day's newspapers bore sensational headlines. The *Sun* had a huge cartoon of General Kitchener with his famous handlebar moustache blaring out the famous line 'Your Country Needs You!' Underneath was an editorial praising the Queen for her far-sightedness.

The pro-Establishment *Daily Telegraph*'s banner headline read 'Random selection of Parliamentarians will wreck country.' Below it the political commentator prophesied the collapse of sterling within six months and the stock market within a year.

The *Daily Express* with its historic Crusader logo was phlegmatic: 'The New Crusade!' was its headline with ten pages of analysis of who, statistically, might lead the nation into this new, visionary Elizabethan Era. Its computer model of 'The Draw' led readers to believe that RADO, the acronym for Random Automatic Democratic Order, would select over a hundred citizens 'good and true' across the shires, glens and valleys of the kingdom. The paper even tried to register RADO as a trademark until somebody on the staff told them it was actually a brand name of a Swiss watch manufacturer. But the name RADO still stuck with their readers. It was easy to remember and rolled off the tongue.

Like the *Telegraph*, the *Financial Times* shared the doom and gloom prophecy. As did *The Times*, *Guardian* and *Independent*. The *Mirror* had a front page cartoon of a busker at Waterloo railway station strumming on a guitar to the lyrics of 'Land of Hope and Glory' with a caption underneath reading 'Can you imagine HIM being your MP?'

Television programmes were full of speculation. Who would actually lead the Government? Would all the selected names then be put into a 'super-draw' to determine the Prime Minister, Foreign Secretary etc.? Days turned into weeks amid a sea of prophecies. Existing MPs prepared to clear their desks. The House of Commons had an almost end of term feel about it. To a man, and woman, they were convinced that by Michaelmas they would all be back and a grateful nation would forgive them all their trespasses and misdemeanours. One hundred and two randomly selected Members with not an ounce of governmental experience between them would not be able to run the country for a week, let alone a full parliamentary term.

But Her Majesty and the Permanent Head of the Civil Service thought otherwise. Plans were laid. If this was going to be a People's Parliament then Joe Public had to approve and be kept informed. Weekly, one step at a time, snippets of information were released to feed the growing national interest in what was about to happen. One week, it was how the selection system would work. The next, when it was to start. Other important details were released on the new website www.yourcountryneedsyou.org and every day millions of ordinary people clicked their mice to take a look. It was a revolution and a revelation at the same time.

Other details came out. Like how much a new Member would be paid. The salary was a fixed twenty-five thousand pounds a year plus weekly travelling expenses to and from the constituency and the cost of accommodation in London.

As a temporary measure over a hundred rooms had been pre-booked at the old but newly refurbished Russell Hotel in Russell Square. There were to be no phoney secretarial allowances which had been squandered on mistresses. No wives doubling up as salaried secretaries and no fancy offices on which to claim fancy rents. Those days were over. Any Members who for whatever reason could not use their own PC or laptop for corresponding on constituency matters could avail themselves of a central Commons typing pool manned by twenty new girls recruited from a London secretarial school on salaries of fifteen thousand pounds a year for a thirty-five hour week over thirty five weeks. The website received over a thousand applicants for any vacancies. The civil servant in charge of the Treasury reckoned that running Parliament this way would save eighty million pounds a year. The only other perks members would receive were £3,600 a year into a Stakeholder Pension of their choice and a guaranteed 'Death in service benefit' of a hundred thousand pounds.

Her Majesty went on live television to announce that she would be dissolving Parliament the following week.

The Department of Social Security's Newcastle upon Tyne office had been tasked with feeding every citizens' National Insurance number into a new computer whose software had been designed along the lines of the old ERNIE. Except that RADO would be selecting Members of Parliament and not Premium Bond winners. Across the entire nation reality started to sink in. In clubs, pubs, colleges and factories there was only one topic of conversation and one question. 'What if my country needs *me*?'

The 'draw' would be live on all TV channels at prime time. Seven o'clock on a Saturday evening – around the same time as the old Lotto which since the extra efforts to revive it had failed had been moved to a wet Wednesday afternoon. Advertising rates for the commercial channels soared for the night in question. The viewing figures would be astronomical. The estimated audience figure was over fifty million. To some, selection would be a disaster. To others it would indeed be like winning the Lottery. Twenty-five grand a year plus perks was a king's ransom to some and a pittance to others.

As D-day approached every man and woman in the nation over eighteen years of age made sure they had their National Insurance number handy. Only the numbers would come up on the screen, not the names. One hundred and two individuals would know immediately that for the next four years at least their lives would change. The nation as a whole would not know who their new MPs were until the list was officially published a week later. Then the swearing in would begin.

The day after the Queen dissolved Parliament the Italian Government sent an executive jet to Heathrow which returned to Pisa International Airport later the same day. The now ex-Prime Minister had always liked Tuscany and now he could enjoy sun-dried tomatoes and Valpolicella until the cows came home. If they came home.

An air of anticipation hung over the nation. It was like waiting for the result of a General Election but this time there was no 'swingometer', no red, blue or yellow icons on a computer-generated mock-up of the House of Commons. In fact only real political comment could follow a week later when the names were published. What a nail-biting week that would be!

In Newcastle the final quantities of data were being downloaded into RADO. Over 40 million National Insurance numbers! The system had to be checked to take into account people under eighteen years of age who were ineligible and thus rejected but had to accommodate those who were exactly eighteen on the day of the Draw. At the other end of the scale checks were made on recent deaths. It would be most distressing if a family discovered that Grandad, who had just passed away, had been selected.

On the eve of the 'Draw' Sir Michael de la Nice went on to live TV during the six o'clock news. It was a little bit like a Party Political Broadcast without a Party. He was unused to cameras and it showed. But he did his best partly reading from an autocue and partly from notes he held in front of him. He started with the words – 'I am commanded by the Queen to inform you....'

He revealed more details of the due process that was about to follow. After the Draw all selected members would receive a letter, rather like an old fashioned telegram, from Her Majesty. The List would become public knowledge within a week and Members would be expected to report to the House within ten days after that. All of them would be required to swear an Oath of Allegiance – there would be no exceptions. Failure so to do would result in imprisonment. In the new order hard labour was being reintroduced. As was penal servitude. The House of Lords was to stay intact. As was the Judiciary. The previous Government had tried its damnedest to severely curtail its powers but now its true value would be tested if the new People's House failed to measure up. His speech was interesting just as much for what it did not reveal. How would a Cabinet be selected? Who would be Leader of the House? Who, effectively, would be Prime Minister? Who would act as the Speaker? Viewers got the impression he knew more than he was letting on. They were right.

On the morning of the Draw, all the Saturday papers were full of it. The *Sun* had done a computer model of a possible result and published a pull out supplement with no less than one hundred and two cartoons of profiles of likely Members. The Member from County Armagh in Northern Ireland had been selected by their computer to be a priest and a part-time pig farmer and the cartoon showed him wearing green wellies and drinking Guinness at a bar whilst practising his sermon for the following day. The Member for Somerset was depicted by a cider apple

8

grower drinking scrumpy in an orchard. The Member for Glamorgan was depicted by a Welsh miner complete with lamp and pickaxe. More members. More caricatures. It was a cartoonist's dream! Surely it wasn't really going to be like this. Was it?

The bottom line was that nobody really knew.

Chapter 3

It was like Armistice Day in November at the eleventh hour of the eleventh day. The whole country came to a halt just before seven in the evening. This was new ground and political commentators had no idea how to handle it. Current affairs channels had booked prime time to cover the 'Draw' for three hours before and three hours afterwards. Then the programme directors, realising that they would only be faced with a mass of numbers and letters, cancelled their plans and replaced them with previously scheduled itineraries. It was bizarre and unparalleled.

At seven o'clock precisely GMT the TV channels all switched to a hastily convened studio. Where was it? In Newcastle at the DSS? At the Home Office? The BBC? Nobody seemed to know – but it must be coming from somewhere.

A single, solitary man dressed in an immaculate pinstriped suit was seated behind a gleaming polished desk. He was perspiring slightly under the warmth of the studio lights. It was Sir Michael. Once again he was being called upon to perform his duty. Whoever had window dressed the studio had done an awesome job. Before the cameras zoomed in for the close ups viewers could clearly make out a Gainsborough depicting Elizabeth the First knighting Francis Drake. There was a print depicting a Fairey Swordfish taking off from *Ark Royal* to attack the *Bismarck* in 1941. A picture of the late Queen Mother giving shamrocks to the Irish Guards on St Patrick's Day. A portrait of Nye Bevan, the founding father of the Health Service. There was Florence Nightingale attending to dying soldiers in the Crimea. A dying Lord Nelson was painted on the deck of the *Victory* at Trafalgar. Another painting of a field of Flanders' poppies with the caption 'Lest we forget.' and signed Artist Unknown to emulate the Unknown Warrior. And finally, sat on the desk itself, was a bronze bust of the great man himself. Churchill – the man so recently voted 'the Greatest Briton ever' in a hugely entertaining national poll that had been turned into a successful TV series. There was something for everybody of all political persuasions and from whichever part of the kingdom. The whole set should have won the Turner Prize for art but only dead sheep and dirty knickers won that sort of thing anymore. At that precise moment every viewer in the land wanted the whole idea to work. The cameras slowly zoomed in.

'Good evening, Ladies and Gentlemen.' He spoke for two minutes that seemed like a lifetime to him. He finished with the words '*and Her Majesty hopes that this will be a new beginning for the whole nation. A Second Elizabethan Era. Her hopes and prayers will be with all of you selected to be Members of the House. She asks only one thing of you – that you do your very, very best. I bid you all good night.*'

The cameras moved through ninety degrees of azimuth to a huge plasma screen that seemed to fill the whole of one side of the studio. It was split into a hundred and two identical squares containing the names of each county of England, Wales, Scotland and the Six Counties of Ulster alphabetically from Aberdeenshire to Yorkshire West Riding. Beneath each name was a space sufficient for one National Insurance number each consisting of two letters, six digits and a final single letter.

Nationwide a hundred million eyes focused on the screen as RADO commenced its work. The name Aberdeenshire started to flash in a red neon colour then turned to amber and stopped flashing. It made a curious electronic bleeping sound like the old football scores tele-printer used to do at five o'clock on a Saturday afternoon. Then suddenly, there they were, the first nine characters! All glowing in green like a traffic light on GO! GO! GO! Only Murray Walker was missing. The first Member of the House of Commons ever to be randomly selected by a computer. Who was it? Of course nobody knew. Not yet. Then Argyllshire started to flash, then Bedfordshire. By nine o'clock it had still only got to Kent. But every corner of the kingdom had to wait its turn. Every pub and club in the land was jammed to capacity with people clutching a beer mat with their own National Insurance number scribbled on it. In Cornwall a thousand fishermen threw their losing tickets away when they realised it was not their lucky night. Betrayed and bankrupted by years of European Union fishing regulations, twenty-five thousand a year was a fortune to all of them. They'd have to go back to doing Lotto and signing on the dole. It was the same in North Yorkshire with a thousand steel workers from Redcar. And the same in Leicestershire with a thousand textile workers. In County Durham five hundred employees who worked at a bank call centre that was being transferred to India watched attentively, hoping it would be them. Slowly but surely RADO moved down the list. Essex. Flintshire. Gloucestershire. Down south things were a bit different. RADO was just about to deal with Surrey then Sussex. What some people used to call BBCs – big buck counties. Here in the affluent south only a handful of people were hoping to win a seat in the Commons. Twenty-five grand a year plus a few rail tickets? No way José! A shelf-stacker at Sainsbury's could almost make that without having to listen to boring speeches and dress like a tailor's mannequin. It was a different story in

Yorkshire and the North East. The working mens' clubs in the old industrial towns and mining villages were jammed to capacity. They hadn't sold so much ale since New Year's Eve. Everybody wanted to be a winner! Everybody.

There was only one real flaw to this new democracy. Whilst the draw was truly random different citizens stood different chances of winning depending on where they lived. The one member per county rule was absolute but that applied equally to Middlesex with a population of some 3 million and Lancashire with 5 million as to Rutland with a hundred thousand. Still it was a whole lot better, for those that wanted to win, than doing Lotto with a one in ten million chance. You couldn't 'fix' your residence either. The information had been taken from the 2001 Census.

There had in the past been cries from the English taxpayer that Scotland was over represented in Parliament with a disproportionate number of MPs in relation to its population. This would be even more the case under the new system with Scotland having 33 members out of a hundred and two. The Queen had discussed this at some length with Sir Michael who had given the matter considerable thought. Between them they came up with two marvellous ideas. Although English, with no Caledonian pretensions of any sort, Sir Michael had suggested that the new system should go ahead but that the number of English seats could be artificially increased by a further five seats by allowing Yorkshire to be split into the three ancient Ridings and Lincolnshire to be devolved into the 'olde Engle' regions of Kesteven, Holland and Lindsay. Lastly, Sussex could be split into East and West just like they used to be.

'What a capital idea' she had replied. Her Majesty would also use this newly acquired Scottish People Power as a perfect excuse to dissolve the new Scottish Parliament in Edinburgh for good. What a colossal waste of taxpayer's money it had proved to be. This ghastly blot on the landscape had cost over 400 million pounds and had proved to be simply a talking shop for overpaid, egocentric isolationists who tried their best to render the Act of Union of 1707 a worthless document. It was a disgrace. But not for much longer. The Scottish Parliament Abolition Act would be amongst the first Bills to be presented in her next Queen's Speech. But she and Sir Michael would keep that under their respective crown and bowler for a while yet. All in good time.

A tabloid newspaper had offered £5,000 each to the first ten new MPs to call their London office and demonstrate proof of selection. By seven thirty they had already received two hundred replies which proved that some sort of scam was going on somewhere. The idea was quickly forgotten and no new stories appeared the following Monday. A commercial TV station had offered a staggering £100,000, equivalent to the whole four years' parliamentary salary, to the first new Member who identified themselves and agreed to an interview. To this end the station had no less than thirty camera crews with satellite transmitter kits strategically placed across the length and breadth of the land. The first call had come in at ten minutes past seven from a sheep farmer in County Antrim of all places. The organisers hadn't realised that RADO was going to work alphabetically. Had they done so they might have saved themselves a great deal of expense by having a single crew in the seven counties that started with the letter A – four in Scotland, one in Wales and two in Ulster. There was huge panic at the TV station HQ in Birmingham. Shit. They'd forgotten the Six Counties altogether. What a cock-up! The farmer had evidently already contacted the *Belfast Telegraph* so they couldn't pretend they hadn't received the call. A deal was quickly arranged with a subsidiary TV company in Belfast and a crew raced north up the A26 to find the farm in the middle of nowhere near Portrush. They needn't have bothered. It was a false alarm. An excess of

Bushmills whisky and the absence of reading glasses had caused the gentleman in question to misread the XX of the National Insurance number on RADO's screen as YY. The following six digits and the final letter were otherwise correct. What bad luck. Oh well, a hundred grand would have been nice but at least he had a half of the bottle left and he had enjoyed his very temporary cult status. The crew drove slowly back to Belfast hoping to a man that they might have won the County Down seat themselves. They weren't that well paid.

But one person did win the £100K. A girl from Essex called Chloe Ledger. She was aged eighteen years and a week and she worked as a sales assistant in the Chelmsford branch of WH Smith's. By 8 o'clock she was being interviewed on live TV. The camera crew and interviewer had to help her get ready for the five minute interview. Her mother Sharon (aged thirty-six) and her boyfriend Wayne (Chloe's father was dead) were down at the local pub – the Slug and Lettuce – watching the Draw themselves on a big screen. The editors of *The Times*, *Telegraph*, *Guardian* and *Independent* groaned as they watched from the comfort of their million pound houses in 'BBC' counties. What on earth was this silly little bitch going to do for her country? What on earth? They would justify their previous predictions for this instant democracy by writing ridiculing leader articles in their Monday editions.

The arc light powered from a battery in the crew's white van provided the only lighting as Chloe stood outside the small but smart semi-detached house that could have been in mediocre suburbia anywhere in England. The interviewer had told her what questions he was going to ask her which gave her a little time to prepare. She didn't need to write anything down. She prided herself on her memory and could remember the prices and stock codes of over two hundred sales lines in the store. She couldn't add up though – fank Gawd for electronic tills!

She'd had only ten minutes to get ready. She'd put on a semi-transparent pale lime green cropped top which showed her pierced navel to perfection. Underneath, the black Triumph 'wonderbra' accentuated her ample bust to a status that would disprove Newton's laws of gravity if only her maths was a bit better. The skin tight pinstripe trousers looked almost respectable. Her golden locks were swept up on to her head and held in place by a tortoiseshell comb clamp. An excess of cheap pink lipstick sheened almost purple under the arc light. She didn't want to look 'naff' on camera. Now did she? The camera started to roll.

'Chloe, congratulations.'

'Fank you. It's an honour. My Dad would have been so proud of me. I know he would. Sadly he was killed in a car accident when I was only five. The driver wasn't insured and me Mum brought me and Ben, my little bruvver that is, up on her own.'

'Well, Chloe, Westminster will be a big change from working in the store in Chelmsford won't it.'

'Dunno, really. S'pose so. 'Aven't had time to fink yet.'

Down at the Slug and Lettuce Mrs Sharon Ledger was already mentally spending the £100K that Chloe had just won. They'd sell up and use the money to buy a bigger house nearer to Westminster. She might even become a bit of a celeb herself. Wayne would have to go of course. With his earrings, tattoos and Ford Sierra he just wouldn't fit in now would he? I mean, now would he?

The editors reached for their laptops. By lunchtime on Sunday their leaders would be e-mailed to the printing sections. This Estuarian Essex girl was going to epitomise the new Britannia. The Queen had made the gravest error of judgement in her fifty year reign. The interview was coming to an end.

'And lastly, Chloe, had there been a proper General Election this year how would you have voted now that you're eighteen? Any idea?'

'Yeah, Green. I'd have voted green I like green. See?' Her right hand momentarily rubbed her other sleeve. They both laughed. It was her first ever televised joke. This smart little cookie wasn't the stupid little bitch those editors first thought she was.

Chapter 4

It was almost midnight by the time that RADO reached Yorkshire West Riding, alphabetically the last county in the kingdom. There had been some sort of a gremlin in the system when it had reached Lindsay. Perhaps it was still searching for Lincolnshire, three out of the first four letters being common to both names maybe confusing its memory. No matter. The twenty minute delay seemed only to add to the expectation and allowed publicans across the land time to change barrels and clear glasses. One of these events every Saturday night instead of every four years would do wonders for the licensed trade. If only!

The known list of new Members was growing steadily. In TV studios throughout the land the National Insurance numbers were being replaced by real people. There wasn't a returning officer as such like in previous elections. No recounts. No hushed town halls just before the candidates' names and votes were announced. By 2 am in the morning most channels stopped broadcasting and so far over sixty names were formally announced. There were no more false alarms from Ulster or anywhere else. There were no celebs or known personalities in the list thus far. A Mr John

Leadbitter, the new Member for County Durham, claimed that he had once played soccer for Sunderland reserves but almost nobody could remember him. This would have been the ex-Prime Minister's seat should he have been allowed to continue in office. A cricket groundsman from Taunton called Leslie Percy in his early sixties was the new Member for Somerset. So much for the predicted apple grower! The Member for the Isle of Wight was a hotelier from Shanklin called Wendy Howlett who looked about 50 from the brief TV appearance. Many viewers thought that she looked like the actress that had starred in 'Are you being served' and 'EastEnders' – blonde, slightly porky and pleasant. The Member for Hereford was a farmer which seemed to fit in with everyone's idea of that part of England. So much for the *Sun*'s prediction that it would be a member of the SAS!

Her Majesty and Sir Michael had taken actuarial and statistical advice from those that should know. The law of random probabilities dictated that, statistically at least, males and females should each make up about half the numbers of Members. If so, this would be a sop to the feminists who still complained that too many hidebound men took up seats in the Commons. Of the Members so far declared males were running slightly ahead but with about forty seats still to be revealed this could soon be put right. The Home Office, to which Sir Michael had delegated the task, started to put together the Commands from Her Majesty that would be personally delivered by courier to all Members. Nobody would be allowed to slip out through the net. You either served in Her Majesty's Parliament or you were detained at Her Majesty's pleasure. It was as simple as that.

By the Tuesday all but six of the Members had been identified – that's ninety-six new MPs. Chloe Ledger's picture appeared on the front page of every newspaper. The *Daily Sport* had offered her another £100,000 to pose topless and her mother Sharon had agreed on the telephone without even consulting Chloe. When a chauffeur driven Rolls Royce arrived at her home in Chelmsford to collect her she went ballistic. 'No way', she said. 'Not me.' Her mother was livid. A hundred grand for the taking and she was turning it down? Chloe had the brains to realise that if she kept her head screwed on then in a year's time £100K would look like chicken feed. In the meantime she would play a sweet little girl.

RADO had turned out a hugely diverse team of Members. Chloe, as expected, was the youngest by quite a long way. Next youngest was a Mr Martin Hemingway aged twenty, an apprentice plumber from Mirfield who was now the Member for Yorkshire, West Riding. At the other end of the scale 99 year old Edith Alice Coates was the oldest Member. She lived in a little village just outside Skipton and was now the Member for Yorkshire, North Riding. Some truly interesting characters had come out of the hat. The Member for Middlesex was one Toni Marconi. He was forty and a fourth generation London Italian. He ran a fruit and veg stall on Edmonton Green, North London. His grandfather had sold ice cream there in the summer and chestnuts and baked potatoes in the winter. The Member for Nottinghamshire was a retired Inland Revenue Inspector called Roy Usher aged sixty-five. There was a photo of him in several papers posing in his garden and genially smoking his pipe with his wife and black labrador. He looked like a man everybody could trust. Pipes and dogs always gave that impression. Ask Harold Wilson.

There were some real characters coming from north of the border. A redundant shipyard worker from Greenock called Ray Grant was now the Member for Renfrewshire. A caravan park owner from Dollar was the Member for Clackmannanshire. At fifty-one Laura MacDonald was still quite vivacious with her auburn hair and well-honed figure. She had been a widow for three years and 'put it about a bit' as they say. The business earned her a lot of money and attending at Westminster would not be a problem as the summer Parliamentary recess would coincide with the busy tourist season when she made the most money anyway. The extra twenty-five grand a year would be a bonus and the chance to explore new men in London was inviting. The Member for Fife was a potato grower from Auchtermuchty called Archie Murdoch. Although sixty he had never once been south of the border. This would be an education for him. He didn't exactly relish the prospect but if an Englishman was going to pay him in coins of the Realm for four years then he would take the Queen's shilling without any conscience. Aye! A Fund Manager from one of those fancy investment management companies in Charlotte Square, Edinburgh called Duncan Gibson had become the Member for East Lothian. At fifty he was experienced in banking and fiscal matters. The New Commons would need people like him to complement those of a lesser business background. Other Scots included a salmon farmer from the Isle of Lewis, Hamish McIver, and an air stewardess in her thirties from Perth called Linda Ross.

Sadly, it was quite a different story in Wales. As Sir Michael had remarked to Her Majesty, 'Thank the Lord there are only twelve counties in the Principality, Ma'am.' Reluctantly she had to agree. All 12 Welsh Members had now been identified. One was an unmarried single mother aged twenty-two with no less than four illegitimate children. Mari Jones had never had a proper job. She had one talent, apart from procreating, and that was singing. She could also strum on a guitar as long as no more than the five chords she knew were involved. Mari did a very passable imitation of Mary Hopkin and she played down at the local pub on 'live music' nights. When she was seventeen the drummer in the support band had put her in the family way – followed by the lead guitarist when she was nineteen, the bass guitarist when she was twenty and the landlord's son when she was twenty-one. Now on income support and every other benefit a 21st century Welfare State could muster, before being declared the Member for Merionethshire she could see no way forward in life. At least not beyond the damp green valley that her council house clung to beneath a slag heap that looked like Aberfan Two. Who knows – maybe Mary Hopkin had been mistaken? Those Days of hers were still to come. The Member for Pembrokeshire ended out to be a union rep from the giant oil refinery at Milford Haven. He'd been on TV before a few years before as one of the prime organisers of the fuel blockade that had tried to force the Government to reduce fuel tax. Dai Williams wasn't exactly a rebel by nature but a pro-Government newspaper had tried to wrongly depict him as some sort of communist subversive. He wasn't. A civilian aircraft maintenance engineer from RAF Valley was the Member for Anglesey. He was a bit of an aviation 'anorak' and spent his spare time watching aeroplane videos and listening to pilots speaking on VHF frequencies. Nick Grindlay was appalled at having to move to London. Still, he could always nip down to Heathrow or Gatwick for a jet fix if required. The rest of the Welsh MPs were totally indescribable. Just nobodies. One was a brewery worker, another unemployed and another an administrative assistant at the Royal Mint which had long since removed from London to Llantrisant. The occupations of the remainder were a mystery. A rumour circulated in the *Cardiff Evening News* suggested that the Member for Glamorgan might even have a criminal record but the story was so far unconfirmed.

Worse was to come. Despite all the efforts of British politicians to bring peace to Ulster over three decades whenever there was an election the voters seemed to polarise. In the new order it was hoped that six moderates would be selected by RADO. Some chance. Defying the laws of statistics the Members for all Six Counties were male and Nationalists. That well known Protestant priest with the voice that could be heard in London without the use of a cable or satellite immediately demanded an investigation and an audience with the Queen...She declined for the time being but sent him a personal message urging him to give the new system a try. Who knows, in four years time RADO might pick six Orangemen. Or even six orange women.

One by one five of the six remaining seats were filled. The seats of Holland, Lindsay, Kesteven, Yorkshire East Riding and Sussex East all had different but valid reasons for declaring late. Most of the press followed up a rumour that it was the splitting of Yorkshire and Lincolnshire into separate parts that had probably caused some problem with inputting National Insurance numbers into RADO. Quite probably, but that was definitely not the case with Staffordshire, the very last county to declare its Member of Parliament.

In a flat above an Asian 'takeaway' on Walsall Road, Wolverhampton a Bangladeshi man in his mid-thirties didn't know what the bloody hell to do.

Chapter 5

Zia Ali Mohammed Akbar was actually a most pleasant guy to know. He had been the friendly face behind the counter when the local population had popped in after the pubs closed to order a chicken Madras, poppadums, special pilau rice and a garlic naan bread to take home before watching a video or giving the girlfriend a good 'seeing to'. Or both. He had a major dilemma on his hands and by golly did he know it. It was midnight and he had just shut the shop downstairs. He looked down at the local evening paper showing the headline 'So who IS our new MP?' Actually it was him!

His problem was that he had bought his identity, complete with valid National Insurance number and passport, from a contact in Sylhet, Bangladesh five years earlier. It had cost him ten thousand sterling, a small amount of money in relation to what his whole family connections made in England from takeaways each year. There were five of them with the same National Insurance number which was fine as long as only one of them claimed benefits at any time. But Zia wasn't interested in benefits. He was only interested in making money. Amazingly he was an illegal immigrant with a legal national identity.

He just couldn't believe his bad luck. His mind wandered back to the day he had left Bangladesh for good. After purchasing his British Passport, National Insurance Card, National Health Insurance Card, a Visa credit card, two utility bills for the previous quarter already in his name at a bona fide address in Leicester he had travelled by train to Calcutta. In a back street leather wear store he bought a battered Delsey suitcase that looked as if it had made a dozen return trips to the United Kingdom. That's because it had. It was plastered in airline stickers and luggage labels from BA, Air India and Qantas – all airlines that flew between India and London. For an extra ten pounds (payable in Sterling only) you could have an authentic BOAC label as well if you wanted to predate 1973 when it became part of BA. But that would have been over egging the pudding – or in his case over spicing the tandoori. In case the bag was searched there was even a soccer programme from a Leicester City home match dated two years earlier to add an extra touch of authenticity. How easy it had all seemed. It was!

And here he was. At the incredible odds of two and a half million to one HE was the new Member for Staffordshire. Five days had passed now since the Draw on TV. He had actually watched it live on a TV that was perched in the corner of the takeaway shop. Normally it proved temporary entertainment for customers while they waited for their orders but last Saturday it had been deserted so he watched it alone sat behind the formica counter. Not many people know their own National Insurance number off by heart. With nine digits and letters to remember altogether it can never exactly roll off the tongue in anybody's language. But Zia knew his allright. He had memorised it on that first flight into the UK all those years ago. He'd figured that no genuinely illegal immigrant would know what such a number was let alone remember it perfectly. In the event of him being questioned by immigration officers at Heathrow

25

he would be able to demonstrate within seconds that he was one of them. He'd even memorised the previous Saturday's Premiership scores. Nobody would be more English than him! When RADO's flashing light moved to Staffordshire on that screen and his combination came up he almost had a fit. He had weighed up the pros and cons for five days now. He would just have to come clean and own up – say he had been poorly for a few days or something. Self inflicted Delhi belly maybe. He didn't want to go to Stafford Prison for four years by declining the seat at Westminster but he didn't want to be discovered as an illegal immigrant after all these years either. Maybe once he had been sworn in as an MP he would be safe. Keep his head down and just vote with the general sway of opinion. Yes, that's what he would do. Just be a neutral.

For the umpteenth time he unfolded the official communication from Buckingham Palace that had been contained in a gold envelope bearing the Queen's Royal Seal in wax on the fold. And for the umpteenth time he read it aloud to himself;

'You are commanded to sit as the Member of Parliament for the County of Staffordshire according to antient lore.'

That was a load of water buffalo shit for a start! Dear God, what a country this was. It continued: *'Pursuant to Her Majesty's instructions it is Her wish that you do Swear an Oath to Her Parliament and Her Sovereign Provinces Overseas etc etc.'*

The next day's *Staffordshire Gazette* had his photo and a story on the front page. 'Asian takeaway proprietor is new MP in Powell's old seat.' Zia was confused. He didn't know that the old head of the Scout Movement had been an MP as well. He'd been a Scout himself when Bangladesh was still called East Pakistan and he remembered a picture of Baden Powell on the wall of the scout hut taken in the Fifties. When time allowed after he had settled at Westminster he would look at some of the old records and see what sort of MP

Baden Powell had been. In the meantime he detailed a male cousin to look after the business for the next few weeks in his absence. He was almost excited!

In another week he would be sworn in as a bona fide MP. Can you imagine that? An illegal immigrant with a purchased Nationality would be able to vote in the Mother of all Parliaments. He was quite at home in his adopted country. He followed Wolverhampton Wanderers Football Club (through good times and bad) and was even considering buying a season ticket next time. He was rather hoping that he would not be the only 'ethnic' MP in the new House. He needn't have worried.

Chapter 6

RADO had been kind to ethnic minorities. Or rather one type of minority. Mr Kareem Khan was the new Member for Leicestershire. The City of Leicester was believed to be the first City in England to be more than fifty per cent 'ethnic.' This ancient Roman town was a melting pot of races. At least that was what the race industry purists would have one believe. In fact it was a dumping ground for Asians from the new Commonwealth. After the partition of the Indian sub-continent in 1947 and the last Viceroy had become a brand of cigarettes, Muslim Pakistan was born, devolved from India and split into East and West. In 1971 revolution in East Pakistan gave birth to Bangladesh and a curry gravy train of immigrants to the UK. Many of them came from the district of Sylhet in the north east of that new nation which had traditionally supplied the great Port of Calcutta with the bulk of its seafaring men. As the late Lord 'Bill' Deedes had written in one of his weekly columns – 'Travelling through impoverished Bangladesh some years ago I formed a bond of sympathy with the people of the region. Deprived of their traditional livelihoods, despairingly, many Bangladeshi people decided to come here.' The great humanitarian that he was, Bill Deedes was right. It was one of the great tragedies of Partition.

If Zia Akbar was the acceptable face of immigration then Kareem Khan was the antithesis. He'd been one of the lucky ones. After his parents had been expelled from Uganda by the despotic Idi Amin his family had settled in the Midlands amid a sea of goodwill and assistance from the British people who demonstrated beyond measure that a British Passport was not a worthless document. But Mr Khan was not one of those to sit back and soak up British culture. He left high school with only three 'O' levels but by the time he was twenty-five he owned three corner shops. By the time he was thirty he owned two supermarkets. By the time he was forty he owned a whole street full of terraced houses – all earning extortionately high rents from the tide of new immigrants from Asia. He became a Labour Councillor and a Rotarian to boot. And now he was an MP! Truly, all his Gods had been good to him. He was looking forward immensely to see what sort of scams and rackets he could operate when he was an MP. Goodness, he had read about so many of them over the past few years. The opportunities would be almost limitless. Inshallah!

In fact, RADO had been very, very kind to Asians. The new member for Gloucestershire was Chinese, or rather Hong Kong Chinese. Her name was Alice Tam, she was twenty-eight, highly educated and the daughter of the owner of the Hong Kong Chinese restaurant in the Montpelier district of Cheltenham. She was honoured beyond measure. She wanted to make a real contribution to the country that had given her family protection. Her father, Paul Tam, had been employed by the British Government in Hong Kong in a very sensitive position in internal security and well before the handover to communist China the whole family had moved to England with passports, money and a warm welcome. Paul had been a keen race goer in Hong Kong at both Sha Tin and Happy Valley and he had seen races from

Cheltenham on HKTV. He would have to get used to races 'over the sticks' though. None of that lark in Hong Kong. The ground was far too hard and dangerous in Hong Kong's bone dry winter. Cheltenham seemed like a nice place to live and the family settled easily. The restaurant was bought as a going concern from another Chinese family that wanted to retire. Alice was an only child who worked hard at school and university. She had qualified as a chartered accountant and specialised in corporate taxation. Her English friends called her 'Abacus Alice' as she was as quick on one of those as most people were with high tech, high speed electronic calculators.

Alice was nobody's fool and woe betide anyone who tried to outsmart her. She just couldn't wait to get to Westminster.

The Member for Sussex East was perhaps the most unwilling of all the new Parliamentarians. What wretched bad luck he was having of late. Bob Meadows was on the Board of one of the biggest High Street banks in the country – the Dogger Bank plc. Less than a year ago his then wife had discovered he had two mistresses when she had accidentally picked up his mobile phone one day instead of hers and retrieved two incoming texts – one from Honeybun and one from Puss in Boots. From that moment on his game was up. The subsequent quickie divorce had cost him a staggering nine hundred thousand pounds after her cute overpaid barrister had calculated the value of their two houses, one in London and one in Brighton. Then just for spite he'd added on the accrued value of his Dogger Bank pension, his Bank shares, his share options and the value of his beloved Jaguar E Type that he kept mothballed pending his retirement. Puss in Boots was no longer attracted by his halved fiscal status but at least he still had Honey. She, at least was loyal. And great in bed too, which helped. Not that he needed help. At fifty-six he was twenty years Honey's senior but the lead in his pencil would have done any Red & Black salesman proud.

They had just got back to Brighton after a week's spring break in Madeira. It was their favourite destination and they always stayed at Reids. In fact that's where they had first met when both were on holiday with their first respective spouses. Honey's first husband was also a banker in the City but he had died two years earlier from a suspected cardiac when they were attached to a Bermudan subsidiary. Although married, Honey had flirted outrageously with Bob whenever his wife wasn't around. One day she would have him to herself she thought. She thought right.

The Bank car, with driver, had picked them up at Gatwick for the thirty minute drive to Brighton and their secluded home in the smart Kemp Town area. They had missed the Draw whilst away but on the plane home Bob saw an article on the front page of a complimentary *Daily Telegraph* in the First Class section of the Airbus A320. 'Few seats left to be declared – Sussex East...Kesteven...Holland...etc.' He hadn't taken much notice. He thought the whole notion was going to be a disaster anyway. He'd seen the interview with Chloe Ledger on satellite TV and laughed his socks off.

The bank Rover 75 purred its way onto the gravel drive of their splendid detached residence. Barely had it slowed to a halt before the driver was ejecting from the front seat and had miraculously opened the rear door for Honey Meadows before she had time to realise the car had actually stopped. Such were the skills taught by www.chauffeurs. com in this the 21st Century equivalent of footplatemen. com! They were soon inside their comfortable home and as soon as coats were off and cases left by the stairs the pile of mail on the hall side table was next on the list. There was the usual assortment of junk mail from the *Reader's Digest*, a few mail order offers, charity begging letters, a post card from a neighbour visiting New Zealand and one small hand-written note. It was from Mary, the daily help, who had been doing some spring cleaning in their absence. The note read 'I had to sign for one letter. It looks ever so important. I've put in on the Welsh dresser in the breakfast room. See you on Monday then. Mary.' Less than a minute later Robert Ernest Meadows knew that he was the new MP for Sussex East. He was appalled. Tomorrow morning first thing, he would call his private lawyers in Mayfair. There must be some way out of this. Surely!

A few days before the Queen was to officially open the new session of Parliament in the time honoured way, Her Majesty spent a whole afternoon with her most senior civil servant.

'Sir Michael, how is it all looking? The new House I mean – the Members?'

'Well Ma'am, it's looking a lot better than it was a week ago, certainly. Fortunately, the law of random probabilities has looked upon us with a little favour. I was beginning to wonder if we could make up a team but now...'

Her Majesty interrupted. 'Perhaps you could run through the principal Members for me.'

'Certainly, Ma'am. I'll start with Scotland.'

Sir Michael rattled on for a few minutes while an attentive Monarch listened and took notes.

'So, Sir Michael, of the thirty-three Scottish Members, who are going to be the most useful as possible Cabinet Members? Initially at any rate.' A corgi fussed around her ankles and she threw it a fig biscuit.

'Mr Angus McLean, the Member for Aberdeenshire, Ma'am, is a retired Justice of the Peace. A landowner and businessman, albeit retired, he will bring a firm hand to the tiller. He's only sixty-two and in good health seemingly. With your permission, Ma'am, I thought he would make a good Speaker. Traditionally that is a non-voting role so it would have the added advantage of reducing the Scottish numbers by one.'

'Yes, quite. Good thinking. And do you think that the chappie who looks after money in Edinburgh, er Mr Gibson is it? Would he make a good Chancellor?'

'Possibly, Ma'am, but fate has awarded us the opportunity to put a senior English banker at the helm of the nation's finances. A Mr Robert Ernest Meadows from Brighton is the new Member for Sussex East and he is on the Board of the Dogger Bank plc. In the circumstances, Ma'am, he's an automatic choice for Chancellor. We are very lucky.'

'Indeed we are, Sir Michael. Indeed we are.' Her little scowl at the mere mention of the Dogger Bank went unnoticed by the forelock tapping civil servant.

Chapter 7

Her Majesty opened the new session of Parliament with all the pomp and pageantry that only the United Kingdom could muster. This truly was a day for 'The People' and almost as many thronged the streets of the capital as had done for the English rugby team on their triumphant return from Australia with the World Cup. The Queen's carriage was accompanied down the Mall to Westminster by a mounted detachment from the Blues and Royals of the Household Division which had fortunately remained unscathed by the last round of defence cuts. She wondered how long that would last. The last lot had taken away her beloved yacht, Britannia, out of sheer spite she thought. Sheer spite. She rather hoped he would remember that as he languished in his Tuscan exile.

The scene in the House of Commons was almost surreal. With the former six hundred plus Members now replaced by just one hundred and two there were oceans of space and the place looked almost empty. It had been decided to create vastly more space for ordinary members of the public to watch democracy at work. The Speaker's chair was still intact, as were the despatch boxes and the mace but both 'sides' of the House had been reduced to only about eighty of the plush green leather seats so familiar to viewers of 'Today in Westminster'. Tomorrow in Westminster would be another story.

Black Rod performed his usual duty and banged three times on the door of the Commons and all the Members then traipsed into the Lords to listen to the Queen's Speech. It was a lot different this time because she had actually written it. Normally it is the custom for the Prime Minister and the Leader of the Opposition to walk side by side as they meander into the Upper House but today there was no PM – not yet anyway. Thus a crocodile of a hundred and two men and women sauntered into the House of Lords. Their Lordships couldn't quite believe it either.

Octogenarian gentlemen on the edge of their red leather seats craned forwards to try and catch a glimpse of Chloe Ledger's skin tight black trouser suit as she was ushered into one of the seats reserved for Commoners. Dressing conservatively was not one of Chloe's talents, hidden or otherwise, but she had tried with her mother's assistance to look less provocative than she had done on that first TV interview. Gone was the wonderbra and the high heels, and wearing her hair tied back with a pearl choker she could have passed for an office girl in a smart London bank.

Edith Alice Coates was in a wheelchair and accompanied by a nurse provided at taxpayers' expense 'just in case' she was taken bad and had one of her funny turns. This was truly the greatest day of her life. Robert Meadows was wearing his usual dark pin stripe suit just as if he was attending his Head Office in Lombard Street. He looked decidedly pissed off but Honey had made him promise that he would smile if he spotted a camera zooming in his way. The Member for Glamorgan was having a field day. This was his golden hour. Three weeks earlier Darren Davies, 'Daz' to his mates, was selling the *Big Issue* outside Cardiff railway station. His several convictions for petty larceny over the previous year had not disqualified him from taking his seat. If only his father could have seen him now – he would have been so proud. His father had been a Bevin Boy during the War but exposure to coal dust in one of the Rhondda's deepest mines had resulted in an early death from emphysema. Purely by accident he had been tuned into Radio 2's 'Good Morning Sunday' programme two years earlier and had listened to a man called John Bird. Mr Bird had founded the *Big Issue* magazine here in the UK and Daz was impressed no end by what he had heard. That bit of fate had given him his first little break and now fate had intervened again. Daz actually lived in another former Prime Minister's seat and for the next four years he would do as Her Majesty commanded. Simply, he would do his very, very best. His mother had bought him a suit with her store card so that he could look smart until his first month's pay cheque came in. Back home in Merthyr Tydfil she was glued to her TV set to try and catch a glimpse of her boyo.

Laura MacDonald was dolled up like never before. The Member for Clackmannanshire was used to tarting up for the hunt but today she had excelled herself. She wore a tight fitting dark grey suit with dark tights. Her auburn hair was 'up' like a red coconut on her head. The tight white blouse with a narrow black pinstripe accentuated her ample bust. She carried a Gucci handbag and the matching shoes added three inches to her already adequate five feet six. A whiff of her favourite Rive Gauche and she was ready to go. The richest and most privileged men in the land were all within two hundred feet of her. This was surely her Serengeti and over the next four years this Caledonian lioness would eat her fill.

Linda Ross, the Member for Perthshire, was all dolled up just as if she was about to serve drinkipoos in the First Class section of a jumbo jet. At thirty-six she was over the moon at coming out of the draw. She had tired of being a trolley dolly or the 'tart with a cart' and the settlement from divorce number two had not been overly fruitful. Four years at twenty-five grand plus expenses wasn't a fortune but, who knows, there should be rich pickings for sucker number three at Westminster. She'd already started to eye up her fellow Members. The guy from Anglesey, Nick Grindlay, looked like he might be a ladies' man – slim, tall and darkish with just a hint of grey, probably about forty. She'd chat him up soon. Probably back at the Russell Hotel over a few drinks. She flicked her dark curly tresses from side to side as she peered around the Upper House. Jesus, some of these old codgers looked as if they were mummies. No wonder the old PM had tried to abolish half of them.

Mari Jones, the Member for Merionethshire, wore a red suit for the occasion and was almost camouflaged amid a sea of red leather seats. She had started chatting to Dai Williams from Pembroke just before Black Rod had interrupted their conversation and she had thought he was 'quite nice' really. That was Mari's problem. She thought most men were 'quite nice' and that was why she already had a large family. Would Westminster prove any different from her green Welsh valley? Only time would tell. The omens were not good. Dai Williams was no oil painting.

Silence descended on the Upper House as her Majesty began her speech. Normally it began with the time honoured phrase 'My Ministers and…' and then droned on for ages as she simply regurgitated a speech written for her by the Prime Minister's script writer. But this was hers and hers alone. Nobody, but nobody, knew what she was going to say. In over fifty years on the throne this was by far her shortest but most important speech.

It was all over in eight minutes. She explained that she did not want to over-burden her new House of Commons with too much legislation. She reminded everybody that centuries earlier Parliament assembled but once a year, to fix taxes, but that over the years its business had grown and become more demanding. She acknowledged that the world was a more sophisticated and dangerous place today but affirmed her belief that there was 'too much government' and not enough concentration on the real issues that affected the lives of real people. She expounded again on why she had dissolved the previous Parliament. She reminded them that the responsibility on their shoulders was awesome but they could give only of their best.

'And finally, I am not laying down any formal legislative programme for the foreseeable future. God bless you all.'

Sat high in the upper mantle of the Upper House, Sir Michael knew now exactly what he had to do.

There was no debate on the Queen's Speech since there was no formal opposition to oppose it. Instead all one hundred and two members assembled in Committee Room 14 which was just large enough to hold them all. The doors were closed and Sir Michael, sitting at a huge desk slightly elevated above the masses, tapped his gavel firmly on the solid oak top. He felt the great weight of history on his shoulders. He was ready.

'Good afternoon, everybody.' Sir Michael's manners were always impeccable.

'Firstly, Her Majesty has asked me to convey to you her thanks for assuming office.' Everybody smiled and most nodded.

'The purpose of this meeting is to establish a team – I won't call it a Cabinet, we are trying to reduce formality to a minimum. As the Permanent Head of the Civil Service it is my duty to inform you that every Department of State is at your service and every civil servant within those departments is there to help you. Having said that I believe it is my duty also to help you establish that team and some sort of initial framework within it. Thus there are Offices of State that have to be filled in order to protect the ongoing governance of the nation. I'm sure that you will understand that.' There were favourable mutterings all around.

'Having had the opportunity to meet with you all over the past two weeks I have thus drawn up a list of those Offices together with the names of those of you who, I honestly believe, would be best suited – initially at least – to assume responsibility for that post.' The silence was deafening.

'Firstly, let's start with the position of Speaker shall we? For those of you unfamiliar with parliamentary procedures the Speaker is a sort of Chairman, sorry Chairperson, who makes sure that the rules of debate are broadly followed and that everybody gets a chance to say something. Mr Angus McLean' he nodded towards the Member for Aberdeenshire, 'would you be willing to assume this pivotal role?'

Angus rose from his chair and nodded slowly to Sir Michael. 'I would be deeply honoured, Sir.' There was a ripple of applause from the rest and 'Daz' Davies even let out a whistle as he shouted out 'Nice one, Jock.'

'Order, order!' barked Angus, emulating the late George Thomas, arguably the best ever Speaker the House of Commons has ever seen. He was getting into the swing of it already. Sir Michael would tell him later over a dram or two in the Members Bar that he would lose his voting rights. Right now he didn't need to know.

Sir Michael peered down over the half-moon reading spectacles so favoured by the late Sir Alec Douglas Hume, a former Prime Minister and the last Scottish Statesman to lead the United Kingdom. It truly was a 'united kingdom' in those days too. None of this devolution nonsense. 'The position of Prime Minister I want to leave aside for a moment. So, moving on to the three great Offices of State, let's see about the Chancellor of the Exchequer.' He nodded towards Bob Meadows, the senior London banker from the Dogger Bank plc. 'Mr Meadows, are you willing to assume that office?'

'Delighted, delighted.' There was another polite ripple of applause. Things were looking up. Honey would be pleased.

He could see her now standing alongside him as he posed outside Number 11 on Budget Day holding aloft the bright red dispatch box. He couldn't wait to call her on his mobile later.

Sat right at the back, Roy Usher the Member for Nottinghamshire with a fondness for dogs and pipes was deeply disappointed. He'd thought that with his knowledge of taxation the job of Chancellor was in the bag. His disappointment was short lived. Sir Michael resumed his task.

'I'm sure I don't have to tell you just how sensitive the job of Home Secretary is at this point in the nation's history. Crime up. Asylum seekers inundating the welfare system and the NHS, police corruption, prison reform – you name it. Mr Usher you are, may I say, a senior citizen and in your long career at the Inland Revenue you gained a reputation for being fair but firm. Are you willing to assume this great office?'

'I am. I am!' Four years as Home Secretary! What a story to tell his young grandson.

Methodically Sir Michael completed his task until the main Ministries were filled – Education and Science, Foreign and Commonwealth, Agriculture and Fisheries (DEFRA had been dissolved), Trade and Industry and Defence. 'And finally, ladies and gentlemen, the position of Prime Minister I have deliberately left until last. It is most tricky. Her Majesty has indicated that she would not be unamused if there were no Prime Minister at least for the first session of Parliament. In fact, privately, she has admitted to me that she was so appalled by the Presidential style of the former incumbent that she actually would prefer the country not to have a single leader as such but be represented by her as Head of State supported by her Ministers. She might actually have a point. If there is no official opposition in Parliament then the role is redundant, at least in the Commons. Let's look at it again in a few months shall we?' An hour later and

Sir Michael was taking tea with the Queen.

'Are the various Ministers now in place, Sir Michael? At least the main ones?'

'Yes, Ma'am. And as you suggested I told them in confidence what you had told me in private – about the PM's situation, or rather the lack of a PM's position.'

'Excellent, excellent. One step at a time, Sir Michael, one step at a time.'

'Precisely, Ma'am. Precisely.'

Chapter 8

It was a Thursday night and the day had proved quite long. All the Members bar one, Bob Meadows, had taken advantage of the free accommodation at the Russell Hotel and the trolley dolly was already plying Nick Grindlay with expensive wine – all on the bill of course. Meadows had sped back to Brighton via Victoria to celebrate his new Chancellorship with Honey. She had nearly wet herself with happiness on hearing the news. His greedy ex-wife must be green with envy. Serves the bitch right. But Honey hadn't forecast the problems that were coming their way from the Bank.

A Bank courier had hand delivered an envelope to their home in Kemp Town. That in itself was unusual. Meadows tore it open. Bloody cheek, why couldn't it wait until the Board Meeting next week for God's sake? Within two minutes he knew why. The Board had already met – without him, on the day Parliament was opened. Inside the envelope was a personal missive from the Chief Executive.

'Dear Bob. Your fellow directors congratulate you etc. etc, however it is felt that the Bank is now in a situation whereby it could be construed etc. etc. and accordingly the

Board feels that in order to avoid any unfair criticism and for you to act as Chancellor with total probity etc. etc. that it is better that you resign as a Director for the next four years. We trust you will acquiesce to this arrangement and accordingly a Form 286 b is enclosed for your signature for onward submission to Companies House in Cardiff. It has been arranged for your Bank car, and driver, to be made available to whomever the Board appoints as your successor. Head Office Payroll Department have been instructed to cease salary payments forthwith and a Form P45 will be forwarded to the Pay Office at the House of Commons without delay. Under Head Office Rule 323(b) you will not be eligible to exercise your share options this year and unfortunately under Rule 425(c) options previously allotted that fall due for being exercised over the next four years will not now be eligible etc etc. ...' The bastards!

He screwed the letter into a tight ball and hurled it into the hearth of the expensive Portugese marble fireplace. As sure as eggs were eggs he would get his own back. He was privy to all sorts of scams and insider 'goings on' within the Dogger Bank plc. Honey calmed him down as only she knew how and an hour later they were dining at his favourite seafood restaurant in town. The waiter brought the menu and they sipped at an excellent bottle of Muscadet as they chose their food.

'You know, Honey, those bastards have got a bloody nerve. There were eleven of us on the Board – all of us earning over three hundred grand each and two earning over a million. I'm going to be over a million out of pocket just on salary. And as for the share options!'

'Darling, look, be positive OK? I'm sure there isn't a Chancellor dead or alive who hasn't managed to considerably feather his own nest whilst in office. Just think for a minute. When your term is over you'll command a whole string of Directorships. Plus the earnings from your memoirs. We'll write them together.'

43

Bob Meadows slowly started to brighten up. Maybe Honey was right. He would have to stop thinking as a pinstriped conservative banker and toughen up a bit. Become a predator! Two hours later back at home Meadows demonstrated why the spam e-mails selling viagra were wasted on him. He and Honey could indeed make a bomb over the next four years. Mind you though, as soon as the opportunity arose to shaft the Dogger Bank plc he would do it. Oh yes!

Back in London it was like party night at the Russell Hotel. Linda Ross was all over Grindlay like a rash but he didn't seem to be responding. Maybe being appointed Secretary of State for Defence had gone to his head. Returning from the Ladies' room she soon saw why. Mari Jones had sidled up to him at the bar in her temporary absence. The former Lady in Red was now wearing a skirt in the pattern of a Welsh flag that was so tiny that there was hardly any room for the dragon. Bitch! She would get her own back. He would soon get bored with her anyway as soon as he found out she had four kids to four different fathers. She'd had more lovers than hot dinners but at least she didn't have any baggage. She'd bide her time. One day Grindlay would be a notch on her crotch even if he was now in charge of the defence of the Realm.

Laura MacDonald was reclining in one of those huge leather armchairs that make you feel as if you're going to fall backwards forever. It had rucked up her skirt to upper thigh level and across from another table only a dozen feet away the Member for Somerset was doing his damnedest to get an eyeful of her nether region's attributes. She spotted him smiling at her with his glass of ale raised as if he thought he was in with something of a chance. She'd had just enough to drink to mouth a silent 'foxtrot oscar' and he looked away slightly embarrassed. Leslie Percy was not a bad guy, just a bit green. Maintaining a perfect wicket at Taunton Cricket Ground didn't prepare you for anything like this but he'd taken up the position in good faith like everybody else. He would apologise to the nice Scottish lady when he was less inebriated. Meanwhile he'd have another Indian Pale Ale at four quid a pint at the taxpayers' expense.

Propping up one whole corner of the bar were Dai Williams from Milford Haven and Ray Grant, the Member for Renfrewshire from Greenock. A Celtic Conspiracy if ever there was one. The waitress was having trouble clearing the empties, so fast were they drinking. Archie Murdoch, the potato grower from Fife, soon joined them. He was having a ball on this his first venture to the capital. Noticeable by her absence was young Chloe Ledger from Essex. She was actually having an early night and from the outset wanted to cultivate an innocent image. She would enter the limelight when she wanted to and not when her mother said so. Most of the Members were mingling with each other and trying to generally socialise. In practice it wasn't unlike those informal 'bonding weekends' that certain failed politicians tried to organise where everyone has to turn up in a 'woolly pully' and pretend that they don't have any money. A fat lot of good that did them.

Sir Michael had decided not to be at the hotel on this the first night. He wasn't needed but tomorrow he would brief them again on the proposed legislative programme. Easter, and the customary week's recess, was only a week away and he wanted to make strides before the break. Her Majesty had indicated that the main areas that concerned her were with the proposed European Union Treaty (which she rightly viewed as a threat to her authority) and the connected issues of monetary union and immigration. They would be the biggest challenges facing the House and as such were probably best dealt with first. Following them would be Bills relating to finance and taxation followed by the New Act of Union. This last Bill would cause uproar north of the border and it was best kept till last. Sir Michael slept badly. He had a nightmare about Hadrian's Wall being rebuilt along the lines of the old Berlin Wall and he was mightily relieved to wake up to face Clarissa bringing him early morning tea. Of all the forthcoming Bills it was the Act of Union that troubled him most. Her Majesty had been adamant. She was Queen of the United Kingdom and Great Britain and Northern Ireland and she was going to put an end to all this devolution nonsense as soon as possible. Their little ploy to decrease the Scot's vote by one in the House by having a Scottish Speaker might not be nearly enough. What if the Scots, Welsh and Irish all ganged up against the English? Their combined votes of six plus thirty-three plus twelve added up to fifty-one! Exactly half the total! Could the Speaker use his casting vote? Did the Speaker have a casting vote? Would the three Asians in the House necessarily vote for 'England?' He'd already had reports of the Welsh and Scottish Members starting to socialise together. The six Nationalists representing the Six Counties might do absolutely anything. They might have to be bought off. But how?

The next morning brought a hand-delivered message from another civil servant. It was from Vernon Gardner. Gardner was overseeing the drafting of the early Bills to be put to the House and basically he wanted to know if the Members were ready to debate and pass the first Bill – the highly contentious Immigration Bill. Sir Michael thought that barring accidents the House would be ready and replied accordingly to Gardner. He then picked up the phone to speak with Roy Usher, the Home Secretary. After all, this would be largely his baby. He knew he could trust Roy to do a good job. It was important that the first Bill be handled properly as there were still elements of the press, not to mention failed former politicians, who were only too eager to sniff blood and go for the jugular if things went badly. Only time would tell and the next week would be crucial.

Chapter 9

The next morning Angus McLean, Speaker of the House, rose early in his suite at the Russell Hotel. He wanted to make preparations for the start of the debate on the Immigration Bill. But he still had the problem of how to seat the various members within the House itself. His first inclination was to ask all the English Members to sit on one side of the House and all the rest on the other. That would split them equally assuming that all the Members were present. But they never would be of course. Somebody would always be absent through illness, family circumstances or whatever. But from the outset he wanted to avoid the 'England versus the rest' scenario. Maybe he should just divide them into two camps alphabetically. Say, the A to L's on one side and the M to Z's on the other. Would that work? He opened his Compaq laptop to the Members Database that RADO had (eventually) provided him with. It wasn't quite even with fifty Members in the A to L's and fifty-two in the M to Z's. But on the other hand if he changed it to A to M and N to Z it would be further unbalanced as there were no less than five Members whose names began with the letter M. Why did there always seem to be a preponderance of names with the letter M? It cast him back to his old school days and geography lessons. There were fifty States in the U.S.A. and no less than eight of those began with letter M. Then suddenly he thought that maybe he could split the Counties alphabetically as opposed to the Members. He picked up his laptop again and pressed a few buttons and the one hundred and two constituencies rearranged themselves. Mmm. All the first six were either Scottish or Irish! No, sod it, he would stick with the former idea. He didn't want to have to change it later. Mr Murdoch and Co. would go with the M to Z's. And that was another thing about doing it this way. He didn't want all the Scots on one side of the House either. He knew only too well how clannish his own mob were and he wanted free and open debate. That was his job. He didn't want the battle of Culloden re-enacted, particularly when it came to the Act of Union debate. Sir Michael had tipped him off privately that this would be coming before the summer recess and he wanted a well drilled and orderly House in place as soon as possible.

Having satisfied himself that he'd got it about right Angus printed off two separate lists of Members via his table top printer then sent them down to the secretarial pool to get copied – fifty-one copies of each. He would use these to inform all Members on which side of the House they would be assuming their seats. If the previous House was anything to go by then Members would become creatures of habit and regularly assume the same seats. He would ask that those awarded Ministerial status sit at the front, actually on the floor of the House. There were no disabled or blind Members but if Edith Alice Coates was feeling a bit frail then she would have to sit at the front to avoid steps. Now there was a point he hadn't thought of. What if one side had more Ministers than the other? Would it be unbalanced? Would it matter anyway? He wasn't sure but quickly scanned the two lists. From memory he couldn't yet remember who all the Ministers were but it looked like there would be about four on each side. Mmm. He'd have to wait and see. It was intended that television cameras be allowed into the House as before but perhaps it might be better for all concerned if the first day or two remained 'in camera' just in case there were any mishaps. He would speak to Sir Michael on that point. Rather like a racing commentator doing the Grand National who learnt all the owners colours and numbers he would very soon have to learn all the Members' names and counties to avoid any embarrassments. He didn't want to look a prat when a Member waved an order paper to speak and he got it wrong by saying something like – 'Miss MacDonald, the Member for Clackmannanshire' and then a Chinese girl stood up to speak. He would have to do his homework before the TV cameras started rolling. He didn't think it would take him too long to remember them all. Some were more instantly recognisable than others either by skin pigmentation or hair colouring. Most of the national newspapers had published one of those photographs of all the Members taken on the green outside Westminster accompanied by a drawing of the body outlines all with numbers so the reader could identify his or her own Member. He would study one of those until he got it about right.

The great day arrived. This was day one of the new order. No less than a thousand members of the public queued for hours to get one of the four hundred free seats in the public galleries. A still largely sceptical press corps took up their own positions and waited. Would it all work? If it didn't then it would almost certainly mean the end of the Monarchy as well, so prominent had been Her Majesty's involvement.

The morning session began shortly after 11am. Solemn prayer had been abandoned. Although Defender of the Faith, the Queen had actually suggested that in deference to non-Christian Members the Speaker should simply welcome all Members present and could add a few well chosen words of his own if that was his wish. It was indeed Angus McLean's wish and everyone there present was absolutely startled by his delivery.

'Good morning, everybody. Please be seated.' He sounded almost as if he was on a Court bench again about to deliver a sentence on a criminal.

'I am sure that I do not need to tell any of you the historic significance of today's proceedings. Ever since the great Act of Union in 1707, men and women have travelled the length and breadth of this proud nation to attend Parliament. From the glens of Scotland, the valleys of Wales and the meadows of England people have attended at the capital to steer the Kingdom through the centuries, decades and years of war and peace. In the earliest days, before universal sufferage, only men of wealth and property were entitled, literally, to vote in this, the Mother of all Parliaments. Today the situation is different and you are all here because you have been chosen, albeit by a computer, to represent your county and therefore the residents of that county. Your responsibility to them is awesome. Just as it is to yourselves. The very future of this nation is effectively in the hands of just one hundred and two people, one hundred and one if you discount me.' He paused for effect. It worked. The House was hushed. Nobody uttered a syllable.

'You have all been provided with a draft of the new Immigration Bill to study prior to today. I know that some of you, and I won't mention any names, have asked me for guidance and clarification of some of the words and phrases used. There is nothing wrong with that. It is only because I have been involved with the Law as a Justice of the Peace that I am familiar with all too many of the Latinisms that have crept into our language over the centuries. Phrases like "inter alia", "quid pro quo", 'ipso facto' and many others too numerous to mention have rendered our legal system unfathomable to the average man or woman in the street. I would like to think that one day we will play our part in bringing newer, more understandable language to the legal system.' There were a few 'hear, hears' from several Members who had watched too much of 'Today in Parliament' on TV but to his credit Angus McLean did not even look up from his text. Chloe Ledger smiled inwardly to herself. She was probably the only Member who knew what 'ipso facto' actually meant. She remembered it from the lyrics of a hit pop tune by a band called Badly Drawn Boy. The Speaker continued.

'So, today then, we are to commence work on the first piece of legislation – the Immigration Bill. Home Secretary, you will speak first.' He nodded towards Roy Usher, the Member for Nottinghamshire who rose from his seat on the front bench of the M-Z's. He cleared his throat, adjusted his gold-rimmed reading glasses to the bottom of his nose and tried to pitch his voice to add a touch of gravitas to the proceedings. Only he and his wife knew that he had been practising for days for this moment. They'd reckoned that with a good performance in this first Bill he might be in the running for Prime Minister whenever the time came for one to be selected. He rose to the occasion like viagra.

'Mr Speaker. Thank you, it is indeed my honour and privilege to address the House.' He spoke for eleven minutes, a minute longer than his rehearsals. The slightly slower pace added to its meaning, he thought. Others thought so too and the journalists were scribbling like fury onto their notebooks. When he had finished he sat down. Most people looked pleased. In fact everyone except Messrs Khan and Zia was smiling.

The first editions of the London *Evening Standard* were favourable. The chalk boards of the newspaper vendors outside all of London's commuter stations had more or less the same headline. 'Future Immigration to be banned for ten years! Crackdown on illegals!'

For the Members for Staffordshire and Leicestershire the omens looked bleak. In fact they were far worse than bleak but it would take a little longer yet for either of them to have to face the consequences of their misdemeanours. Mr Zia had known all along that his residency in the UK was illegal but thus far luck had been on his side. It wasn't his fault that RADO had picked him out of all the population of Staffordshire. Was it? He would just have to swim with it for the time being and hope that the promised 'crack down' would not extend too far. He would keep his head down just as he had promised himself before. In the meantime he wanted to be a good constituency MP and play a full role whenever he could. Once the Immigration Bill had been passed he would feel more confident. He also wanted to find out more about Mr Powell, the Scout Leader, who had been MP for Wolverhampton South West. Promising himself the time to research Commons speeches in the extensive library he settled into the pattern of life at Westminster.

Arriving back at his half million pound home in Leicester for the weekend break, Kareem Khan was less than enthusiastic about the Bill. Successful crackdowns on illegal immigrants could prove costly to him. He reckoned that over half his terraced houses were let to people who had slipped through the various failed immigration and asylum controls. He might have to start up new legitimate businesses instead.

Chapter 10

Back at home in Nottingham that same weekend Roy Usher was very pleased with himself. He watched 'Newsnight' on BBC2 with Jeremy Paxman interviewing several broadsheet editors on how they saw the new Westminster. Overall their opinion was best described as muted praise. About six out of ten on the infants' school scale. The reality was that to a man they were jealous that they were not Members themselves and that the first opportunity they got to rubbish the new system they would jump at the chance. Gone were the cosy chats with MPs in the Commons tea rooms and the 'leaks' and snippets of information here and bits of gossip there. The fancy, overpriced restaurants in Westminster suffered a huge downturn in trade as journalists with expense accounts no longer took over six hundred MPs to three hour, fifty pound lunches in return for favours and information. One male hack from a red top tabloid had tried to entice Chloe Ledger to dinner at the Caprice but she had told him to 'naff off you perv.' Instead she had a margarita pizza with her Mum at a Pizza Express near Liverpool Street washed down with a diet coke. She didn't want to become the first MP to be date raped by some jerk with a digital camera, a phial of Class B drugs and a bottle of Chateau Legover 2004. No way. The same hack had then invited Mari Jones to the same venue but she had returned early to the valleys as one of her four kids had gone down with chickenpox. If only the hack in question had realised it his best bet would have been to ask the Caledonian Lioness but already someone else had beaten him to it. By the time Mr Paxman had said 'goodnight' to all the viewers Laura MacDonald was already well on the way towards her first Serengeti kill. But she was nothing if not discreet. Nobody knew yet and nor would anybody know for a long time, if ever.

Most of the Scottish MPs had left early for the weekend, one or two flying on the BA shuttle to Glasgow for onward destinations but most by train. Linda Ross was back at her little house in Perth overlooking the River Tay. She had bought it years ago when she'd first started the long haul flights with Gulf Air. Originally with British Caledonian she had opted out of joining BA when it got bought out. A wise move. She had saved most of her high, tax free salary and put it into property. Another wise move. It was worth more than five times the forty thousand she'd paid for it. Add her divorce proceeds to her assets and she was quite a catch our Linda. She was enjoying London even if the Secretary of State for Defence hadn't fallen to her charms yet. She'd noticed that Laura MacDonald wasn't on her train to Edinburgh Waverley. She must have stayed the extra night in London. Maybe she'd pulled already. On the Saturday night she was having dinner with an ex-boyfriend at a Chinese restaurant in the town. A penchant for Chinese food was something Linda had picked up on the old 'B Cal' route to Hong Kong in the late Eighties. Men apart, it was her only other vice. At thirty-eight she had plenty of mileage still left in her.

Most of the Members spent a relaxing weekend at home with friends and family as the reality of their jobs and associated responsibilities started to sink in. Edith Alice

Coates went back to her little village in the Yorkshire Dales and was descended upon by almost the entire population as she told everybody what it was like. Next week they would all be able to see for themselves as the TV cameras were going to be allowed again. She wanted to buy a new frock to show off so her neighbours kindly took her into Skipton and she bought one at Rackhams department store and immediately on returning home she packed it into her big Delsey case ready for the trip to London. The Speaker, such a nice man she thought, had whispered in her ear that unlike the rest he didn't expect her to arrive until Monday afternoons. 'It would be quite all right.' She bought him a little box of hand-made chocolates from Yorkshire's oldest chocolatiers as a little thank you. She was like that. She spent Sunday catching up on the *Yorkshire Post*s she had missed during the week and made a mental note to have them sent on to the Russell Hotel in future. She didn't think it would be available south of Sheffield and she was right. The start of the cricket season was coming up and although ninety nine she was still President of the Carleton in Craven Cricket Club tha' knows! She read through the list of home fixtures for the coming season and kept her fingers crossed that her Parliamentary duties would not mean missing any important matches.

In North London Tony Marconi, the Member for Middlesex, was busy making arrangements for his fruit and veg concession on Edmonton Green to be looked after mid-week while he was 'down the other end.' That meant anywhere in posh parts of London south of Highbury. He was already working on a little scam to obtain the contract for the Commons catering contract, or failing that the supply of fruit and veg for four years. Two years earlier he'd had great sympathy for a Sunderland market grocer who had been heavily fined for refusing to price his wares in kilograms as well as pounds. In fact he'd sent him a donation of twenty pounds towards his fine, so strongly did he feel. That was the trouble with this country he thought. The little man didn't count any more. Big Brother and the European Commission just trampled over everybody. It was almost like the previous Government hadn't cared at all. Just you wait till we go into the Euro he thought. English Cox's orange pippins priced in Euros per kilo? Not on his bloody fruit stall mate. Not while he was an MP!

Down in Newquay the Member for Cornwall, Adrian Kristiansand, was getting ready for the summer season which started early in that milder corner of the kingdom. Little wonder that a former PM with his pipe and dogs had spent most of his leisure time on the pretty little islands just offshore. Kristiansand was what a bank manager would call an amusement caterer. In reality what he did was operate fruit machines and one-armed bandits. Thousands of them – in pubs, clubs, caravan sites, hotels and the newly licensed casinos that had sprung up all over since the Gaming Act was amended. There was nothing he didn't know about them since leaving school at sixteen. He had worked as a Saturday job and in the summer holidays as an arcade manager for an owner who spent too much time in the pub in the summer and most of the winter in warmer climes. Kristiansand knew how much money he was making even allowing for a little shrinkage from dishonest employees. His old boss had been making more than twenty grand a year even before decimalisation when the old pennies and threepenny bits were still in use. After 1971 and the introduction of the new five pence pieces, the old shilling, his profits went through the roof because people soon got used to slotting the new coins into new machines without thinking about it. So Adrian had decided at a very early age to get into that side of commerce himself. He started off by installing six machines in six different pubs on a fifty-fifty split with the landlord. They were emptied every Saturday morning before the pubs were open and the money was counted in private over a coffee. Half of the takings were paid in banknotes to the publican, Adrian taking away all the heavy metal in the boot of his Ford Cortina. Little wonder that Led Zeppelin was his favourite cassette in the car! He had a little arrangement with an old school pal who worked as a cashier at a Building Society. Every Saturday afternoon he would drop off all the coin, still uncounted in canvas bags, at his pal's house who would then sort them, bag them up in proper denominations and take them in to the office on the Monday morning. He would then pay ninety per cent of the take into Adrian's personal account, not his business one. The remaining ten per cent was his 'cut' for services rendered. Eventually the rear suspension and shock absorbers gave out on the Cortina and when the number of pubs involved in his growing enterprise reached several dozen it was not possible to work the little scam at the Building Society. He was forced to go 'legit' or 'semi legit' at any rate and open a proper business account at a proper bank and incorporate a Limited Company with a proper accountant and all the other associated misery that went with being an entrepreneur. But old habits die hard and the original six pubs remained outside the system. It was Adrian's little flanker with the Inland Revenue. From a personal point of view he was just pleased that the former Tax Inspector, Roy Usher, was Home Secretary and not Chancellor. He'd already shared a beer or two with Bob Meadows and thought there might be some common ground even if he was a banker at heart. Over the weekend Adrian had a few meetings with some caravan park operators about some new money-spinning games he wanted to install before summer really got underway and then prepared to pack for the trip back to London via Paddington on the Great Western Railway. He had initially been annoyed at his name coming out of the RADO hat but the more he thought about it the more he liked it. He would turn it to his fiscal advantage that's for sure if he possibly could. At fifty-one he would take any opportunity going to bulk up his nestegg over the next four years.

Down in Brighton, Bob Meadows and Honey were having an early night. He was sat up in bed putting the finishing touches to his own maiden speech in the House. The Finance Bill that followed his first Budget wasn't due for a month or more but pressure was being put on him by the Press to set out his views on the currency markets which were causing some exporters more than a little concern. Sterling was at its highest level against the dollar for over ten years, in fact since the UK left the ERM, the absurd system that had all but brought John Major's government down. He didn't have to worry too much though. His predecessor had made the Bank of England totally independent and it was the Governor of the Bank of England and his nominated committee that fixed interest rates now. He thought that he would put the finishing touches to his speech in the bank car en route to London first thing in the morning. Then he suddenly remembered that he would be on the train along with all the other commuters. Damn! He resolved, again, to effect all the damage he possibly could to the Dogger Bank plc and those former colleagues who had shafted him. But he would bide his time and obey the old adage that revenge is a dish best eaten cold. He put down his file, turned out the bedside light and snuggled into Honey's warm back. Tomorrow was another day.

Chapter 11

The US dollar had been in decline for weeks, if not months. Sterling was back up to over $2.00 and heading even further north as the jargon has it. Most sterling related crises that Chancellors had to deal with were caused by the reverse scenario. The pound was now very expensive against the greenback which made it more difficult for British exporters to sell their goods in the States. This was a problem that had not occurred for many years. Bob remembered the time he was at college and seeing a former Chancellor have to turn his car back from en route to Heathrow because the pound had lost four cents whilst his car had been stuck in traffic on the Chiswick flyover. What could he actually do to help? As the only female Prime Minister had once said – 'you can't buck the market!' How right she was.

The Speaker nodded towards the Chancellor as if to give him the cue that his time had come.

'The Chancellor of the Exchequer.' The House hushed and Bob Meadows stood up at the front row of the M–Z's, his notes in his left hand as his right pushed his reading glasses into the most comfortable position on his nose. Back in Brighton Honey was watching on TV. It was the first televised live session and she was nervous for him.

'Mr Speaker, I am sure that all Members of the House rejoice that for the first time in decades we do not have a sterling crisis on our hands that adversely affects the man in the street. The reality is quite the reverse. However, I do share the concern of the Members for Derbyshire, Flintshire, East Yorkshire and Lancashire who all have aerospace industries in their constituencies and who are fighting for crucial orders in the US. These are trying times for them as they compete for vital work against foreign compet...' He didn't finish his sentence. The Member for Yorkshire East who was seated four rows behind him was on his feet shouting.

'It's those Frogs again! Undermining our industries! The Frog government has subsidised their own...'

'Order! Order!' Angus McLean was annoyed. This was the first time he had had to use his gavel in anger. 'Let the Chancellor finish his statement.' The Member for Yorkshire East was startled by the Speaker's intervention and did as he was told. He sat down again. The whole House had just learnt how firm a disciplinarian Mr McLean was going to be.

Meadows recommenced his speech. It was a good one. He gave details about how the Government would monitor the situation but pointed out to howls of mirth all round that now was a good time to buy some dollars and visit Disneyland. 'Go and see how a truly free economy actually works,' he said. 'But don't bring any Mickey Mouse ideas back to the House with you.' Bob sat down after fifteen minutes. He'd explained that he was looking forward to implementing the first Finance Bill before the summer recess. The Speaker took questions from the floor which were all fairly simple for Meadows to answer. Hamish McIver asked him if there might be some Government assistance for the Scottish salmon farming industry which had just been hit by a health warning from a top US food scientist. Meadows said he would look into it. This was a time to make friends not alienate people. A housewife from Elgin who was the Member for Morayshire asked about possible ramifications for the whisky industry. The US was the biggest market for Scotch Whisky and if sterling was too expensive then distilleries in her constituency could suffer badly in the short term. Meadows replied that he had some 'measures' up his sleeve which caused more merriment in the House. He did too, he wasn't fibbing. After the session had finished John Didcot, the Member for Yorkshire East, approached Meadows in the tea room and was a little sheepish. He bought him a cream bun and sat down beside him.

'Mind if I join you? Sorry about my outburst, but I get so pissed off with...'

'No, not at all.' Meadows shuffled to one end of the chesterfield and Didcot sat down.

'I'm afraid I get a bit het up about the French. My constituency takes in the aerospace factory at Brough near Hull and right now thousands of jobs are on the line. The French can't wait for our planes to be so over-priced – then they just dive in with their own government subsidised Mirages. Happens all the time!'

As a banker this sort of real world economics was new to Meadows. All the Dogger Bank plc ever did was make money out of everybody. With subsidiaries the world over it was cushioned against currency movements. What it lost on the swings it made on the roundabouts. And they were big roundabouts. Meadows listened.

'You see, the problem, Bob, sorry may I call you Bob...?'

'Of course.'

'The problem, Bob, really is that there are too few orders and too many manufacturers chasing them. The last big plane order that factory got was from India. And from what I'm led to believe it nearly didn't come off! Some toe-rags in Delhi spun the contract negotiations out for years, literally. Just when thousands of people thought their jobs were secure back the Indians would come with changed specs, new prices and just about any excuse to delay the deal actually being signed. If this latest order for the US Marine Corps doesn't come off then the factory will close.'

'Do you have a personal interest, John? Say shares in the company? Mind me asking?'

'No, twice. No shares. Probably just as well, their value today is only a third of five years ago. I think the average guy in the street has given up on them. I believe that it's just the institutional investors now that effectively control it. You know, pension funds and the like.'

'If you don't mind my asking, John, what is your line of business outside of the House?'

'I'm an egg producer in Holderness.'

Meadows laughed, genuinely. 'And what did you buy first when you set up? A chicken or an egg?'

'Which would you have bought? You're the money man!'

Meadows wasn't sure so he bought Didcot another bun. He liked Didcot. Seemed like he played with a straight bat. A bit dour maybe but there again he was from Yorkshire. Thus from his first effective day as Chancellor Meadows had learnt that you have to try and please everybody from salmon farmers to whisky distillers to egg producers to plane makers. Still, today he had made three potential allies. If all the plans he had for the Dogger Bank were going to come to fruition he would need many more allies. Fifty-one to be precise.

After the tea interlude he quickly called Honey on his mobile, keen to ask how he had come across on TV. The ever loyal Honey was always complimentary and would have sung his praises even if he'd made a hash of it.

'Darling you were marvellous – honestly. You actually looked just like Nigel Lawson when he was Chancellor.' Immediately she realised she had put her foot in it. 'After his diet that is!'

'Really? I sure was nervous! Any other news? Any mail?'

'Oh yes there is. A Recorded Delivery letter addressed to you. I haven't opened it. Do you want me to?'

'Yes please. It's almost certainly from those bastards at the Bank. Probably my last pay cheque and a P45!'

'I don't think so, the envelope is handwritten and postmarked Lincoln, not London. Hang on a sec I'll just get the paper knife – it's Sellotaped as well. Just a mo. Right, there's a very formal letter inside from a Mr Reg Martin who is a Director of Martin's Water Systems Ltd. of Lincoln. It's printed on the firm's letterhead. Hang on.' Fifteen seconds passed before Honey spoke again. 'Bob, this Mr Martin says his company is insolvent thanks to the Bank's negligence and that he intends to sue the Bank and all its Directors personally.'

'How interesting. Look just pop it on my desk and I'll look at it tomorrow. I'll be back on the noon train. Pick me up?'

'Of course, darling! Lunch first or...?'

'I think you know the answer to that, Honey. Bye.'

Chapter 12

Lunch did actually come first, once again at their favourite restaurant – English's Seafood & Oyster Bar in Brighton. Honey had brought the letter from Mr Martin with her and Bob pored over it again and again. He wasn't a director of the Bank anymore so why had he been contacted, and at his home address as well? Was there something here he could use to his advantage? There was only one way to find out. Lunch over they drove home. The sex would have to wait. They had decided on a plan. Honey telephoned Martin's Water Systems and pretended to be Bob's secretary. The girl answering the telephone gave her name as Louise and was very polite.

'Mr Reginald Martin? Yes, he's my father. I can put you through, he's free at the moment that I do know. Hold the line please – putting you through now. Thank you.'

To Honey's experienced ear Mr Martin sounded in his late fifties or early sixties. 'Good morning, my name is Honey and I'm Mr Meadows' secretary, from the Dogger Bank.'

'Oh right. I wasn't expecting a reply so quickly. You know what banks are usually like.' There was a deliberate note of sarcasm in his voice. 'But thank you for calling anyway. You people going to make me an offer then? Before I go to the Press!'

Honey tried to remain collected despite being slightly taken aback by the turn of the conversation. She thought quickly.

'Mr Meadows would be happy to have a meeting with you. Without prejudice of course and at a time to suit you. I have his diary in front of me.' She lied at that point. 'Would next Friday be OK, say 2 pm at the Russell Hotel in London? Or would you prefer to...'

'That'll be fine. Two 'o' clock next Friday then. I'll make myself known to reception. I'll bring all my notes and file with me. I'll come down by train.'

'Thank you Mr Martin. It's in Mr Meadows' diary now. Let's hope the situation can be resolved amicably. Thank you again. Goodbye.'

The whole conversation was over in less than a minute. Reg Martin walked from his desk through to the little reception area where Louise, at twenty-two his eldest daughter, was busy churning out invoices from a computer. Her efforts would probably be in vain. The company was insolvent and it would take tens of thousands of pounds from debtors to be paid within days to prevent the firm's creditors, especially Her Majesty's Revenue & Customs, from issuing a Winding Up petition in Court. The forthcoming meeting with this Mr Meadows was probably the firm's last chance. He looked up at the old black and white photo of himself and his late wife Nancy and his eyes filled. What a happy day that had been, the day they had moved into their new premises almost thirty years ago. Louise and Lisa, still at sixth form college, were still sparkles in his eyes when that photo was snapped. If Nancy was still alive today her heart would be broken.

Bob quizzed Honey. 'So what sort of a guy was he? Could you tell anything at all?'

'Only that it seems like a small family-owned business. The daughter answered the phone. Mr Martin sounded, well, pissed off I suppose is the right expression. Like he just didn't give a shit. A man at the end of his tether. So what do you do now?'

'Quite simple. I meet Mr Martin as arranged and pretend that I'm still a Director of the Bank. See if I can dig up anything dirty to use against them.'

'That's hardly fair on Mr Martin is it. Come on now! He's travelling all the way down to London from Lincoln to meet a guy he thinks is going to solve all his problems and you're no longer able to. That's not cricket, Bob.'

Bob put his hard-nosed banker's hat on. 'No it isn't. But he might prove to be a useful ally if he's really got it in for the Bank. I'll play it by ear. Now, remind me why you excite me so much....'

Up in Wolverhampton Zia Akbar was counting his blessings – and his takings for the week. So far he had been lucky! Not as lucky as the football club he followed though. They looked doomed to relegation. Oh well, there was always next season. He was almost beginning to enjoy being an MP and if it wasn't for his own personal tricky position he would revel in it. He had already held his first 'surgery' for constituents who were asking for his help and was beginning to feel quite important. All sorts of constituents had approached him. Little old ladies moaning about how low pensions were. Young mums complaining about inadequate safety measures for their kids walking to school – a little boy had been knocked down by a supermarket 'dotcom–delivery' van on his way home from school recently. He lost count of how many letters he'd had complaining about Council Tax rises and had had a meeting with a spokesperson from a newly formed pressure group. His constituency of Staffordshire was one of the most multi-racial in the whole country and every colour and creed had come to his surgeries. The absence of political parties in the whole process had dictated that local libraries make some space available for surgeries. He had thus far only held them in his home town of Wolverhampton but he expected to hold them in other libraries in other towns across his county on a type of rota basis so that no constituent could validly claim that their MP was inaccessible. The towns of Stafford and then Walsall were next on his list. He was only just managing to keep on top of his letters and correspondence with the aid of the new secretarial pool at the House.

He had not yet made his maiden speech in the House and was wondering when his time would come. Needless to say he would steer clear of anything that was even remotely connected with immigration or asylum. It was a Friday evening and in years past he would have gone down to the local mosque for evening prayers. It wasn't that he wasn't a Muslim anymore but well, his religious habits had diluted somewhat since his residency in Britain. Besides Friday, the Muslim sabbath, was a very busy day in the Raj Balti Takeaway and before he became an MP he could not afford to employ anybody to fill his job. The fact that he now could had not prompted him to repent and attend prayers. Without realising it he was fast becoming a member of the new multi-racial middle class where money took preference over religion. Not that he was an avaricious man. Far from it. He was a generous contributor to the Commons Hardship Fund which had been set up before the Second World war to assist former MPs who had fallen on genuine hard times.

The Speaker had nominated 'Daz' Davies to spread the gospel about the Fund amongst his fellow Members and he had adopted the task with alacrity. If anybody knew about hard times it was he. Daz had achieved one hundred per cent success. There was not a Member who had not been persuaded to sign a modest banker's order. So charming were the lilting tones of the Welshman who when he put his mind to it could recite Dylan Thomas with a Richard Burton impersonation at the same time. Even Archie Murdoch from

Fife had offered twenty pounds a month. Archie would normally be hard pressed to give twenty pence to anything other than a fruit machine. Anybody who could sell the *Big Issue* in pouring rain on a wet Wednesday in Cardiff in the middle of winter could sell anything to anybody. Ten out of ten to Mr Speaker. He was already learning who could do what best in this New Democracy.

Angus McLean was also starting to feel at home in his new position. Things were starting to settle down nicely but he knew that it was only a matter of time before a crisis blew in from somewhere unexpected that would really put the new House, and its Members, to a real test. It was not long in coming – the next day in fact. A Sunday. Were it not for the fact that the House would reconvene the next day anyway the House would have had to have been recalled.

Chapter 13

The crisis started somewhere over the Mediterranean Sea north of the island of Corsica. The AirBrit Boeing 757 was at about thirty thousand feet heading almost due north for the French coastline and its onward destination of London Heathrow. It was just under two hours from home when mayhem broke out in the economy section of the cabin. A stewardess had noticed for some time that a queue had started to build up at the toilets. This was noticeable because the plane was only about half full. The sector had originated in Naples and at this time of year, before the holiday season was in full swing, this was not uncommon. Suddenly, a male passenger jumped up from his seat waving a piece of paper above his head and screamed at a stewardess in bad and broken English.

'Ere. Geev thees to the capitan...yes. Now!' He thrust the paper into her hand and remained standing, shouting at the other passengers in the toilet queue to sit down. Remaining calm the stewardess walked to the front of the economy section and through the curtain separating First from Economy and drew the curtain behind her. She handed the paper to the purser who went white as soon as he read it.

He read it again. It was written in perfect English, obviously by somebody else.

'I am an Albanian. I have two friends, also Albanian, who are right now locked into the two toilets at the rear of the airplane. They are armed with a small quantity of plastic explosive which has been fixed already onto a bulkhead joined to the airplane's fuselage. You are to order the Captain to fly to Humberside Airport not Heathrow. When the plane has landed it is to be parked on the apron right alongside the terminal building so that a jetway can be attached. The Company will receive further orders when the plane has landed. No harm will come to the plane or its passengers as long as our orders are followed.'

The purser picked up the intercom phone and spoke to the Captain.

Within ten minutes the news was flashed to the newly formed Department of UK Security (DUKS) which had been modelled on the same lines as the American Department of Homeland Security. Its Director was not a civil servant but a serving Army officer who had been seconded to the position for twelve months.

Colonel James Goodman had been at the front end of nearly all the recent skirmishes and small wars that the British Army had been involved in for the last twenty years. After serving in Iraq he had decided to resign, claiming that the Army was being reduced to a platoon of Home Guard nancy boys by a government more concerned with health and safety and political correctness than real soldiering. An adoring Press had conducted 'phone-in polls' to ask the public what they thought. Had the vote for 'Head of State' taken place a few months earlier he would have been top of the tree. But what an adoring public didn't know was that the name of the head of DUKS was a secret. Not public knowledge. Unlike the previous government's much trumpeted 'Cobra' committee which went into session whenever there was a perceived threat to the nation, DUKS met in secret. It consisted of only four men, the Director (Goodman) and a seconded officer from the Royal Marines, the Navy and the Royal Air Force. They were responsible to, and had to report to, two men only – the Defence Secretary and the Home Secretary. There were no other civil servants involved.

Goodman's code name was 'Bwana', given to him after one of his own units had wiped out to a man a renegade battalion of rebels in Sierra Leone a few years earlier. The fact that they didn't speak Swahili in West Africa didn't matter. It was the thought that counted. Bwana despised London and had set up his DUKS HQ in Imphal Barracks in York. Apart from being in his native Yorkshire it was handy for fast trains south to London King's Cross – wrong snow and leaves on the line permitting. He had reported to London every Monday since being appointed by the former Government but thus far had not met Grindlay or Usher.

The call to his mobile phone came when the AirBrit jet was still in the air over southern France. He was probably the only senior serviceman who fully grasped the situation and its implications. With Albanians involved he guessed correctly that the aim was to free over a hundred Albanians temporarily imprisoned at the Wolds Prison in East Yorkshire. Hence the request to fly to Humberside, the nearest airport with a runway long enough for a 757. They had been suspected of being involved in a newly formed terrorist cell and that their applications for asylum were a red herring. Under emergency regulations the previous Government had locked them up pending a forthcoming case in the European Court of Human Rights. That was always asking for trouble Goodman had thought. A right load of bollocks! Just bloody asking for a hostage type situation.

Bwana didn't like Albanians. He'd been shot at several times in Kosovo by Albanian mercenaries. He also remembered the infamous 'Radio Tirana' from the days of the Cold War when Europe's only communist state had broadcast the dogma of Mao and the revisionism of Lenin. It was time to hit back. Via the Home Office and the MOD he quickly managed to establish contact with Nick Grindlay and Roy Usher on secure mobile connections. He informed them both of his predictions. The Albanian spokesman on the plane would soon ask for the prisoners to be bussed to Humberside. Usher was a nice guy but this sort of thing went right over his head. He gave Goodman total discretion in the circumstances but asked to be kept informed. Grindlay was a different kettle of fish.

'The Boeing will be able to land OK at Kirmington, sorry Humberside.' The aviation anorak that he was Grindlay still called it RAF Kirmington – a World War 2 bomber base.

'There's also lots of space beyond the runway, all flat land, cabbages probably, just in case it overshoots. In fact let's make them overshoot.'

'Why?'

'That way they can't get near the terminal. In fact there isn't one anyway in the conventional sense. No walkway. Just tarmac. Humberside is very underdeveloped.'

'You mean isolate the plane – in the cabbages?'

'Absolutely. To do that you'll need to bring the plane in on, hang on a minute.' Grindlay consulted his UK airports manual. 'Runway two zero. That way in the plane is pointing straight into the countryside and open fields. Get the Captain to falsify a brake problem and deliberately take it into the cabbages at about twenty knots. It won't damage the plane much. What then?'

'Leave the rest to me Mr Grindlay. If you would be so kind. But how much fuel do you think will be left on board?'

'Probably not too much by the time they've gone up north a couple of hundred miles. Maybe ten thousand pounds – twelve hundred gallons to you. Why? Does it matter?' Maybe not. Bwana kept his thoughts to himself. He was like that when it mattered. And right now it mattered a lot.

By the time the jet had entered UK airspace Bwana was already at Humberside Airport in the control tower talking to the Captain direct. He was also talking in real time to Grindlay who was at home in Anglesey whiling away the afternoon playing Monopoly with his kids. Until now that is.

'AirBrit 209, this is DUKS, do you copy?'

The Britair Captain and his First officer were on the ball. Their Union's failure to accept Sky Marshals on board had resulted in the airline coming under the direct control of DUKS when in UK airspace. He had no option but to comply with Bwana and he knew it.

'I copy. Over.'

'What is your fuel status, position and heading?'

'Thirty thousand pounds, 51 North 2 East and bearing three five five magnetic. Over.'

Bwana spoke to Grindlay. 'Why is there so much fuel on board, I thought you said...'

'It's the VAT racket. The UK Government put VAT on AVGAS last year. So the airlines all top up overseas now and buy as little as possible in the UK. They'll have taken enough on board for the next sector – back to Naples probably.'

'AirBrit 209, this is DUKS. You are to vector zero five zero out into the North Sea and dump fuel down to ten thousand pounds then commence your finals into Humberside on runway two zero. That's an order.'

Twenty minutes later the 757 was at a standstill in a field full of kale. Ten minutes after that all the tourists just back from Capri, Amalfi and Pompei were in the terminal building relieved that the 'brake problem' had been a minor one and were praising the airline for having the good sense to land at a safe airport in the countryside.

All three Albanians were dead. South Humberside wasn't the Balkans but the principles were the same. Bwana slept soundly that night.

The general public would never know what had happened. After the plane had come to a standstill all the passengers had executed an emergency exit down the yellow plastic slides. The three Albanians waiting for their compatriots to join them for the journey home never saw them again. Six minutes after landing, Army special forces had detonated huge amounts of plastic explosives under both wings igniting what fuel was left and turning the plane into a fireball.

Grindlay was amazed. 'Congratulations, Bwana. I have only one complaint. I've got shares in AirBrit.com.'

'And I've got shares in Boeing. They'll just have to buy another one.'

On the Monday afternoon Her Majesty had requested that she met her Home Secretary and Defence Secretary. It was probably more daunting for her than the two men, they being commoners in the truest sense of the word. They arrived at the Palace in time for afternoon tea as was the Queen's custom. After the initial rather stiff formalities conversation soon became easy. Grindlay was the most apprehensive fearing that an overly curious corgi was about to pee on his right shoe but it soon trotted off when no biscuit was on offer. Her Majesty opened the dialogue.

'Jolly good news about the aeroplane wasn't it. No home casualties. Just one elderly jet that was soon to be replaced anyway I hear.' Neither Usher nor Grindlay were sure whether it was a question or a statement. Not that it mattered. She asked them both about their families and how they were enjoying the House. It was all over in twenty minutes and they departed for Westminster feeling a little puzzled. She rang for her personal equerry.

'Pass on my best wishes to Colonel Goodman will you. A good show. Tell him I'll roast a simba in his honour.' She chuckled at her own little Swahili joke. One of her grandsons had been trying to learn Swahili. She didn't know what the word for a unicorn was but she would try and find out.

After supper that evening Her Majesty telephoned the President of the United States. He had recently had his wristwatch stolen in Tirana when Air Force One had made a goodwill stopover and he had glad-handed a section of the welcoming crowd. Some welcome. He was mighty pleased with 'Betty's news. Served those assholes right. Just as well it was a Timex not a Rolex. Or even a Rado!

Chapter 14

Business resumed at the House the next day as if nothing had happened. There was just a report in the papers that a passenger jet with a mechanical problem had diverted to Humberside and that a quick thinking pilot had saved many lives. There was not even a vague inference to terrorist connections. Usher wanted to go public as a deterrent to others not to hijack British planes but the security services were adamant that the message would get back when the Albanians failed to return. In the meantime extra facilities were being set up at Humberside Airport to deal with any future incidents. If possible all planes in that kind of trouble would be diverted there. It was away from the glare of publicity tucked into a corner of England that rarely made the news. Bwana set up a facility there for his own team's use – just in case. Nothing that would set alarm bells ringing. Just a small office away from the public terminal with secure lines to the rest of the outside world. And a hanger for a chopper.

Angus McLean was keen that the projected legislative programme be adhered to – national emergencies apart. Immigration had been sorted out thus far and next in line was money! The Finance Bill. Taxes still had to be raised and the Government still had to pay its bills. McLean was wondering how Meadows was getting along and summoned him to his office. Meadows could just do without anything from McLean at the moment. Not that he didn't wish to do his job, far from it. But he had just got his final pay details through from the Dogger Bank plc and the meeting later in the week with Mr Reg Martin from Lincoln was uppermost in his mind.

The latest figures from the Treasury had shown that the economy was still growing fast so all things being equal taxes were still coming in commensurate with that growth. What had riled him (and most of the public) were the huge numbers of so called 'stealth taxes' that had crept in. He wanted to abolish as many of them as possible during his four years in office. He might be fiscally out of pocket during that time but the more friends he made the better his chances of picking up some juicy directorships afterwards. In the meantime it was McLean who was asking the questions.

'So, Bob, is the new Finance Bill anything like ready? You know – to be put to the vote?'

Meadows lied, knowing that McLean was not a money man. 'Nowhere near I'm sorry to say. Still waiting for lots of answers from the Treasury. Stats on manufacturing, productivity, inflation – you name it in fact.'

'Are we talking days or weeks?'

Meadows lied again, knowing that most of the answers were already on his desk. 'Weeks I'd say – maybe six.'

McLean was genuinely appalled. 'But Sir Michael has expressed a wish that the Finance Bill is next to go through.'

'Just tell him that so fundamental are the changes in the taxation system being proposed that I need another two months. Say up until the summer recess.' On that point Meadows was telling the truth. But he didn't tell McLean that he needed the time to shaft the whole banking system and one in particular. Only he and Honey and the duvet knew about that. So far.

McLean consulted his diary or in his case a huge year planner on his wall and marked off a week in early July for the Finance Bill. This was tiresome. He would have to bring something else forward to fill the gap. But what? It was far too early to bring in anything remotely controversial. The RADO system had to be seen to be working in the public eye. Then out of the blue he had a brilliant idea.

The old system of Private Member's Bills had fallen into disuse, mostly because so few such Bills became Acts as there simply wasn't enough time for them within the legislative programme. Every time an MP had come up with something half decent that had broad appeal in the nation something went wrong. Either the Member himself gave up or the Government couldn't find the debating time in the House or something. Almost every Member had a bee in their bonnet about something. Maybe, with only a hundred and two Members, time could be found for every single one of them to have a Private Bill within the four year term of office. There would always be some who would decline he thought. Maybe their names should go into a hat, a sort of 'baby Rado' to determine whose should go first for possible inclusion into the Statute Book? He would run the idea past Sir Michael as soon as he could. In fact he would call him now and arrange a meeting as soon as possible. He did so and they agreed to meet the next morning over coffee at Sir Michael's Whitehall office.

To his surprise and disappointment Angus McLean found Sir Michael only lukewarm at the idea.

'The problem, my dear Angus, is that all sorts of cranky ideas might come up and who knows what, or who, might be behind them in reality.' He had a point. 'Do you remember that awful Radio 4 phone in programme where a Government MP actually volunteered to bring a Private

Member's Bill on any subject voted for by the listeners? Of course it had to be stopped – totally out of the question. Totally! Suppose that little tart from Essex – what's her name...?'

'You mean Chloe Ledger?'

'Yes, her. Just suppose she wanted to legalise street prostitution for example. Westminster would look like Bangkok at night. Dreadful. Just dreadful.'

Unlike Sir Michael, McLean had actually been out on the town in Bangkok and several other Asian cities when his golf club had organised a different kind of 'matchplay' on a Far East tour a couple of years back. Men only of course. One or two of the younger members had come back with an embarrassing rash as well as a tan but overall he thought it had been a good crack. He immediately started to hum to himself the old pop tune by Murray Head called 'One night in Bangkok and the world's your oyster.' Somebody had once told him that it was about street vendors selling illegally produced Rolex Oysters but it sounded like one of those highly improbable 'true or false' pub quiz questions to him. The problem was it was just the daft kind of question that could be 'true'.

'I suppose it could be open to abuse. Like say a big corporation paying a Member to promote a Bill in their own commercial interests you mean?'

'Precisely. Just imagine for example that a company illicitly paid a Member a bribe to bring in a Bill making something that they manufactured compulsory. And that company had a monopoly or say a Patent on that product?'

'Like what?'

'Well, I don't know exactly...but I'm sure that there must be something like...' Sir Michael was starting to lose the initiative so McLean pressed him.

'In any case the Member's name would have to come out of the hat so no company was going to bribe a Member on a one hundred and two to one chance. That would be commercial folly.' He told him about his 'baby-Rado' idea. Sir Michael started to mellow a little. Maybe the idea had some merit. He promised to think about it seriously and said he would get back to him at the weekend after he had consulted the legal and constitutional experts. In point of fact there was only one person he was going to discuss it with.

Sir Michael took afternoon tea with Her Majesty that same afternoon and with the pleasantries and social niceties over in minutes he launched into his sombre, pious, hand wringing mode that only a British civil servant could make look half respectable.

'Ma'am, I think I've come up with something that your subjects would find most attractive....'

That's what she liked about the Permanent Head of the Civil Service. So reliable and so sensitive to the real issues at stake. She gave him carte blanche to get the ball rolling and organise a press conference. The Great British Public would soon start to take more interest than ever in the affairs of Parliament. Arrangements were made. 'Baby-Rado' would perform on live TV just before the draw for the next round of the FA Cup. It was decided that two Members' names would be selected every month when Parliament was in session. The newspapers were having a field day again and every Member was bombarded daily by a hungry press wanting to know what Bill they would introduce if their name came up. Who would it be? Everybody would have to wait.

In the meantime Bob Meadows was getting ready for his meeting with Reg Martin from Lincoln. The Finance Bill was not even on his back burner. He had other fish to fry and they would all be caught on the Dogger Bank. His lower lip curled at his own little joke.

Chapter 15

Most Members called it a day at lunchtime on Fridays. Most had a long way to travel, particularly those from Scotland and Ulster. Bob Meadows waited slightly anxiously for Mr Martin. Sometime between their second and third coital union that previous night Honey had persuaded him to come clean about his Directorship of the Dogger Bank. Reluctantly he had agreed but he wanted to suss him out first. He didn't have long to wait. Martin was early as he had got an earlier train than expected.

The lobby of the Russell Hotel was almost deserted and mutual recognition was swift. Reg Martin wore a smart dark grey suit. His eldest daughter had insisted. 'You don't want to look like a schmuck, Dad, and nothing too funky either, OK?' Reg Martin considered himself to be a fairly 'with it' sort of guy but whilst he thought he knew what a schmuck was the adjective funky was lost on him. When the same daughter had dropped him off at the station in Lincoln in one of the firm's vans and had added he looked 'cool' he was even more confused. It was, he thought, quite a mild day and he had decided not to take a top-coat. If anything he felt rather warm. Oh well.

'Mr Martin? Bob Meadows – how do you do?'

'Reg Martin – pleased to meet you.' Meadows grinned to himself. After two months of a proletariat Parliament he was used to hearing the northern version of 'how do you do' more often than not.

At Honey's suggestion Bob Meadows had dressed down slightly for the meeting. Gone was the pinstriped suit and waistcoat to be replaced by his Sussex Cricket Club blazer of which he was immensely proud. He'd played as a junior at county level and surprisingly it still fitted him after all those Dogger Bank expense account lunches. Reg Martin was impressed when he asked him about the badge on the breast pocket. It broke the ice instantly and Reg felt less in awe about the whole occasion. Bob steered his guest through the lobby to the left and into the magnificent brasserie which, like the rest of the hotel, had been returned to its former glimmering glory.

They took a table in the corner. Not that there was anybody around to pry. Four blue-rinsed elderly ladies were cackling at another table. Looked like a birthday lunch or something. It was a quiet time with everybody winding down for the weekend. They both ordered a beer whilst looking at the simple but pleasant menu. Lamb cutlets for Meadows and Cumberland sausages and garlic mash for Martin.

'So, Mr Martin. Your grievance against the Bank. How might I be able to help you?'

Reg Martin's obvious sincerity and meticulous detail for facts took Meadows completely by surprise. He started by telling him about the firm's origins and how he and his late wife Nancy had scrimped and saved to get the firm up and running. He explained how Lincolnshire was a notorious area for hard water and how in addition the run off from excessive use of fertilisers into the local water supplies in that primarily agricultural county had given a boost to their business. Clean water was the name of the game. Martin's Water Systems Ltd. had increased its turnover by a margin of no less than thirty per cent every year since incorporation over twenty years ago. They had started manufacturing water softeners suitable for domestic as well as industrial use and some years ago had moved into much bigger premises assisted by a Dogger Bank commercial loan secured not just on the factory but also on the family home. The Bank had insisted on this added collateral as well as personal guarantees from himself and his now late wife. The firm had prospered immeasurably in recent years thanks to a multitude of contracts from various local authorities wishing to install softeners and purifiers in schools, hospitals, nursing homes and the like.

Meadows listened but was puzzled. 'I don't get it! The bank grants you a new loan and your family gets richer. Where's the rub?'

Martin sighed a long one as if to poise for a verbal marathon. 'Well, it all started when we went into the Bank for the annual review. Things were going very well but the only hiccup was those new contracts with all those local councils.'

'Problems? With councils? They're blue chip – they have to pay their bills.'

'Yes, within thirty days according to statute but, well, in practice we could wait ninety days or more and some of the contracts were so juicy that we couldn't start the next one until we'd been paid for the previous one. The average value of those contracts was about ten thousand and we were maybe doing one a week but the cash flow went haywire.'

'So you asked the Bank to increase the overdraft facility? That shouldn't have been a problem. Not with payments from councils.'

'Well that's what we thought we should ask the Bank to do but before we could start to even ask he was reaching for a glossy little brochure which he passed across the desk to me. It was called "Sail Forward with Dogger Factors" and there was a logo of an old fashioned schooner in full sail heading for the Dogger Bank.' Meadows knew instantly what it was. Dogger Factors Ltd. was a wholly owned subsidiary of the Bank and it made millions of pounds a year towards Group profits. Over fifty million last year if his memory served him correctly. He kept shtum and let Reg Martin continue.

'Anyway, the manager said that by signing up to a service from Dogger Factors all our problems would be solved. Apparently it works like this. When the job is completed you assign the invoice to Dogger Factors who then pay you seventy per cent of its value up front. They then collect the money and...'

Meadows knew what was coming next almost verbatim but he let Martin continue with his tale of woe.

'All went well for a few months then one Friday Lisa, my youngest, went to the bank to cash some wages cheques. The cashier refused – there was insufficient funds in the account! She went back to the office and phoned the regional office of Dogger Factors. They said they would telex funds through that same day and they did. There was no explanation for the hiccup at all. Then a couple of weeks later the Bank bounced several cheques to suppliers and we started to really worry...' Meadows knew exactly what was coming.

'I contacted the three biggest councils that we did business with and they all asked us to deal direct with them on account of problems with Dogger Factors. So we did. We had no option. Then out of the blue we got a letter from Dogger Factors saying that they were closing our account with them as we had broke the contract! At that point we were still owed over a hundred grand as far as we know. We still don't know exactly where all the money is. It seems to have been lost in some huge black hole. The bottom line is that the firm is now insolvent and the Revenue are threatening to Wind us Up in Court within a month unless we pay up to date PAYE and National Insurance. It's a nightmare.'

The food arrived at the table which took the heat out of the conversation and the waiter brought two more beers.

'We brought in some fancy accountant to investigate who said that the whole thing was a total mess. He said that in his opinion we had been sold the "wrong type" of factoring contract and that we were doomed as soon as we signed up to it. How were we to know? We just trusted the Bank!' Reg Martin could hardly eat, so upset was he and reached for a handkerchief.

'I'm so sorry. Years of hard work for all this. We'd just patented a new domestic combined filter and softener too – a world beater, a gem. It would have sold by the million if only we...'

Meadows decided it was time to come clean. 'Reg, sorry, may I call you Reg? I have a confession to make. I am no longer a Director of the Bank. I was effectively dismissed as soon as I became an MP. The bank has treated me very shabbily.'

He told him how his wife Honey had lured him to London on false pretences in the hope that they might be able to help each other – a common enemy and all that. He told Reg how he would get his own back on those bastards and how he would do his level best as Chancellor to bring about their downfall.

'Reg, I notice you've brought what looks like a overnight bag with you...'

'Yes, if time allowed I was going to pop over to Ealing to see a relative I only see once a flood. Why?'

'Come back to Brighton with me instead and stay as our guest. I'll call Honey now. We'll put a few plans together.'

Between them they would put a scheme together, firstly to save his family firm and secondly to sink the whole Board of the Dogger Bank plc if not the bank itself. It might take a year or more but between them they would do it. If the Chancellor of the Exchequer couldn't do it who could?

Reg Martin smiled for the first time in months and suddenly bangers and mash never tasted so good.

Chapter 16

Sir Michael had discussed the arrangements for the new Private Member's Bills with the Speaker at some length. They too had met over a very late lunch and their discussions were becoming more streamlined, so well were they working together. They were probably the two most important men in the whole country in the New Order of things but being modest individuals by nature they didn't realise it at the time. One person did though and Her Majesty was only too painfully aware just how much she depended on them. The coffees were arriving and Sir Michael then broached the Private Member's Bills in more detail. The Draw for the first two names was to held on Monday at 1:30 pm and by arrangement with the Football Association the two former England managers whose task it was to pick the matching teams for the next round of the Cup would also be asked to perform a similar task for the Private Member's Bills. It was the Queen's idea and it was her way of trying to make modern politics as popular with her people as possible.

Sir Michael leaned forward across their lunch table as if to say something semi-private. 'It is Her Majesty's wish that the first two Member's Bills are sensible and well, you know, in the greater public's interest.' McLean recalled Sir Michael's incredulous and somewhat snobbish remark about the legalisation of street prostitution and grinned. It was a damned shame he wasn't a full Member. He'd bring in a Bill forcing all Scottish pubs to open twenty-four hours a day just to upset some little tossers in the Free Presbyterian Church he'd had a run in with over some planning dispute on his land. He grinned inwardly. Now that would open up a social chasm between England and Scotland! There would be mass migration of Englishmen to the Borders where they could nip over to Scotland for a forty-eight hour bender at weekends. Now there's a thought. The clinking of a spoon as Sir Michael stirred the sugar into his coffee awoke him from his temporary daydream.

'Right then, I'll send out an e-mail to all Members within the hour informing them of the arrangements and to be prepared to introduce their own Bill should their name come up. It might be quite interesting. We have some unusual characters in the House, that's for sure.' Sir Michael didn't comment, sipped the last of his favourite Kenyan filter coffee and bade him farewell and a pleasant weekend. Angus McLean repaired to his office to prepare the mass e-mail to all Members. Many of them would be home by now. They all had computers installed at home at the taxpayers' expense to facilitate speedy communications and McLean guessed correctly that over the weekend many Members would be giving consideration to their own Bill. It would all be very interesting he thought.

Five hundred miles to the north-west, on the geographical periphery of the United Kingdom, the twin-engined passenger plane from Glasgow City Airport was about to commence its final approach into Stornoway, the principal town and capital of the Isle of Lewis. The plane was full, not a single spare seat. Commuters who worked in Glasgow and surrounding Inverclyde were going home for the weekend. All the passengers were in a jovial mood and looking forward to seeing their friends and family and just generally chill out after the hectic pace of the working week. That is all the passengers except one. Hamish McIver, the Member of Parliament for the Hebrides, was close to tears and staring forlornly out of the window down at a cold grey Minch that divided Lewis from the Scottish mainland. Weeks earlier the American inspired health scare on farmed salmon had caused the price to drop to less than a pound a pound. A year earlier it had been as high as three pounds. His family salmon farm business was in deep trouble and he knew it. His wife Shona had been on the phone during the week in a distressed state sobbing her heart out. They had received a letter from the bank informing them that unless matters improved financially in the short term then the bank would have to consider putting the business into receivership. How different it all was from a year ago when smoked salmon became within the price range of millions. Supermarkets and drugstores sold oodles of 'smoked salmon and mayo' sandwiches every day in the triangular plastic cartons that every office worker seemed to clutch together with a bottle of designer water. Today? Today salmon was left on the shelf as the eco-brigade's message came across that farmed salmon was polluted with mercury, cadmium, radioactive isotopes and anything else that sounded as if it had come from a leaking nuclear power station. It was all so unfair. His salmon farm was washed clean by the chill waters of the north Atlantic tides twice a day and he wouldn't hesitate to feed his own fish to his own kids twice a day every day. Any justified criticism pertained only to salmon farms in relatively still and calm waters – most of them in Norway not Scotland. But such was the influence of the internet these days that once a wrong message went out to consumers it took forever to put it right. It didn't seem to work in reverse.

The 'bong bong' of the seat belt sign jolted him back to the present and he snapped his belt on. Ten minutes later and he was inside the terminal where Shona was waiting for him. She had picked him up every Friday since he had become an MP. They hugged and kissed a little longer than usual as if both didn't want to say anything. Two minutes later they were in the family Jeep and heading south for Stornoway town itself and the dormer bungalow that was the family home at the top of Goat Hill Road. Twelve minutes later they pulled into the drive to be met by son Andrew aged twelve and daughter Ailsa, eight. And the family dog – a border collie bitch called Mollie. The kids, and dog, had been shopping in town with neighbours while Shona had been at the business all afternoon. They employed more than a dozen men and women and she had been in tears when she told them that their jobs were in danger as the bank was getting anxious. What she didn't know was that there had been a Recorded Delivery letter arrive about lunchtime and that the same neighbour had had to sign for it.

Shona was half way through cooking Hamish's favourite supper (after salmon) of local venison casserole and dumplings when there was a soft knock on the kitchen door. It was the neighbour clutching the white deluxe envelope that was franked and bore an Inverness postmark dated the previous day. She knew by the small printing on the back that it was from the Regional Office of the bank. In total dread of its contents she placed it on the wooden dining table that dominated the open style kitchen and carried on as if nothing had happened. She was in total denial. Five minutes later Hamish walked in, refreshed after a wash and a change of clothes. He spotted the envelope immediately.

'Hello – late post eh?'

'Aye, Maureen's just brought it round. Came earlier apparently. She had to sign for it. Leave it till later eh dear?' Her voice trailed off into infinity and Hamish sensed her nervousness.

But Hamish McIver wasn't that sort of guy. He reached for a sharp kitchen knife and slit open the envelope holding it up to the light so he could read it without his reading glasses.

'The Bank, with its Registered Office at Lombard Street, in the City of London do hereby demand the full and immediate repayment of all outstanding loans, overdrafts and all unsettled letters of credit etc. etc. etc.' It was a Formal Demand from the bank. The Dogger Bank plc.

Shona was inconsolable and later she cried herself to sleep, her Gaelic auburn tresses awash with tears from both of them. It was the end. They would lose everything – the business, the house, cars, pensions. Everything. Bloody banks!

Chapter 17

It was a different picture down in Brighton. Things were looking up. After getting Bob's phone call that Reg Martin was coming to stay overnight Honey had thrown herself into the hostess role. She had freshened up the single guest room and switched on the electric blanket to air the bed. Would they eat out as usual on a Friday night? No, she thought. She would make an effort to entertain. Besides it would be good practice for hosting the forthcoming social soirées that the Chancellor's wife would be expected to host sooner or later.

They arrived by taxi from the station shortly after six. Honey showed Reg up to his room and pointed out the guest bathroom, towels and the like. He changed into more casual clothes and a quarter of an hour later the three of them were sipping glasses of wine in front of the gas fired imitation log fire in the drawing room. Honey had decided on simple fare of mushroom soup with warm baguettes and a beef goulash helped on a little by the addition of one of those Jolly Handy brand packet sauce mixes. That bit was her little secret.

While the food was getting to the aroma stage the three of them discussed the day's developments. Reg was quite happy for Honey to be privy to everything. Bob retold the whole story as far as he knew it but he needed to know a bit more.

'So, Reg, did you submit a formal complaint to Dogger Factors? You know, to the Head Office?'

'Oh yes, and all seemed to go well at first. I even got a letter from the Chief Executive saying that he had appointed a Director on the Board to review my case and...'

'Don't tell me. He came all the way to Lincoln to see you. Let me guess his business card said that he was the Risk Director?'

'How on earth do you know I mean to say...'

'It was standard procedure at Dogger Factors. Probably still is.' He topped up Reg's glass with more wine. 'You see, Reg, that was all part of the delaying process. Don't tell me he was a really nice guy... promised to report sympathetically to the Board... wrote you a nice letter starting Dear Reg... wrote to you again three weeks later to apologise for the delay but he has been abroad on business and that the matter was in hand... then nothing for weeks... then finally a Dear Sir letter denying all liability? All told about ten weeks since you first complained. Am I right?'

Reg Martin was staggered. Meadows had got it right almost to within a day. 'But what's the point of all that game playing? Why not deny liability straight away for God's sake?'

'Because, Reg, Dogger Factors will have known just what dire straits your firm was in. They would have access to all sorts of information like whether any of your creditors had obtained Judgements against you in County Courts. A phone call to the bank itself would give them your bank balances – don't forget they are both in the same Group. That so called Risk Director came to see you for two reasons. Firstly, to delay the whole thing and secondly to assess the chances of your firm being Wound Up by one or more of your creditors before any action you brought against them succeeded.

Sounds unbelievable doesn't it but believe me that's exactly how it works. Exactly. You didn't stand a chance, Reg. Not a snowball's chance in hell. At least not until now.'

Honey clicked her fingers so hard she almost broke one of her expensive nails. 'Come on boys. Din dins.'

Reg sliced his baguette right down the centreline like he was filleting a herring and buttered both halves liberally with Lurpak butter – his favourite but now banned from the table by his two daughters and replaced by some white looking tractor grease with an Italian sounding name. Honey smiled. She'd tried to put Bob on the same stuff herself but he had also rebelled. Maybe it was a man thing.

Bob recommenced the tack. 'So, Reg, did you also complain to the Bank itself as well as Dogger Factors?'

Reg looked surprised. 'I did, verbally, to some little tosser in a call centre somewhere. I didn't ever see my old bank manager again. Apparently he has been superseded by something called a 'lending team' now – in Peterborough I think. To be honest I hung up. I could barely understand the person I was speaking too. It used to be Geordie accents usually but I couldn't decipher this one.'

Meadows interjected. 'The old Sunderland call centre closed six weeks ago. It is now in Bangalore, India. It cut staff costs by eighty per cent overnight.'

Reg had stopped laughing now and slurped the last of the excellent soup from the bowl, wiping the rim with the last crust of the baguette. 'So what do I do now? Cave in? The Revenue will only wait so long then serve a Winding Up Petition. I can't defend it. There is no defence.'

'How much do you owe them?'

'About eight grand plus interest.'

'Is there any spare in the account?'

'None. But on top of that the bank has now issued a Formal Demand, so effectively the firm has no bank account anyway.'

'It's standard procedure, Reg. They try to get you in no man's land – then wallop! If a creditor doesn't Wind you Up then the bank will. Wammo! Seen it a dozen times. Dogger Factors earns a cosy fortune for the Group as a whole and it's almost regarded as a licence to print money.'

'So how come it doesn't get into the press like when the bank got done for mis-selling investment Bonds? Isn't this mis-selling as well?'

'It sure is. But it's usually small firms that suffer. The bank wouldn't risk the wrath of say ICI but your little firm is fair game. Little firms don't have the sort of money needed to take a big bank to the High Court and they know it. And even if you did and you won the case the bank would instantly lodge an Appeal. Then you'd have to find another thirty grand or so to contest the Appeal. And all the while they know you don't have that sort of money!'

'So what on earth are we going to do?'

'Reg, we will put together a package of measures that will buy the firm a lot of time. Trust me. Also, we can lodge a complaint against the bank itself. So far you've only responded to Dogger Factors. Factoring companies aren't actually regulated by any official body – that's why they get away with murder! But the Bank is regulated by the Financial Services Authority who can fine them tens of thousands for mis-selling. On top of that the Financial Ombudsman can order the bank to compensate your firm up to a hundred grand...'

'With respect, Bob, they can't. They can't assist Limited Companies – it's outside their remit and...'

'Did the Bank tell you that?'

'Yes, I had a letter to say that...'

'Reg, the Bank lied to throw you off the scent. You swallowed it hook, line and sinker my friend. So have hundreds of other small companies. If the firm's turnover is less than a million then the Ombudsman can help you and...'

'It was about a half a million last year.'

'Then just relax. You will have your day I promise you. The Ombudsman can and will help you. By the time we've finished with them they'll wish you banked somewhere else. Now, tell me more about that new water filter you patented.' Honey brought in the main course and started to serve it out. It was delicious and three clean plates later they settled with coffees back in the drawing room. The new all singing, all dancing 'ProAqua' filter was obviously Reg's little baby. For ten full minutes he waxed lyrical about how a combination of reverse osmosis, ion exchange and a new anti-bacterial injected ceramic core had resulted in his dream product. It looked a bit like one of those new stainless steel thermos flasks that were all the rage and it weighed just less than half a kilo. About a pound of bananas to Tony Marconi. Well fed and watered they retired at about eleven o'clock.

Reg Martin slept like an asylum seeker on maximum benefits.

Chapter 18

The next morning Reg took a convenient train up to Victoria, paid a quick visit to the relative in Ealing then headed for King's Cross. He was home in Lincoln by tea time. Daughter Lisa could not believe the change in him. Maybe he'd met some fancy woman!

Down in Brighton, Honey was tidying up the breakfast pots. 'Are you listening, Bob? I forgot to mention last night. I checked your e-mails for you. There are two new ones in your inbox. Are you listening?' He wasn't actually. Just giving a creditable impression of listening – like most men. She teased him. 'So what did I just say then?'

'Snails for tea or something.' He was teasing her now and she swished him around the head with a tea towel. Snails was his pet euphemism for e-mails. 'Who from?'

'One from McLean and one from Hamish McIver. Who's he anyway?'

'He's the Member for the Hebrides. Nice chap – had a dram or two with him one night when I went out of my way to meet some of the Scottish Members. I didn't want any of them to think that a Sassenach Chancellor was going to usurp them in some way. You know how sensitive our

Caledonian cousins can be. I suppose I'd better take a look myself.' He threw the racing section of the *Daily Express* onto the coffee table and walked into his den cum office off the hallway. It was a man's world in that hundred square feet of chauvinism. On one wall were autographed photos of Ted Dexter and John Snow, both former Sussex cricket heroes. On another wall was a Pirelli calendar and a black and white print of Marilyn Monroe. A ship's decanter of finest port finished off the 'men only' message that was taken as read by anybody who entered. Even Mary, the daily help, felt uncomfortable in there.

Bob flicked the switch on his computer and waited for it to boot up, the red anti-virus logo dominating the screen for several seconds whilst all the spam sandwiches and viagra offers were scanned for bugs. He clicked onto 'Outlook Express' for his mailbox and waited. Sure enough, just two messages. He clicked on the one from McLean first. The subject matter simply said 'Private Bills' and he spent three minutes digesting its contents. All Members would be expected to introduce a Private Member's Bill during the four year term of office in the interests of the whole country and that the names of the first two MPs would be decided by a draw on Monday lunchtime at the same time as the FA Cup draw. Meadows laughed out loud. He might not have laughed if he'd known it was Her Majesty's idea. Not a bad idea though he thought. Not bad at all.

He clicked onto the second message from McIver. The subject matter had said simply 'Please help.' Meadows read McIver's message three times. He couldn't believe it. Another firm was being shafted by the Dogger Bank plc. A minute later and he accessed the database of all Members' addresses and phone numbers and called McIver direct at his Stornoway home. Fortunately he was in and Shona was out with the kids and Mollie the collie. Hamish's voice was not his usual happy chirp.

'Bob, thanks for calling back. I'm in desperate straits. We could lose the business and the house, everything. I'm just so...'

'Hamish, just calm down OK? I think the bank has issued the Formal Demand as a sort of precaution, just in case this salmon scare doesn't blow over and...'

'Bob, I know you were a Director until recently and therefore you know how the Bank works but, seriously, this scare will not blow over for months. If at all. Three other farms have folded already. It's just terrible. My two biggest customers have cancelled long term contracts – both supermarket chains that I cannot afford to lose. I just heard today... I haven't told Shona...sorry, Shona's my wife...I think she would have a breakdown.'

'Hamish, I'll level with you. It doesn't look good. But you have to keep your wits about you. And you have to be prepared to lie to the bank OK?'

'Like how?'

'Like this. Call their Regional Office in Inverness on Monday morning – ask to speak to Mr Ronald Forsyth's seceretary – and tell them that all your corporate customers are awaiting the outcome of forensic tests before entering into new contracts. Tell them you're optimistic and that with prices so low you've had an e-mail enquiry from a Japanese sushi firm in Kagoshima called ANS Inc. that supplies the Junko Shimada chain throughout Japan. Get a pen, write it down.'

'But that's not true and I can't...'

'Hamish just do it. First thing Monday morning.' He repeated the details. 'Then meet me in my office at two o'clock at the House and we'll put some plan together OK?'

'OK, Bob, and thank you. I owe you one. See you on Monday then. That's junko as in junk bond is it? OK. Thanks again. Bye.' Hamish McIver had never heard of Kagoshima let alone Junko whatsitsname but it sounded very impressive. Already he felt a little better. He would try and relax with

Shona and the kids over the rest of the weekend and looked forward to seeing Bob Meadows on Monday. He knew that if anybody could help him it would be Bob. Not a bad chap for a Sassenach. Aye!

Bob settled down to watch the racing on Channel Four. Sod the Private Member's Bills. And sod the Dogger Bank.

Chapter 19

Monday morning and the start of a new week. The whole country was quite excited all over again by the new draw on live TV. For the public it was the real start of the New Order – when real people get to change the way the country was run.

There was a stiff tailwind blowing down from Iceland and his feeder-jet from Stornoway to Glasgow allowed Hamish to connect with an earlier than anticipated shuttle to London Heathrow. He was in Westminster by 12:45 and decided to drop into Bob Meadows' office ahead of the arranged time. With luck he might be in. He was and Big Ben was just striking the hour when he knocked on the door of the old fashioned but adequate Chancellor's office.

'Morning Hamish, or good afternoon rather.' They shook hands. 'Good flight?'

'Aye, quicker than normal but a bit turbulent thanks to a freezing tailwind from Iceland.'

'Nothing good comes from up there does it? Remember the old Cod Wars? What a bloody carry on that lark was.' Right now all that worried Hamish was the salmon war.

'So, Hamish, how did Mr Forsyth take to your new opportunities in Japan?'

'He was impressed I can tell you! That Junko Shimada bit floored him. It floored me by the way as well. What is Junko Shimada?'

'It's an up-market Japanese store. A sort of cross between Harvey Nicks and Harrods. They have these incredibly expensive food halls where you can sit and eat sushi at a billion yen a gobfull.'

'How the hell do you know all this?'

'Last year a Japanese bank that was interested in a possible merger with our Far Eastern subsidiary Dogger Asia invited all the Board Members, and their wives, on a little freebie tour to the Land of the Rising Sun. You know, cherry blossoms, bullet train trip, Kyoto and all that geisha crap for the lads while the girls are away for two days at some retreat learning how to tie up a kimono knot while playing a violin and serving tea!' They both laughed.

'Well anyway, the last day was completely free to ourselves and Honey, bless her, spent a bloody fortune on my Company charge card in a Junko Shimada store on Tokyo's Ginza Strip. I've still got the receipts. She spent over a grand sterling on souvenirs in that store.'

'What on?'

'Junk, just junk!' They laughed some more. 'I couldn't help but notice the prices they were paying at the sushi bar. It was just the first thing that came into my head when we were on the phone. Between you and I, Ron Forsyth who is now Regional Director for the Highlands & Islands Division of the bank was put out to grass there about a year ago. He'd dropped a bollock on a couple of big lendings in Glasgow that went tits up and we felt it was best to send him somewhere he couldn't do any real damage before he retired. I can just see him now looking for Kagoshima on his Encarta World CD Rom and wondering what ANS Inc, stands for!'

'What does it stand for?'

'I made it up – let's call it All Nippon Sushi shall we – if ever you get asked! Now, seriously Hamish, you do not have to worry about the Bank for a long, long time. Trust me. Before I forget, did you and Shona give the bank personal guarantees on the business loans?'

'Sadly we did. That's why we could lose the house eventually. I remember the day we signed and posted them only too well.'

'You posted them? Why?'

'We were due to fly to Inverness to sign them and everything at the Bank's Regional Office but the weather was terrible – force ten gales – and the flight was cancelled. They ended up posting them to us the following week. We signed them and posted them back. Why?'

'Who's a lucky boy then? Those guarantees are not legally binding! They must be signed and witnessed by a Bank Officer at the time they are executed!'

'What? The bank never mentioned that. We just took it as read that...'

'Well of course the bank wouldn't tell you that! But even Forsyth will know it. Even he's not that daft. That's why he's sent the Formal Demands early. He knows the guarantees are worthless and therefore your own house is not at risk.'

'The bastards. I'll phone them and tell them what I think and ...'

'No don't. Keep mum. In the meantime we'll spoon feed him some more sushi shite so that he won't touch the salmon farm either. Has the bank got a debenture on it – you know fixed and floating assets larky?'

'Aye. Does that matter?'

'Not yet but it might later. But it's no problem in the short term OK? Trust me I'm a banker!'

Suddenly there were rapid knocks on the door and Angus McLean burst in almost out of breath. 'Ah, Hamish, there you are at last. Congratulations!'

Hamish looked puzzled. 'The draw – you know, for the Private Member's Bill. Yours was the second name out of the hat! Didn't you watch? Got any ideas? Regional aid for poor depressed Scotland I think would be in order don't you?' He winked out of sight of the English Chancellor.

Meadows and McIver had been so engrossed in the merits of sushi that they had forgotten to turn the TV on. McLean departed still amazed those two had missed the draw.

'Goodness, that's a turn up for the books! All I've got to do now is introduce the Compulsory Salmon Consumption Bill and sit back and get rich!'

'Say that again, Hamish, slowly.' Hamish did. 'My dear, dear friend. You and I are going to make a fortune – a bloody fortune. Listen, give me half an hour will you while I just collect my thoughts. Meet me in the Tea Room – say fourish?'

'Aye, four it is. Buggered if I know what sort of Bill I'm going to introduce though. Any ideas?' Meadows was in a world of his own and didn't even hear him, let alone reply. McIver left for his own office.

Meadows picked up his phone with one hand and reached for his electronic diary with the other where he stored all important phone numbers and quickly dialled eleven numbers on the handset of his cordless phone. He heard the familiar ring tones at the other end then suddenly he pressed the red 'end' button to cancel. Phew! That was a close one. Can't take any chances. You never know what phones are bugged in this day and age with all the anti-terrorist precautions. He tapped the same digits in to the memory store of his personal Motorola V70, a birthday present from Honey, and pressed 'call' and waited.

'Martin's Water Systems – how can I help you?' Lisa soon put him through.

'Hi, Reg? Its Bob...Meadows. Fine thanks, yourself. Listen, can you come back down to London as early as tomorrow? Yes, that's right. There's been a development. ...Rather not say on the phone. You can? Great. Did I watch the draw on TV? No, to be honest I missed it. A Scots chap you say?' He played dumb. 'And who? The line was a bit fuzzy and the signal a bit weak from the mobile. He thought he said 'Middlesex' but wasn't sure. Tony Marconi might be making us buy our apples and pears by the pound again shortly. Good chap. One in the eye for those sprout eaters in Brussels!

Less than a mile away at Buckingham Palace, Her Majesty was taking afternoon tea with Sir Michael again. These informal little get-togethers had replaced the rather stiff and formal weekly audiences with the former Prime Minister. She so much preferred the new arrangement. She didn't have to listen to all the spin and claptrap anymore. They talked animatedly about how well things were going. Even the broadsheet press were beginning to come on side. Sterling was strong and the stock market doing fine. The Footsie 100 was heading back to 6000 again. Security matters were always a worry but she had the utmost confidence in the Chiefs of Staff and 'The Bwana' was defending Her Realm almost single handedly. She poured them both more tea.

'And I am so pleased with the names of the two Members who were picked to introduce the first Private Bills. It couldn't have been better could it? One English, one Scottish and one male, one female. How fortunate!'

Sir Michael almost coughed the last sip of tea back up. He'd missed the draw too. Not a football fan by any stretch of the imagination he had clean forgotten. 'Apologies, Ma'am, but nature had called at the apposite moment, perhaps you could enlighten me...'

'Of course, I'm sorry I hadn't realised. Mr McIver from the Western Isles was one and the little lady from Essex was the other...er...Chloe St.Leger or something. Isn't she involved in horse racing?'

For Sir Michael de la Nice, KCMG, his worst nightmare had come true.

Chapter 20

The next morning's papers all had pictures on the front page of Hamish McIver and Chloe Ledger standing side by side on the grass with Big Ben in the background. They'd both been on live TV the evening before during the six o'clock news. The BBC's political editor Andrew Marr had been detailed to speak briefly to both of them. For Chloe, being interviewed was now becoming second nature and she handled Marr like an old trooper who'd been in the Commons twenty years.

Gone was the transparent lime green top and the black wonderbra. She wore a splendidly cut pinstriped suit, white blouse and a fashionable Burberry scarf tied like a cravat. She could easily have passed for one of those high flying fund managers from one of those fancy banks that was known only by letters like BANRO or ZDZ brokers. She rounded on him straight away.

'Why should I tell you what I've got in mind for my Bill? That's my business for now see? All I'm saying is that it will be sumfink very close to my heart', and she pointed to her breasts that looked as if she had received implants prior to being nominated for one of those Jungle Celebrity TV shows. For once the usually capable Marr didn't know what to say so he backed off but he was temporarily relieved by Big Ben striking the quarter hour.

Bob Meadows was watching from his office. Suddenly he realised he'd misheard Middlesex for Miss Essex. Blimey what a turn up for the books. He waited for Marr to turn the microphone towards Hamish McIver who he had briefed well at their four o'clock meeting.

'Mr McIver, congratulations. Can I ask you what your Bill will be about? A Scottish connection no doubt. Relief subsidies for industries in distress?'

'Not at all, Andrew, not at all.' Hamish was totally relaxed. 'Do you remember the Clean Air Act of 1956 which eliminated factory smoke and grime from our cities and towns for ever? It made a healthier environment for future generations. Did it not?'

Marr grinned, he was too young to remember. 'Yes I do...very well.'

'Well I'm going to introduce the Clean Water Act. It will make it compulsory for all domestic houses in the United Kingdom to be fitted with special water filters. We just cannot have our children drinking polluted and possibly contaminated water these days. Especially with terrorists threatening to put ricin and God knows what into reservoirs. Now can we?'

'Thank you both and now back to the studio. Fiona.'

Bob Meadows smiled like a cat with all the cream. So did Reg Martin. Wasn't democracy just wonderful? Over in his own private office Sir Michael winced. Lord only knows what was coming from the Essex Girl. He shuddered to think. If Her Majesty is expecting a reform of the laws regulating the Sport of Kings she has another think coming. Oh dear me.

Young Chloe knew exactly what she was doing, at least in theory, but she needed some high powered advice that's for sure and she wasn't sure where to get it. She didn't know anybody in the House with the expertise she needed.

Where on earth was she going to get it without spilling the beans about her intentions?

Walking back inside the Palace of Westminster after the TV interview she decided to put her trust in Hamish McIver and ask him for his advice. She thought that, like her, he had the wider interests of the general public at heart with his proposed Clean Water Act. Such a public spirited notion she thought. A nice Scotsman, a family man and a person she might be able to look up to. If only she had a Dad like that to keep an eye on her. If only. She opted to give it a go.

'Hamish, er sorry – I mean Mr McIver. Can we have a little chat over a coffee. Fink you might be able to help me with my Bill, maybe and I ...'

McIver's paternal instinct took over. In another few short years his own daughter Ailsa would be Chloe's age and he knew that she had grown up in a single parent environment. In any event how could he refuse? Bob Meadows looked to have all his own problems under control in under a day. Of course he could spare some time to help somebody else. He steered her towards one of the several Tea Rooms that now catered more for the visitors to the House now that there were over five hundred fewer Members. It was her treat and she came back to the little table with two cappuccinos and some shortbreads. She thought he might like that little touch.

'So, Chloe, how can I help? I'm just as inexperienced as you, you know, with legislation and all and...'

'Yes, but I don't even drive and I need to know about motor insurance and...'

'Chloe, you need to pass your test first. Look get some lessons at weekends – does your Mum drive...'

'No, look let me explain. Remember that poor little boy who got knocked down and killed by a bogus asylum seeker earlier this year?'

'Vaguely, aye. An African or something who...'

'Algerian actually, but he had no insurance or nuffink.' She reached for her little bag and drew a tissue from it. 'Don't you see? I'm sorry I'm getting all upset.' A tear drop left both eyes and she wiped them, smudging her mascara as she did so. 'Silly old moo...now look what I've done.' She sipped some coffee and regained her composure. 'Thing is, that's what happened to my Dad...hit and killed by a tearaway in a stolen car. I can only just remember him and my little bruvver Ben was born after Dad was killed. Mum got almost no compensation because that yobbo had no insurance.'

'I'm sorry Chloe, I can recall now. That's what you said when you were first interviewed on the night of the big Draw when we all came out of the hat. I saw you on live TV not knowing that I was going to be the Member for the Western Isles myself. Because it is so far down the alphabet I didn't know until almost midnight.'

'Please help me, Mr McIver, please.' She sniffed some more, memories of her Dad exploding like a technicolour video in front of her eyes.

'How? What exactly do you want to do?'

'I want to introduce the Mandatory Motor Insurance Bill in my Dad's memory. OK?'

Tears came to Hamish's eyes too. What a little cracker this girl was. So much for Sir Michael's fear for the legalisation of street prostitution. Come to think of it 'One night in Bangkok' might do him a power of good! At least he might learn how some people have to earn a crust in the real world.

'So will you help me – please? Just between me 'n' you?'

How could he refuse. He smiled, nodded in the affirmative and munched on a shortbread. She almost jumped over the table and gave him a big hug and pecked him on both cheeks. Looks like he had a second, adopted, daughter on his hands. Ah well!

Chapter 21

Hamish telephoned Bob Meadows at his home in Kemp Town later that evening. 'How did the interview come across, Bob?'

'Just right I thought, just right. We've got some serious thinking to do now. Before your Clean Water Bill comes before the House we have a frightful amount to do. You, Reg and I will have to get together soon – just the three of us of course and outside London. You and I are now nationally recognised figures and there must never be any perceived link between us and Martin's Water Systems for obvious reasons.'

'Agreed on that one! So when and where shall we meet?'

'Well as we speak Reg is doing some costings on his ProAqua product – you know, a bit like a forecast for the Bank! Sorry to mention that, I didn't mean to...'

'Yes, I know what you mean. But look we can buy a bit more time on all of this if Chloe Ledger introduces her Bill first. But she needs help OK? She seems to be relying on me to help her with her Bill.' Hamish explained to Bob about Chloe's late father's death by an uninsured hit and run driver. Bob listened.

'The problem is a national scheme like that is probably too big a thing for any one organisation to handle. It needs to be underwritten – you know, by a huge insurance company or...'

'Say that again, Hamish, that last bit.'

'I said it needs to be underwritten by a big...'

'That's it! That's it! We'll leak the details of the forthcoming Bill to a bank with an insurance subsidiary who will mysteriously come up with a national scheme within days.'

'Any ideas?'

'Hamish, wake up my Bonnie Boy, wake up! Which big bank do you know that owns subsidiary companies in just about every aspect of finance and insurance?'

'You mean Dogger?'

'Right on! Look, my brain is almost going into overdrive on all this.' Meadows wasn't exaggerating at all. He knew damned well that insider dealing as it was called was illegal and punishable by imprisonment. But he wasn't on the inside at the moment, far from it. Another piece of a huge jigsaw suddenly fell into place in his revengeful eye.

'Listen, Hamish, I think we can stuff the Dogger Bank directors totally over this. And when I say totally, I mean each and every orifice. In the meantime you, my friend, are going to book an appointment with Ron Forsyth at the bank's Inverness office on say Friday – yes, Friday afternoon on your regular trip back to Stornoway for the weekend. Get the first train on GNER from King's Cross to Scotland on Friday morning. Got a good laptop?'

'Aye. Shona insisted for personal and family e-mails – a birthday present, before the bad news on the salmon scare!'

'Excellent. We will almost certainly have to get some fictional statistical bullshit on ANS Inc. for you to pass on to Forsyth. I'll get Honey onto it straight away OK. But the real reason I want you to meet with Forsyth is because you are

111

going to leak him some information on Chloe Ledger's Bill. He will have seen you on TV with her being interviewed by that Marr guy but nobody knows what her Bill is about yet. So you, Hamish, are gonna tell him! Unofficially of course and in exchange for the bank taking a more optimistic view of the prospects for salmon farming!'

'Will it work though? Will he swallow it?'

'Totally. I guarantee three things. Firstly, he will accept the info we give him, because, secondly he will want continuing access to the information on the Mandatory Motor Insurance Bill. You will only spoon-feed him the initial, broad brush outlines for the first meeting. Thirdly, he will be on the telephone to Head Office in Lombard Street before you have arrived at Inverness Airport for the onward flight home.'

'You sure about this? I mean...'

'Look, old Ron almost got the heave ho from the bank after those two foul ups in Glasgow. It was only the fact that his wife's family is well connected that saved his bacon. He will still be a worried man lest compulsory early retirement is dangled before him. He won't want that at fifty-four, believe me...'

'So we tell him lies about the salmon industry and lies about motor insurance?'

'No, no! We tell him the truth about the forthcoming motor insurance legislation for two reasons. One, we want Chloe's Bill to become law don't we? But, two, once genuine information has been leaked to them about something that makes them a whole pile of dough they won't be at all suspicious about the next leak. It's the next one that will be the bank director's personal downfall. Trust me. I know just how to do it!'

Hamish was more than a little perplexed by the turn of events but slept easily that night. Chloe had gone back to Chelmsford to see her Mum after the TV interview. She wanted to tell her what her plans were but also she wanted to avoid the press who were pestering her for more information. She just knew her Mum would help her with the information she needed to gather to prepare her Bill. The financial and actual insurance side of things she would leave to the nice chap from the Scottish Islands to sort out for her. She thought she might bring him a little pressie from Essex. Some nice jellied eels maybe, or some pease pudding. In the bar at the Russell Hotel the talk all night was of the Clean Water Act. What a good idea and how unselfish of McIver to think of a national as opposed to just a Scottish matter.

At Buckingham Palace Her Majesty was almost euphoric. This was just the start she wanted to her new Elizabethan Era. Ordinary people governing the nation in the interests of the whole Kingdom. Once the wider public had a taste of how just and benevolent the New Order was she would instruct Sir Michael to lay down the 'New Act of Union' and that horrid Devolution would be a thing of the past. All the Queen's corgis got an extra fig biscuit that night. But all the Queen's Horses and all the Queen's Men didn't know what was coming.

Chapter 22

The fortunes of the two male Asian Members could not be moving in two greater opposite directions. In Wolverhampton, Zia Akbar had settled down well to Parliamentary life and his Saturday morning surgeries were swollen with constituents seeking his help and advice. His business was also booming following a charity curry lunch he had laid on at The House one Friday morning, in aid of flood victims following a disastrous cyclone in Bangladesh. It had raised over £2,000 in two hours and raised his own personal profile even higher. *Hello!* magazine had covered the function and donated their fees to the appeal. He was becoming a man to be seen and be seen with. The Raj Balti was now a major hot spot for curry fiends and he decided to open a proper sit down restaurant in Westminster as soon as funds allowed. The way his luck was running that would not be long and with leases on Westminster restaurants going for a song now the future looked good – Inshallah!

He had toed the official line on the Immigration Bill. How ironic that a real illegal immigrant should be in the House at all, let alone voting for extra curbs on immigration. Still, he paid his taxes – well most of them anyway – and the country's welfare system was starting to get overloaded so why not vote like a True Blue Tory. Not that there were any anymore of whatever hue, true or false. He just kept on hoping that if ever his real status was revealed then his good citizenship would count in his favour. So far, so good.

One thing had however puzzled him beyond measure and he hadn't managed to have a word with anybody he thought might be able to help. He had looked up in Hansard, the official book of records of Parliament's daily affairs to find out what he could about Baden Powell, the old Member from his own constituency. He had found nothing! Perhaps he might ask the Speaker one day when he remembered to do so. He had been around a long time. Yes, he felt sure he was the man to ask.

In Leicester, Kareem Khan was starting to get the feeling in his waters that a dam was about to burst. The new controls on illegal immigration were beginning to bite into his profits. Over thirty of his dingy back to back terrace houses were unoccupied, the tenants having moved on after establishing themselves into the British black economy and the so called underclass. Following the horrendous human disaster of the Morecambe Bay tragedy when twenty illegal Chinese immigrants lost their lives, the clampdown on illicit smuggling of people had been overwhelming. He was tempted to sell the unoccupied houses but having in effect created his own ghetto selling them all at once would simply force the prices down – perhaps below the original purchase price. He also didn't want to draw attention to himself any more than was absolutely necessary. Because there were now only one sixth as many MPs as previously just about every newspaper in the land tended to follow their fortunes. Khan was beginning to envy Zia with his new found charitable status – the country's first philanthropic restaurateur and a fellow Asian to boot! As if his problems weren't bad enough a recent story in the *London Standard* had speculated about 'an unnamed MP' being involved in a cash for passports racket. Surely it couldn't be him. Could it? His original tracks had been well covered, not just with the greasing of palms with silver, but with the passage of time as well. All the same he felt uneasy. It was time to keep his head low. Very low. He decided to spend the summer recess abroad, well away from any prying reporters should the situation get even more squiffy. There weren't any more of those fact finding overseas junketing missions when scores of the old Members would avail themselves of all expenses paid trips to 'study this and study that' in some nice location that was guaranteed to be at least twenty degrees centigrade warmer than the UK. In the old days could you ever find an MP when you needed one during a holiday period? Could you heck! Those days were over and the modest salary of twenty-five grand wouldn't allow most new Members the luxury of the Red Sea in January or the Med at Easter. Khan decided that the south of France was sufficiently 'away from it all' and booked a villa in the little town of Agay on the Côte d'Azure for ten weeks. It would cost over ten grand but it would be worth it. Oh yes. His wife bought a little French phrase book from WH Smith's and over dinner they would practise ordering the finest food and wines in the local tongue. In fact Mrs Khan bought two of the little pocket sized books, one each, and slipped one into her husband's briefcase. He could practise on the train to and from Leicester. She hand wrote his name on the inside cover lest he mislaid it in the House. It would get handed in to 'lost property' along with all the umbrellas, gloves and scarves. Roll on the summer recess! They wouldn't need scarves and gloves in France in July.

The third Asian MP 'Abacus Alice' Tam had been deeply affected by the Morecambe Bay disaster. It wasn't just the fact they were all Chinese that upset her – she was from a very different part of China to those that had died. But what had really got to her were the plethora of unkind jokes that

116

suddenly screamed out of the ether by e-mails and texts seemingly within hours of the tragedy unfolding. A couple of weeks later she had watched David Dimbleby chair the TV programme called 'Question Time' when members of the public ask a panel of so-called celebrities their opinions on current issues. The very first question had been 'Are racist jokes ever acceptable?' and she had watched intently as one by one the panel gave their answers. The panel were unanimous that racist jokes were always unacceptable but when one of the panellists immediately told an Irish joke which had the whole studio in stitches, perhaps for the first time since she had arrived in the UK Alice began to realise that the UK was exactly that, a United Kingdom, and that jokes about the Irish made by Scots, Welsh or English were fine. Or vice versa. She remembered that back in Hong Kong it was OK for Chinese to say dreadful things about all foreigners. In fact they had derogatory slang terms for just about all non-Chinese races. Particularly the Indians whom they called the Yan Do Yan or the Dirty People. To her, and all Chinese in fact, Bangladeshis also came under this category. Not that she would ever admit to it. Maybe England and the English were not so bad at all by comparison.

Nonetheless, Alice resolved that if ever her name came out of the hat for a Private Member's Bill then she would be ready. In fact she had already started to draft the details. She would pioneer a totally new approach to the hiring of foreign workers and, furthermore, it would earn money for Her Majesty's Exchequer. Firstly though, she would do her research thoroughly and then run some figures past the approachable Mr Meadows. She would take her calculator to that meeting though. She didn't think that as a 'Gweilo' – a foreign devil – Mr Meadows would be much good on an abacus. She was right there.

Chapter 23

The diesel-powered dark blue GNER train pulled into Inverness only two minutes late –not bad for a journey of almost six hundred miles. It was just as well Hamish McIver didn't need a porter because there weren't any. Fortunately he had one of those cases that had two little wheels and an extendable handle so you could pull it along like some sort of Irish golf cart with undersized wheels. It was only five minutes walk to the regional office of the Dogger Bank plc. It overlooked the river and was a compromise between ultra modern and traditional architecture. Visually it was a hybrid of a laird's castle and a modern office building. A compromise of granite and tinted blue glass with little artificial turrets on all corners as a sop to the Braveheart mentality that still tried to pretend that Caledonia still ruled OK! Built at a cost of over six million pounds it represented a drop in the ocean of the Group's profits which had embarrassingly exceeded five billion pounds at the last count.

The automatic doors opened with a 'swoosh' and closed just as quickly behind him with a 'ping' as he proceeded into the main lobby. Just like 'Star Trek'. Scotty would have approved. The lush deep tartan patterned carpet gave under his feet like moss on a lawn in March and he noticed that his suitcase was leaving twin tracks in the pile. A roller blader would have a field day carving graffiti. He wondered how the tea trolley lady managed. Maybe they didn't have one any more what with these awful vending machines and polystyrene cups.

'Good afternoon, Sir. May I help you?' The pretty little twenty-something receptionist was sat behind a pinkish stone reception façade on which was mounted a leather bound visitors' book, complete with a very expensive looking pen laying perfectly parallel to the vertical columns dividing the open page. No sign here of a plastic Bic wannabee dangling around on a scratty bit of chain moored to the surface with a lump of blu-tac, like in all the branches of the bank that Joe Public had to use. It looked like a Parker or a Schaefer.

'Thank you Miss, er...MacPherson.' Hamish gawped towards the girl's nameplate dangling from the left lapel of her smart jacket. Why was a person's name always printed in letters half the size of Bank's logo? 'I have an appointment with Mr Forsyth. The name's McIver, Hamish McIver. From Stornoway.'

'I'll call his secretary. Please take a seat Mr McIver. But would you please sign the visitors' book first if you wouldn't mind.' She placed the pen in his hand the right way round for him and he duly obliged. He noticed that he was only the second visitor that day. She motioned towards the expensive looking leather chairs that surrounded a very ornate onyx circular coffee table and the golf cart made twin railway tracks towards it as if he was headed for the green not a table and a brief read of today's *Scotsman*. Travelling from south to north his complimentary newspaper on the GNER train had been the *Daily Telegraph* and it would be good to catch up on a bit of home news. No such luck. He had barely sat down when Miss MacPherson appeared at his side. 'Actually Mr Forsyth is free now, Mr McIver. I'll take you to his office upstairs.'

What a surprise. From the sparsity of entries in the visitors' book it looked as if the whole building was just a monument to corporate waste. A twenty second ride in a lift later he was being ushered into Forsyth's personal office. It was huge – at least forty feet square. It seemed to be divided geographically into two halves, a working half with a full sized boardroom table covered in green baize and the other with a monstrous hardwood desk on which was sat a computer flat-screen monitor and one of those executive toys of steel balls suspended on a horizontal wire. The man he assumed was Forsyth was sitting at one of those so called captain's chairs behind. Forsyth jumped up from his chair like a scared rabbit and walked from around his desk towards Hamish.

'Delighted, delighted.' They shook hands. Bankers know when to grovel even if this MP was chosen by a computer and not freely elected. This was an important moment for Forsyth although Hamish hadn't realised it. The Board in London had already instructed Forsyth to back off from the Formal Demand which they knew was invalid anyway. His orders were to be as helpful as possible with the difficulties surrounding the salmon farm and to try and ingratiate himself into McIver's confidence. Six hundred miles to the south Bob Meadows sat grinning over a cup of tea. He knew the score. The bank's directors were probably already regretting getting rid of him and wishing they had somebody on the inside of Government – just like they used to have. He hadn't passed on all his thoughts to Hamish. He took the view that Hamish would perform better if he was just a teeny weeny bit nervous. He would come across all the more genuine to the hapless Forsyth.

Forsyth wasn't sure how to open the batting so he rang for tea and biscuits to break the ice. 'So, Mr McIver, do tell me more about the Japanese Company ANS Inc. from Kago...er...Kago...er...'

'Kagoshima!' Hamish helped him along, happy to appear to be in control.

'Aye! Sounds like a dream…at just the right time too eh? I looked it up on the map. Looks like they are well placed to distribute from their homebase there and…'

'Absolutely. Look I've brought you some more details received from their marketing people yesterday. Looks like a one hundred million yen order…for starters you understand!' They both laughed at his little joke, each trying to laugh louder than the other. He removed a sheaf of papers from a zipped document wallet and passed it across the desk that was wide enough to play table tennis on. Half of it was in Japanese the rest in the Japanese equivalent of Chinglish. Honey had done a brilliant job, downloading a logo from a firm in Kagoshima's website together with some sales bullshit. The firm in question built ships but Bob Meadows had assured him that nobody at the Dogger Bank would know, let alone take the trouble to find out. He said he was a hundred per cent certain that following the collapse of the takeover talks for Dogger Asia the bank had dismissed the small team of specialist Japanese speakers. It had cost the bank over a million pounds in contract termination compensation. If the guy with an overdraft and a struggling corner shop in Little Morton on the Marsh knew where his bank charges were going he would be appalled. But that was the way banks worked in the UK.

Forsyth fiddled with the papers that Hamish had passed him and pretended to quickly assimilate the English part of the script. Then he remembered that he wasn't wearing his reading glasses so he put those on as well to appear even more deeply investigative. The old duffer hadn't even found Kagoshima on his Encarta map. He was looking near to Tokyo and Osaka for the city of Kagoshima which wasn't even on the same mainland island! Had he known that Kagoshima was the most southerly Japanese city and stuck out on the island of Kyushu he would not have made the stupid off the cuff remark about how centrally placed ANS Inc. was for distribution purposes. Kagoshima was to Tokyo what Stornoway was to London!

'Well, Mr McIver, that seems very interesting indeed, very interesting.' He never even reached the bit about Junko Shimada. He placed the documents flat on his desk, doubting if another human being would ever read them again. And then he started.

'So, how is the new Westminster shaping up? I saw you on the TV eh? With that wee lassie from Essex! Lucky you. And what about your new Clean Water Act? Very commendable I'd say, very commendable. Up here of course we take that sort of thing for granted. Aye, very much so.'

He wasn't joking on that one. Millions of litres of highland bottled spring water were sold all over the UK, such was the penchant for expensive designer water labels that were almost becoming a fashion accessory. What a missed opportunity that had been! The French had been the biggest winners with a dozen brands selling all over the world. No doubt John Didcot could tell him a lot more about unfair French competition. Even a major multi-international soft drinks corporation had recently been exposed – selling bottled Thames water in a fancy bottle with a fancy foreign sounding name. Del Boy, eat your heart out.

Forsyth continued, hesitatingly, mindful not to be seen to be too probing but anxious nonetheless. 'Eh, and about the Essex lassie...d'you ken her legislative ambitions? Her own Member's Bill. Any ideas? Off the record...I'm just interested in politics...you know.'

It was the dream opening that Hamish could not have expected in a million years. He munched the last of his first shortbread, appropriately the same make as those Chloe had brought for him in the House that time, and leant forward as if to speak confidentially. Forsyth reciprocated and bent his neck to where the net might have been.

'Mr Forsyth, I think one good turn deserves another don't you. I am most grateful for the Bank's forbearance on the salmon business... and of course, well, I don't have to tell you that this is in the utmost...'

'Absolutely, I can assure you it will go no further, I can...'

'Well Chloe Ledger is planning to introduce the Mandatory Motor Insurance Bill...'

'You don't say... you mean compulsory motor insurance... but that's already law isn't it, I mean...'

'Yes, of course it is but look how many people are killed and injured by uninsured drivers. What I think she's looking at is a national motor insurance scheme whereby every car on the road is automatically insured for third party injuries as soon as a vehicle is taxed. I think that's her angle but it will need some major financial institution to underwrite the whole scheme.'

'You mean an insurance company?'

'A bank more like, with an insurance subsidiary probably.' The trout was on the line. He played it along.

'What about Dogger Re-insurance plc? Aren't they up for this sort of thing? One thing's for sure – whichever company gets the scheme set up first will clean up! Just think of it. Forty million drivers compulsorily insured via DVLC at even a tenner a time is four hundred million quid a year! You're not telling me that un-insured losses will amount to more than a quarter of that. No way. That's three hundred million a year profit. If its twenty quid a head that's six hundred million.'

Forsyth was almost wetting himself. This information would get him off the Bank's hook up to and beyond retirement. He might even make the Board before he was sixty. He tried hard to concentrate.

'So, eh... when does Miss... er Chloe Ledger get to present her Bill? Soon?'

'Oh yes. Within three weeks I'd say.'

'Interesting. More tea? Another shortbread?'

The subject of salmon never arose again during the meeting and when they had finished they agreed to meet again over lunch in a month's time. Forsyth kindly arranged for his car and driver to take Hamish out to Inverness Airport for the four o'clock flight to Stornoway. The flight across the Minch was a darn sight more pleasant than that a few weeks ago when he and Shona had shared the misery of impending doom and bankruptcy.

After the venison supper he called Bob Meadows who was already 'on board' his flight of milk and Honey and was not best pleased to have to come in to land too soon. He soon cheered up when Hamish gave him the low-down. He suspected that by Monday morning the information would already be at the Bank's Head Office.

Chapter 24

That weekend, all over the United Kingdom, the majority of Members were making the initial drafts to their own Private Member's Bill. Some ideas were made public but most remained closely guarded secrets. Down in Cornwall Adrian Kristiansand was working on a new Gaming Bill which would force all illicit fruit machines out into the open. Talk about a poacher turned gamekeeper! But there was logic, and money, to his ideas. He'd figured that as he had a stake in over half of Cornwall's machines he couldn't lose now anyway. The steep fall in popularity of the National Lottery had been primarily caused, he suspected, by the public's deep scepticism on the so called 'good causes' that were supposed to benefit. Kristiansand's idea was to make every fruit machine in the land a source of revenue for good causes. Every machine would have a small disc attached to it nominating a specific good cause and the player would know that half of the takings would go to that end. He reckoned it would ensure a fortune for all the operators as well. He couldn't wait for his name to come up and the Bill become law. He would immediately allocate popular good causes to his own machines to maximise the take like sports facilities for kids and day centres for senior citizens. The one-legged lesbian charities wouldn't get a look in. It would be TIC-TAC-TOE all over again. A jackpot every day!

Up in Scotland Ray Grant, the Member for Renfrewshire, was busy thinking about his Bill to rejuvenate the ship-building industry. It had broken his heart to see the new Cunard liner *Queen Mary 2* being constructed in France and not on the Clyde like her illustrious forebears. His new Shipping Bill would introduce massive tax breaks for British ship owners who both had their ships built in the UK and manned by UK nationals. Not that he had anything personal against the Indian and Filipino crews of British owned ships but somehow it just didn't seem right. At least the two new carriers for the Navy were built in the UK but even they were the subject of much bickering involving the French design team who, unbelievably, were calling the shots. What on earth would Nelson have thought to that? Ray's mind flashed back to the night that RADO had effected the Draw and he remembered the painting of Nelson dying on the deck of the *Victory*. He also remembered the day he had witnessed the first launch of a new ship in the yard where he served his apprenticeship. It was in 1965 and it was called the MV *Benledi* – a fast twenty knot cargo liner for the Edinburgh based Ben Line Steamers Ltd. Aye! Those were the days and if he had his way those days would return.

Also in Scotland, Linda Ross was thinking about a new Aviation Safety Bill. As a former stewardess she was concerned that the whole issue of sky marshals and hijacking was not being taken seriously enough. Far from it. She had seen a cartoon on the front page of the *Daily Telegraph* where two sky marshals who worked for different airlines were having a chat. One was armed to the teeth with machine guns, rocket launchers and bazookas and the other had a Dennis the Menace style catapult. The words from the latter read 'I work for a budget no frills airline!' To Linda this seemed to sum up the whole issue and she was determined to try and do something about it. She had never been on a plane during an in-flight security scare when she had been a hostess but she had several friends who had. Memories of 9/11 were still fresh in many people's minds. The whole notion that some airlines would have sky marshals and others not was totally unworkable. It would soon leak out which airlines were cutting corners. No, there had to be uniformity across the industry and it had to be backed by law. A guy taking his wife and kids for a week's sunshine on the Costa Packet was entitled to the same degree of security as a businessman flying to Washington. The sooner her name came up for a Private Member's Bill the better.

Even the Mother of the House, Edith Alice Coates, was working on her Bill. She had just celebrated her 100th birthday and had a lunch party with one hundred guests to mark the occasion. It was the first time Her Majesty had sent the customary telegram to a serving Member of Parliament. *OK!* magazine had photographed the party and Edith Alice had insisted that they donate their usual fee to the local Carleton-in-Craven Cricket Club. The Club Captain had been detailed to present her with a huge bouquet after the lunch and she was quite overwhelmed. She and the Member for Somerset, Leslie Percy, had decided to jointly introduce the School Sports Field Bill. There had been much press coverage of late about cash strapped local authorities raising money by selling off school sports fields to housing developers and superstore owners resulting in many schools losing their green field sporting activities forever. Once law, the Act would make the disposal of all such land illegal. As a county ground greenkeeper Leslie Percy knew just how difficult it was to replace that type of asset. Once gone, it was gone forever. Like giving a bun to an elephant. You never got the bun back.

In County Down the Member of Parliament, Peter McGympsey, was trying his best to come up with something that had across the board appeal. With no official political parties anymore there were no party political points to prove. The New Order made the old one look positively prehistoric in the province. Ordinary people were just getting on with their lives again. He had seen Hamish McIver announce his Clean Water Act and he rather hoped that he could come up with something equally as appealing to the whole Kingdom. He didn't know about the wider picture of course, let alone the revenge that was about to be taken against the Dogger Bank, but he would try his best. He decided to consult his colleagues from the other Six Counties. Maybe they could jointly put something useful together and arrange for the first of them to come out of the hat to formally introduce a Bill. That seemed a good idea to him. He would phone them over the weekend. In the meantime he would nip down to his favourite pub in Donaghadee - Grace Neil's. It was jazz night tonight and the female vocalist did a great tribute act to Ottilie Patterson - the beautiful and original 'Girl from County Down' as it said in the song. As ever it would be a good crack. Cheers!

Chapter 25

When Jesus Christ threw the grubby money lenders out of the Temple at Jerusalem round about 30AD he could not possibly have known that so many of them would have ended up in Lombard Street, London EC3 in that part of the Roman Empire called Britannia.

Most of the Head Offices of the major UK banks were located in this, the richest of streets in the Square Mile that was the City of London. Named after the Lombards, or more accurately, the Lombardis who were wealthy Italian bankers, it is London's last testament to the presence of those so called financiers and promoters of industry and commerce. In fact they were usurers and pawnbrokers whose unpopularity knew no bounds. In 1338 Edward III pledged his jewels to the Lombardis to finance his Wars against France and Henry V did likewise in 1415. They were finally banished by Queen Elizabeth the First and in doing so she rid England of a parasitic infestation that should never have crossed the Channel. Unfortunately they were replaced by a home grown version known as the London Clearing Banks.

The information received at the Dogger Bank Head Office from Inverness over the weekend had caused much excitement. So much so in fact that the Chief Executive had hastily convened a breakfast meeting for the Monday morning at 8 o'clock. Poor old Ron Forsyth had received explicit instructions that he must be there, preferably by 7:30 to brief the Chief Executive a bit more before the actual meeting proper. God, how he hated the dreaded breakfast meetings. It meant he had to travel down by train on the Sunday afternoon. As usual there was so called 'track maintenance' being undertaken on the Sunday and buses replaced the train between Kingussie and Pitlochry putting another hour on the journey. The instructions had come too late to get a flight first thing Monday morning. Still, no matter, he looked forward to the meeting as he was the lynchpin to the whole thing. He'd booked overnight at the Hilton on the Park which cost two hundred and seventy five pounds (without breakfast). Just as well the man with the corner shop and the overdraft was paying the bill.

The newly appointed Chief Exec was one 'Dan' Ericsson, a naturalised American of Danish extraction. Dan wasn't his real first name which was totally unpronounceable to most non-Danish tongues – hence the nickname 'Dan' which had stuck with him since he emigrated to the States with his family as a young boy. Despite his boyish good looks and reddish fair hair he was in fact sixty years old and the unexpected offer to become CE of the Bank had come out of the blue. He had been President of the Watermelon Bank Inc. of New York and when Dogger Bank bought it to 'add to their strategic international portfolio' as the press release had put it, he was immediately head hunted for the job in London. He had been lured with a 'golden hello' of ten million US dollars bought for when the dollar was strong and once again the man with the corner shop had picked up the tab.

Dan Ericsson was built like the proverbial northern brick shithouse like those seen at the beginning of every episode of Coronation Street. Except that in his case there was no pussycat sunning itself on a warm roof and no confectionery ads to soften the picture. He had short still reddish hair cropped not unlike an astronaut. He was known to his closest associates as Eric the Red after the Danish explorer who had discovered Greenland. He was as hard as nails, or ice pitons in his case and was totally unapproachable. His contract was performance related to group profits and if he had his way his pay cheque next fiscal year would be over twenty million – sterling not dollars. 'When in Rome' he had said to his lawyers negotiating the deal. He might as well have said Lombardi. Elizabeth the First would have thrown him back across the Po or even the Styx if she could have managed it. If only.

The meeting commenced at ten minutes to eight as all those summoned were already present. The so-called breakfast of coffee and bagels had long since been served and cleared away, much to the annoyance of the CE of Dogger Re-insurance who had been delayed on his commuter train from Weybridge, where he lived in his three million pound pad. Mind you he wasn't that keen on bagels which had replaced the traditional toast and croissants since the arrival of the Septic Tank from New York. A bloody imposition he thought. He wouldn't dream of asking his colleagues not to chew gum or drink black coffee all day if the positions had been reversed. He'd been in France the previous week trying to put together a deal with a major French insurance group and had been most impressed by the absence of any meetings whatsoever before morning coffee and chocolates at about eleven. They were the most profitable insurers in the world per capita and their relaxed attitude was in marked contrast to the Americans who seemed to make the most crucial decisions at such a totally uncivilised hour. Maybe it was just New Yorkers trying to get everything stitched up before their opposite numbers in California had even woken up. Oh well.

Eric the Red formally opened the meeting. 'Good morning, guys. As you know this is not a formal meeting as such and not even an extraordinary general meeting. In fact I can tell you that it will not even be minuted and no notes are to made by anybody here present. Do I make myself clear?' Everybody nodded.

'Right. We'll get straight into it then. Ron, I'd like you to give us all a fifteen minute rundown on what you know to be coming on that young lady's Bill... you know the broad from Essex County with the big fun bags...'

Ericsson was unfamiliar with normal London bank etiquette, in particular that normally observed for meetings whether ordinary or extraordinary. The CE of 'Dogger-Re' as he was known inhouse, was not totally surprised however. He'd only met the American once before and that was simply an exchange of meaningless pleasantries at the welcoming cocktail party the Chairman had laid on for him and his awful wife several months ago. It was her first visit to 'Ingerland' and it had showed. She was the daughter of a New York press baron and was totally out of place anywhere outside of Noo Yawk. She had not endeared herself to any of her husband's new colleagues, but like she had said to him afterwards – 'Hun, do we have to actually live here? Maybe you can commute and come home weekends?' Dan had reminded her that Concorde had stopped flying and that it was out of the question. She would have to put up, shut up and just think of the dough they could make from the Limey bank in the next two years! So she did.

Ron Forsyth cleared his throat and began. This was a big moment for him as he had not been at Lombard Street since the investigations surrounding his bad lending and the subsequent formal reprimand. He made sure that he looked at each one in turn as he told his story which he had practised on the train the day before. The position he adopted was a cross between a friendly old fashioned bank manager, which he used to be, and a salesman of the next best thing to sliced bread. He spoke slowly for maximum effect.

'Well, Gentlemen, as you all probably know by now the hand of fate has seemingly delivered us an opportunity that only occurs once in a normal career. At a routine meeting with the Member of Parliament for the Western Isles, Mr Hamish McIver, he just happened to mention that the Member for Essex was intending to introduce a Bill in connection with compulsory motor insurance being purchased whenever a car is taxed. A sort of add-on if you like. This would ensure that no car was ever uninsured – well not if it is taxed anyway and...'

The CE of 'Dogger-Re' interrupted him. 'Excuse me, but that is a huge undertaking, are you trying to tell me that we should...' He didn't finish. Forsyth cut him short like a rapier which did not go unnoticed by Ericsson.

'Yes, we, that is Dogger Group should effectively have the scheme ready before the formal announcement – i's dotted and t's crossed. Then after, say, a notional twenty-four hours we can do a press release to say that we have come up with the answer. We'll leave the rest standing! Like a stalled automobile at the start of the Indy 500.' He had practised that last bit carefully just in case Ericsson thought that Formula One was something that was added to kids' toothpaste or something.

'The finite details will of course take some time to research but you chappies can no doubt get all the info you need from the Bureau of Motor Insurers vis-à-vis the statistics for the number of claims they had to deal with for uninsured accidents. DVLA in Swansea will provide up to the minute details on vehicles, registered owners and a host of other stats you will need like medians of drivers' ages, sex, geographical spreads etc.'

The CE of Dogger-Re had brought three others with him – his immediate deputy, the Operations Director and the senior Risk Director. Within seconds they had started to mutter to each other and Ericsson knew they had taken the bait. To a man they were all on seven figure bonuses and their flared nostrils were already sniffing the truffles just below the surface of the Promised Land.

Ericsson took control. 'Well, guys. Do we have a winner here or what?'

Half an hour later the insurance men were on their way to their multi-million pound offices in St. Mary's Axe just along from Lloyds of London and opposite to where the old Baltic Exchange used to be before the Provisional IRA blew it up. They were already mentally counting the following year's bonuses. For a laugh they had each secretly written on a small folded piece of paper the bonus figure that each thought would prove to be correct and these were sealed in an envelope and secreted safely away. The one who was nearest to the right answer would collect ten grand from each of the other three. This was going to be a stroll but much work had to be done in the next three weeks. Two of them cancelled planned holidays to make sure the project would be finished before 'Miss Essex' stood up in the House.

Eric the Red was in an unusually jovial mood and congratulated Forsyth on a good presentation. This little Scottish Limey wasn't such a dummy as his staff file had suggested. He suspected that he might have been the victim of English public schoolboys ganging up on him in the Boardroom. OK so the guy had a couple of lendings that went bad. So what the heck! Back Stateside if a banker didn't lose money from time to time then he sure as hell wasn't lending enough! He decided to take Forsyth for lunch before his flight back to Inverness. The subject of the salmon farm that was losing money cropped up.

'Shit, Ronnie. Look, just mark a £100k overdraft for that Mac...er...what's his name again?'

'Hamish McIver.'

'Yeah. Just give the guy whatever he wants OK? Even if we lose the whole Goddamned lot it won't matter. Just think of the overall Group picture in all of this.'

Ericsson's smart Manhattan lawyers had negotiated his bonuses on new profits. Losses had to be absorbed by the Bank! The afternoon flight from Heathrow to Inverness via Edinburgh was most enjoyable. Ron Forsyth reflected on the last few days. What a bloody game banking had become. One thing was for sure, Ericsson was going to really need him for the foreseeable future and once McIver was in his pocket who knows what else he might be able to come up with. Thank goodness McIver was in the House for the next four years, well almost four years.

Back in Truffle Street, Ericsson was already trying to make some arithmetic sense of the upside. He had placed no less than nine calls through to 'Dogger-Re' since lunchtime asking them how they were getting along with their research. Talk about straining at the leash. Already he was picturing the summer house his ugly wife had wanted them to buy in the Hamptons out on Long Island. Yesiree! It was only a matter of time.

Chapter 26

The Bull Hotel in Peterborough is the type of place that specialises in reunions. Being centrally located in Middle England on the AI Great North Road and the East Coast Main Line railway it affords easy access from North and South. When Bob Meadows had suggested that he, Reg Martin and Hamish McIver meet there two weeks later to bring each other up to speed he hadn't realised that the hotel was the venue that weekend for the Fiftieth Annual Reunion of the Cutters Association. The place was absolutely heaving. It was the annual gathering of the former crew members of the WW2 cutters that had been borrowed from the US Coast Guards – hence the name of the association. They had been hastily converted to destroyer escorts and served on the dangerous North Atlantic run from Liverpool to Halifax, Nova Scotia protecting allied shipping from German U-boats. All the survivors were getting on in years now, all in their seventies at least with most in their eighties and some even more. Despite their frailness the finest attributes of the Senior Service were still being upheld and the Pussers Rum was flowing like the Severn in flood. At the rate they were quaffing it a signal would have to be sent to Tortola in the British Virgin Islands for back-up supplies.

Bob Meadows had arrived first and tried to fight his way to the bar for a beer. He had no sooner got there than one of the old codgers who looked like a clone of Uncle Albert from 'Only Fools and Horses' slapped him on the back.

'Blimey aren't you the new Chancellor, matey? Seen you on the telly! What about scrapping the duty on rum for us ex-matelots! 'Ere let me buy you a double Pussers to remind you!'

How could he refuse? The old sea dog poured the same amount of water into the dark brown goo to turn it into grog and handed it to the Chancellor.

'Cheers, matey. Down in two! One...two!'

Five seconds later Meadows thought he'd been poleaxed. Mind you Pussers Rum was the proper stuff, Nelson's blood and all that. Recovering his composure Bob glanced up at the ship's name on the 'Admiral's' cap. It read HMS *Totland*. Land of the tot more like. Surely that wasn't the real name of a ship? Actually it was. Formerly the US Coast Guard Cutter *Cayuga* it was renamed *Totland* on secondment to the Royal Navy. It survived the war and Hitler's U-Boats only to sink many years later after a collision in Chesapeake Bay.

His cover and anonymity blown several other old salts were wanting to say hello and shake his hand. He had to act quickly. He could not take the risk of being seen with McIver or Martin. He took a twenty pound note from his wallet and passed it to the busty barmaid 'Here love, a few more rums for the admirals, I've a meeting to get to!' Making a hasty exit to the door he was back-slapped by almost everybody and the words *scrap the rum duty!* were the last he heard before escaping into the relative tranquillity of the hotel lobby. He was fervently hoping that he had their vitality if ever he got to their age and assuming that Honey hadn't bonked him into an early grave first.

He asked the receptionist if there was a quiet meeting room available away from the rum and rabble and was offered a separate function room called Broadway. It was just along the lobby from a huge portrait of King Henry the Eighth. The girl's 'anything to help the Chancellor' surprised him. He still hadn't quite got used to the idea and probably never would. He was just heading for Peterborough's slice of New York when he spotted Reg Martin coming through the front door closely followed by Hamish McIver. Neither had recognised the other as they had never met. The introductions over, Bob walked back to the reception desk and asked for coffee and sandwiches to be sent to them.

Hamish was still very much in the dark about all this from a financial viewpoint so Bob explained to him that Reg had a major problem with the same bank. Except that in his case the bank was totally at fault but had simply denied liability for their errors that had brought Martin's Water Systems Ltd. to the verge of liquidation. So he detailed to Reg how between them they had sold the Dogger Bank a Japanese dummy and how grateful the bank was now to have an MP in their pocket.

'So, Reg, Hamish's so called Clean Water Act is the way to a fortune for all of us. Reg has patented an all singing all dancing gizmo that is the Rolls Royce of water filters and purifiers. Effectively Hamish has donated his Bill to the cause.' He explained to Reg about how the leak of the forthcoming Mandatory Motor Insurance by Chloe Ledger was hush hush and about how the goons at the bank were working hard on it, probably as they were meeting. He was right there. Eric the Red was rocking his subalterns right around the clock. Bill Hayley had nothing on him at the moment!

'So, what we do is let the bank make a killing on the insurance scheme then we leak, excuse the pun, some insider knowledge about the new 'ProAqua' which must of course appear to come from a new company totally unconnected with Martin's.' His brain was working a bit faster than the other two so he slowed down. At that moment the refreshments arrived so they had to stop talking anyway. This was dynamite.

'Reg, you need about three months to get this thing into mass production don't you?' he nodded as he chewed a corned beef doorstep.

'Yes, give or take a couple of weeks. Say early Septemberish. But where the hell will the money come from? It'll cost about two million I reckon to establish the plant, staff etc. Not to mention distribution methods. I just don't know at the moment how...'

'Leave that for now, the dosh won't be a problem. Another MP will have to help us. He doesn't know it yet but we might have to give him a stake in the whole thing. Look, in a nutshell this is the crack OK?'

Bob went into detail about how a new dummy company would be set up that would appear to be the profit centre for the whole thing. It was this company that was going to be the 'sting' and he whistled the opening bars of the 1970's movie starring Robert Redford and they all laughed. However it was the real Martin's that was actually going to make the new gizmo and make the profits for Reg and his daughters. He would have no problem raising the capital required. But the directors of the Dogger Bank were going to be invited to invest several millions of their own money into the sting company. The one that would fold like a house of cards as soon as they pressed the button! Over the next few months they all had to play their part then the grateful Hamish would have another very interesting lunch in Inverness with the equally grateful Ron Forsyth. It was simply just a question of how big a lesson they all wanted to teach the bank. All three of them had the motive and the inclination. A million? Two? Three? They decided to think about it. An hour later and they wrapped up the meeting. The station was only five minutes walk away via the Queensgate Centre – a Seventies designed mall that had recently received a complete refurbishment.

As he waited on the platform for his train south Bob could see a bridge over the River Nene. He remembered that he had once seen a 'birdman' competition on TV where eccentric Britons with balsa wood wings attached took a running jump from a jetty in a vainglorious attempt to reach the other side of the river. They all failed of course and ended up in the drink. Still, at least they hadn't done an Icarus and flown too close to the sun. Fat chance of that even with global warming.

A nice place Peterborough – and the Bull. Quite posh. Honey would like it too. He might bring her back for a weekend and a tour of the nearby Fen Country.

Chapter 27

Chloe had worked so hard on her Bill. Her Mum, Sharon, had helped her with correspondence to the Motor Insurers Bureau and DVLA in Swansea. Everybody was very helpful. 'Amazing what a fancy letterhead wiv a House of Commons portcullis crest could get you innit', she had said to her Mum. Sharon had not disagreed. She was still a trifle out of sorts with the whole thing of her little girl being an MP. Chloe had not gone along with the idea of using the £100k from the TV company to buy a bigger house nearer to Westminster and Sharon was still no nearer being recognised as a celebrity in her own right. But maybe that was no bad thing. There hadn't been any adverse publicity about boyfriends or nights out on the town about Chloe. She was a veritable choirgirl. She had put half the fee money into a Trust Fund for her brother Ben, bought thirty thousand pounds worth of Premium Bonds for herself and given her Mum the other twenty thousand. Her 'Uncle Wayne' had long since disappeared into the sunset along with his earrings, tattoo and Sierra. He'd found another 'Sharon' in another Slug & Lettuce.

The information they managed to gather from the insurers was daunting and Sharon suggested inputting it into her home computer. This she managed quite easily as she had recently been on one of those adult learning courses for the electronically bewildered. It paid off as they were soon able to reproduce statistics into a colourful visual form in the shape of bar charts and pie graphs. 'Rainbow pie' Chloe called it. They were still waiting for facts and figures from DVLA but they promised to send it by e-mail as soon as they could. When it arrived it was startling in its detail. A full account and breakdown of every licensed driver in the UK, year on year for the last twenty years. More charts and more pies. Chloe and Sharon worked on it all weekend, every weekend until the Sunday night before the great day arrived and the first Private Member's Bill of the New Order was about to be put before the House.

The press and TV commentators were having a field day trying to guess what was coming. The night before Sir Michael de la Nice had a nightmare. He dreamed that the Prostitution Act resulted in scores of hookers operating legally inside the Palace of Westminster and that within two weeks six male Members had their photos in the *News of the World* accompanied by 'kiss and tell' stories from impecunious little floozies seeking to make a lot more than their fifty quids a trick. He was so relieved when Clarissa woke him with tea at the customary 7 am ritual. But he was still worried. What was Miss Essex going to do? Why couldn't McIver's Bill have gone in first for goodness sake? Of course he didn't know about the ProAqua gizmo, let alone the coming scam on one of the country's biggest banks. In his case ignorance was indeed bliss. Sir Michael decided to watch the proceedings from the House on television from his Whitehall office. He didn't want any cameras straying in his direction, particularly after the opening speeches. He would keep a very low profile. After all he was only a civil servant and not a politician. He suspected that whatever happened Her Majesty would ask to see him shortly and it was perhaps best to slightly distance himself from the proceedings at this juncture.

Her speech written, Chloe decided to have a fairly early night. She didn't want to look tired for her big day. The proceedings in the House would be shown live on TV, satellite as well as terrestrial. Even CNN had wanted to get a 'look in'. In the Mother of Parliaments, even this was revolutionary. Before she put out her bedside light Chloe had a last, final read through her speech which was printed out, double spaced, and secured in a black A4-sized filofax type binder. At the front of it, in its own separate cellophane dust cover, was a photo of her late father with Chloe, then aged about five, sat on his knee. It was taken on a summer's day in the garden and was one of the last snaps taken of him before his horrific accident. In the photo he was wearing a dark green pilot's shirt with epaulettes on the shoulders. It was Chloe's favourite photo of him and that was why green would always remain her own favourite colour too. She slept a lot more soundly than Sir Michael.

It was just after 2:00 pm and the House was packed. Not a spare seat to be had. Stewards had marshalled those members of the public who had queued for hours into the visitors' seats. Only one Member was missing – Edith Alice Coates who wasn't feeling too well. She usually sat next to Chloe in the second row up of the A to L's and on more than one occasion the Speaker had had to stare sternly at the pair of them to stop their chattering. Chloe had been teaching the centenarian how to text messages on her new mobile phone and just before entering the House the familiar 'double-two' bleeps on her own mobile had alerted her to an incoming message. It was from Edith Alice herself wishing Chloe good luck on her big day. Chloe had texted back 'thanx luv get wel soon' then switched it off before walking slightly nervously through the lobbies and into the chamber itself.

As any viewer of 'Westminster Live' will know, the leather seats of the House of Commons are a mid to darkish green. Not bottle green but Lincoln Green. More Robin Hood than Carlsberg. Thus Chloe's initial idea of wearing her new green trouser suit was out of the question. She would have been almost camouflaged, like Mari's first outing in the House of Lords that day. Instead she had thumbed through some fashion magazines and some recent editions of *Hello!* and *OK!* to see what went well with green, if anything. She came across a stunning picture of the owner of the latest winner of the Cheltenham Gold Cup flanked on both sides by professional models representing the sponsors. Both girls were blonde, like her, and both wore jet black trouser suits with sashes the brightest emerald green you could imagine. Against the background of the greenest turf a damp English spring could produce the girls looked sensational. So, in turn, she would do too. A Hermes silk scarf in green and gold around her neck and affixed with a gold brooch replaced the sponsor's sashes. She looked like a million dollars. The House was buzzing in expectation and she could see Mr McLean fiddling with his papers and getting ready to reach for his gavel. She didn't have to wait long.

'Order, order! Order, I say.' Wood met wood sharply twice and a hush fell on the House.

'The Member for Essex, Miss Ledger, if you please!' Chloe stood up, clutching the file in both hands.

'Thank you, Mr Speaker.' Three months earlier and thank you would have been fanx. This lady was going places. You could hear a pin drop.

'Mr Speaker, fellow Members of Parliament and ladies and gentlemen.' She nodded towards the public galleries as she spoke those final introductory words.

'It is indeed my pleasure and privilege to be the first Member to be asked to introduce a Private Member's Bill. It seems only yesterday that I was standing in front of

144

cameras outside our house on the night we were all elected, or should I say selected!' She accentuated the first syllable of that last word and a ripple of laughter rang around the House. It was polite laughter and didn't even raise a single of the Speaker's million hackles. The gavel stayed where it was.

'Some of you might remember the few words I spoke that night to those journalists. I must admit I didn't remember any of them at first. It was only when I watched the video later that I realised I had mentioned my late father and how he had been tragically killed in an accident by a hit and run driver. I suppose I must have spoken straight from the heart without even realising it.' She glanced down at her filofax, her father's smiling face beaming back at her. She hadn't needed to read anything yet but the file acted as a mental and a physical prop. She continued and got ready to turn a page. Soon, she would really need those notes.

'The driver of the car that knocked down and killed my father was not insured. My mother received a pittance of a settlement from the Fund set up to cover such accidents. Life was a struggle but, single-handedly my Mum brought up my brother Ben and I to the best of her ability and Ben and I never wanted for anything.' Three months earlier and it would have been never wanted for nuffink.

'Accordingly, Mr Speaker,' and she looked directly at him, 'my Bill will introduce measures that will ensure that what happened to my mother cannot happen to anyone else in the future. Sadly, there will always be accidents – that is statistically certain –but we can make sure that every driver is insured as soon as a car takes to the road. I am calling my Bill the Mandatory Motor Insurance Bill. When, sorry I should have said, if, it becomes law, then any vehicle that is taxed will automatically be insured for third party injuries as well.' She paused for breath and wished that she had brought a bottle of water into the House with her. Already her mouth was drying up.

'This can only be guaranteed if, when a car is taxed by DVLA at Swansea, insurance comes as part of the package. It must be done then, at the point of taxation, not later when it might be too late. The new measures introduced by the last Government on the question of ensuring that all cars are taxed will also help us. The number of untaxed, and thus uninsured, cars slipping through the net will be minimal. I have studied not dissimilar schemes in other countries where the rule of law is similar to our own. For example the system seems to work well in the State of Victoria in Australia. It couldn't work however in a place like India where corruption is endemic and most vehicles are unregistered. But here in Britain where all vehicles are registered we have no excuse. The registration and associated taxation administration is already in place. It is the insurance aspect that is the biggest challenge however.' She paused again for breath and took time to turn over the page and scanned it for the bullet points she had highlighted then resumed. She reamed off a dozen raw figures that had all been supplied by either the DVLA or the Motor Insurers Bureau. The computer analysis that she and her mother had burned the midnight oil working on had not been wasted. The rainbow pies came to life before her eyes. She quickened the tempo of her delivery for added effect.

'Uninsured accidents in the last ten years – five thousand four hundred and forty-one. Deaths – eight hundred and five. Serious life threatening injuries – two thousand two hundred and twenty-one. Limbs lost-a thousand and ninety-eight. Eyes lost – six hundred and thirty-nine. Children orphaned four hundred and forty-four. Lives destroyed – incalculable! And all these figures stem from only the uninsured cases. We should all hang our heads in shame.' The entire House including the public galleries was totally silent. Almost guiltily so. An eighteen-year-old slip of a girl, a former shop assistant, was telling the whole country on live television that it had to get its Act together – literally.

146

The cameramen, normally keen to pick out a dozing MP or the Speaker scratching his nose as a diversion from the banality of most career politicians' speeches, zoomed in totally on Chloe. This was a new star in the making and they didn't want to miss one nanosecond.

'The challenge, Mr Speaker, is how best to do this. Governments are tax raisers and tax spenders aren't they? I do not think it appropriate that the taxpayer should pick up the bill for this.' She was temporarily interrupted by a 'hear hear' from the Member for Fifeshire who being as tight as duck's arse was smelling another stealth tax in the making. 'Insurance is a risk business and it is not fair to ask older, safer drivers to underwrite the lunacies of a yobbo who's just nicked a hot-hatch and is out for a spin and high on dope. So whilst the State must put in place the legalities it is up to the insurance industry to come up with workable schemes. Government can only create the conditions for that to happen.' She was beginning to sound like a junior version of the Iron Lady.

'The insurance element of such a scheme will, of course, be susceptible to Insurance Premium Tax at the rate prevailing at the time – currently five per cent. This will also benefit the Treasury. This type of cover will not come cheap. But what price peace of mind?' She nodded towards Bob Meadows sitting arms crossed on the front row of the M to Z's directly opposite. He broke into a broad smile but he was actually mentally about three miles away at that time. He was fly on a wall in a certain bank in Truffle Street.

'Other advantages may be less apparent, at least initially. One of the main reasons, I think, why so many young drivers are uninsured is because of the sheer cost of obtaining cover. As an academic exercise I recently pretended to buy insurance for a car I didn't own. At eighteen and therefore with almost no experience, I was quoted premiums of between £800 and £1,200 pounds. That is ridiculous for any working young person but for say a university student

147

it is just impossible. That is not a valid excuse for driving illegally without insurance but it may very well be the real reason. With my new scheme it will not happen. It simply cannot happen.'

There were mutterings of approval all around the House. This girl had really got into the nub of the matter.

'There will, Mr Speaker, also be changes to the timing of vehicle taxation and thus insurance. I have decided to take a leaf from the Sport of Kings. Those of you who like a flutter now and again will know that all racehorses have their official birthdays on the same day – that is 1st January. By a similar token, starting next year, all cars will fall due to be taxed on the 1st of February each year. Vehicles can of course be registered at any time but the tax will be charged on a 'pro-rata' basis and be valid only until the following 1st of February. A brightly coloured hologram disc like a circular credit card will replace the paper circles currently in use and that are so easy to forge. The colour of that disc will change every year so that a police officer, traffic warden or even a member of the public will know immediately at a glance whether or not a car is taxed and therefore insured. Thus starting next February 1st, if my Bill becomes Law, the colour of the issued disc will be red, followed next year by orange, then yellow until all seven colours of a natural prism have been used when it will thereupon return to red and the sequence will start again.' She had got that idea from her rainbow pies but did not divulge that to the House.

'For those of you unfamiliar with optics or physics that's Richard Of York Gave Battle In Vain.' The Speaker was caught by a camera counting them off on the fingers of both hands as he silently recited the little ditty to himself.

'It will thus take from now until next February to get the system up and running fully in which time any little teething problems can be ironed out. Another bonus to the taxpayer, apart from the reduction of fraud and lost revenue, will be that less Civil Servants will be required to man the DVLA.

Their only really busy time will be January in future when extra temporary staff can be recruited. It will enable them to pay off their Christmas credit card debts.

'It is anticipated that the discs will be extremely hi-tech and contain a microchip capable of being read by a hand-held scanner through a windscreen to enable a policeman or warden to verify the registered keeper within seconds. Penalties for not displaying a current disc will be severe – an automatic six month prison sentence for the first offence. I am convinced, Mr Speaker, that this scheme is the only guaranteed way to keep uninsured cars off our roads. They are a curse that can and must be eradicated.

'Mr Speaker, I understand that the previous Government was very keen on what it called Private Finance Initiatives. If the Bill becomes law then it will be up to the insurance companies to put forward their proposals. I'm looking for national discussion on the subject and for those companies interested to submit their detailed proposals within weeks, not months or years. Remember that those dreadful statistics I just recited to you are continuous, like a ticking clock.' She paused, then slowly closed the filofax as if it were a Bible at the end of a Lesson.

'Mr Speaker, the ordinary decent citizens of this land are entitled to look to the State to protect them. It is incumbent upon us to put taxpayers' lives before taxpayers' wallets. Those, Mr Speaker, are the salient points of my Bill. I commend it to the House.'

She sat down. For almost another ten seconds there was nothing but silence. It was broken by some people in the gallery starting to clap. Then all of them started. Then the hard-nosed journalists. Then all the other Members. After almost two minutes the Speaker decided that decorum had to be reintroduced.

'Order. Order! Order I say!'

Six hundred miles north Ronald Forsyth was watching on his office flat screen plasma TV that had cost the man with a corner shop and an overdraft over two grand. He was beaming from ear to ear. Hamish McIver had been spot on. His job was safe and his position within the bank secure for at least four years, possibly longer. He might even outsee Ericsson who he knew was on an initial two year contract. He took his favourite putter, a Canadian rocker, from out of his cupboard and had a few practice strokes on his office carpet. Perhaps Dan would fancy a round the next time he was visiting the Highlands & Islands Office. In fact he would suggest it to him. He wouldn't mind betting he would be on the phone very shortly. He was right.

In St Mary's Axe the four guys at Dogger Reinsurance were ecstatic. When Chloe had said that such cover 'would not be cheap' they each wished to a man that they had doubled the bonus figure that they had written in that sealed envelope for the bet between them. Any notion they might have had about trying to keep it competitive had gone out of the window. She had even said that it was urgent, 'weeks not months' she had said. Working hard they had completed the whole project only the day before. But they could hardly go public the next day. But how long would they wait? They decided to break out the last four remaining bottles of Dom Pérignon '52 that the French insurance giant they had visited recently had given them as a little souvenir. Each bottle was beautifully presented in a box made from solid hand-rubbed French walnut which looked like the dashboard of a Jaguar in the days before they were mass produced for Mondeo Man. Only the champagne truffles were missing.

In Lombard Street EC3 Eric the Red was on the telephone to his ugly wife. It was ten in the morning in Manhattan and she had just risen. She had a three hundred dollar appointment with her hair stylist at eleven and a five hundred dollar a plate charity luncheon at twelve to raise money for some underprivileged kids' school in the Bronx. Gawd how she hated those charities for those kinda schools.

Full of spics and drug peddlers. Still it went with the job as a senior banker's wife and she wanted to maintain their social status for when Dan came back Stateside permanently. She answered the phone on its tenth ring, her finger nails still glistening with wet polish.

'Yeah. Who is it?'

Eric launched into his bonanza routine. 'Hun. After your stoopid spic lunch go take a ride on the Long Island Expressway. Take a bank car and driver. Hun we are gonna make a bomb! Start looking for properties in the ten to twenty mill bracket. We are gonna be in clover!' After he hung up he danced a little jig – more the Lombardi than the Lambada.

Chapter 28

The evening newspapers were sensational in their praise, not just for Chloe but for the whole new system of Private Member's Bills. Since New Year's Day when a tiny child had been run over and killed by an uninsured asylum seeker the general public had been crying out for something to be done. And here it was in a brand spanking new twenty-four carat Bill. Nobody spoke against the Bill in the House. The vote was one hundred in favour and none against. It would now pass to the House of Lords for ratification and thence to her Majesty for the Royal Assent. It could be law as soon as the end of the week. The Upper House was still dealing with the fag end of some legislative crap left behind from the outgoing Government but it shouldn't take long.

Chloe had posed for both *Hello!* and *OK!* straight after the session. She made the floozies at Cheltenham Races look like they'd been hired for the day by the sponsors, which was exactly how they had been acquired from www. racingescorts.com. Chloe charged both magazines a straight £10K each to be donated to the Commons hardship fund. Nothing was for free anymore.

Hamish McIver and Bob Meadows were sharing a few drams of Isle of Jura single malt in Bob's office. 'So what do we do now, Bob.'

'We wait my friend. Just a few days I suspect. There is no doubt that the Dogger insurance guys will already have done all the work. It's just a case now of when they go public and come up with the scheme. My guess is Wednesday, maybe Thursday.' He was wrong. It was just coming up to five o'clock and he switched his office radio on to Radio Four to listen to the 'PM' programme. He was a minute too late and he had missed the pips. The newsreader was already well into the first story – the unanimous vote in the Commons.

'And a news flash just in...Dan Ericsson, the chief executive of the Dogger Bank Group, has just issued a press release to the effect that his company will be working flat out to produce the Scheme in the spirit of the new Bill within forty-eight hours. He added that, if necessary, it would be part subsidised from the Group's recently announced five billion pound pre-tax profits as a gesture of goodwill to the nation.'

Bob Meadows roared with genuine laughter. He knew exactly what type of contract Ericsson was on. It wasn't a trout on the line. It was going to be the biggest marlin ever caught on the Dogger Bank. But not yet. It was going to put on an awful lot of weight first. He picked up the phone to call Reg Martin then remembered, once again, to use his mobile. Another meeting must be arranged soon. Now that Chloe's Bill was on its way to becoming law there would only be so much time before Hamish would have to present his Clean Water Bill and they must be ready at all costs to move forward. He also had to apprise both Reg and Hamish precisely what his plans were to lure the marlin towards the juiciest bait on the biggest hook that had ever been cast. But first they all had a lot of work to do. Just to add to the pressures he had received an e-mail from the Speaker saying that the Budget could not wait much longer and that two weeks was really his deadline. Her Majesty's Revenue & Customs were keen for either the status quo to be preserved or for any new levels of duty to be programmed before the summer recess. Damn them! Bloody civil servants. Honey would have to help him. He also needed to speak urgently with Duncan Gibson, the Member for East Lothian, and the man who Her Majesty had first thought would have made a good Chancellor. Sometimes he wished it had been the other man. He sent Gibson an e-mail asking him if he could spare him half an hour the following morning. The response was swift and he suggested eleven o'clockish. That was fine by Meadows. He decided not to return to Kemp Town that night but to stay at the Hotel and perhaps gauge a few opinions from his fellow members as to what they would like to see in the Budget in a fortnight's time.

Thirty minutes later and he was having a beer or six with Dai Williams, the Member for Pembroke and Leslie Percy, the Member for Somerset.

'What oi'd loik to see in the Budget,' said Percy in his rich West Country brogue 'is some sort of assistance for sports facilities for youngsters.'

He explained to Meadows that as Edith Alice Coates had so recently become so frail it was more than likely that her School Sports Field Bill would have to be introduced by himself as they had mutually agreed that the first out of the hat would bring it in. But allied to it were some fiscal measures that the Chancellor could perhaps pop into the Budget speech as well. What Les Percy had in mind was extra Government money allocated specifically from central funds which fell outside the remit of Local Authorities so that it couldn't get lost or misappropriated. It was what the man in the street had wanted the National Lottery to do but somehow things had seemed to go haywire since that first night back in November 1994 when the whole nation had looked forward to billions going into sports facilities for youngsters. But what had happened? Had England won the

World Cup again since 1966? Had a Briton won Wimbledon? Were the Ashes safely back at Lords where they spiritually belonged? No, none of those. Skateboarding in pedestrian precincts apart, the most exercise that today's youngsters were getting was going to the fridge in between fiddling with the video's remote control. Bob listened hard and stuck a few ideas at the back of his mind for later. To do for sports what the Lottery should have done would cost hundreds of millions. Governments apart, only one sector of industry and commerce had access to that sort of dough.

Chloe's speech had taken the whole country by surprise in its content and presentation and he didn't want his speech to look second class by comparison. It would have to have some flesh on the bone and be beyond a skeletal effort. More work for Honey! He kept moving around chatting to everyone within reach. He was quite a good listener. That was probably why his first wife had given so much earache.

Dai Williams made his case to the Chancellor for a serious review of the duty paid on petrol and diesel. He asked the Chancellor if he remembered the cartoons in the papers some years earlier when the former holder of the nation's purse strings had been depicted as a Highway Robber in the mode of Dick Turpin springing out from behind garage petrol pumps with his swag-bag. The increases in the rate of duty on fuel had brought about industrial protests by drivers of the huge fuel bowsers that collected at refineries for onward delivery to petrol stations across the whole of the UK. It hadn't stopped the Chancellor though who was coining it in right, left and centre. Dai told Bob after his eighth beer that if his name came up for a Private Member's Bill he would severely curtail duty on all fuels. It just wasn't fair he said, particularly in Wales where a lot of people lived in rural areas. Bob Meadows thought long and hard about this too. It almost certainly applied to a lot of Scots too. He spotted a few of the Scottish Members and went over for a chat. Ray Grant said he wanted to see the tax incentives for UK shipbuilders brought in soon. If another Cunard Queen was going to be built he didn't want to see it coming from France again. John Didcot would certainly have agreed with him there. One news item had caught his ear that day though. The Indian Government had finally signed the deal for the purchase of new jet trainers made at the factory in his county. He would be pleased. Maybe that's why he was back up north tonight celebrating with a lot of his constituents. Laura MacDonald was in a hurry for a dinner date with a hereditary peer who had taken a fancy to her Caledonian charms and said she would call him another time. That was her third peer in as many months now. Lucky peers! Archie Murdoch who was immensely enjoying taking the Queen's shilling was adamant that he wanted to see all income tax abolished north of the border and all whisky bought in Scotland to be classed as Duty Free. Bob wasn't sure if Archie was sober and serious or just three sheets to the wind. Deciding it was probably the latter he moved over the lounge where the normally affable Tony Marconi was sitting in a huge armchair staring into nowhere. He looked deeply upset and on the verge of tears.

'What's up Tony? Are you OK?'

'I'm allright mate but I've just heard some really sad news on the telly.'

'Don't tell me. A hurricane's hit the banana crop in the Caribbean? A late frost on the strawberry crop?' Tony still looked choked and instantly Meadows regretted his attempt to cheer him up with instant humour. He sat down in the seat opposite.

'Worse, mate. It's just been announced that my hero, the Metric Martyr, has died suddenly.'

'The metric what...?'

'Remember him? Steve Thoburn, a market grocer from Sunderland. He'd been prosecuted and persecuted by the Council for selling his fruit, mostly bananas, priced in pounds not kilos. He'd refused point blank to go metric. Remember now?'

'Yes, I do too. What, he's died? Surely not. He can't have been more than forty can he? I saw his photo in a paper a few weeks ago. He lost his Appeal in a European Court or something. Are you sure?'

'Yep. I can't believe it either. I never met the guy but I'd sent a few quid up to him to help pay his fine – you know, being in the same business. He even gave me call to say thanks. Bloody Eurocrats and bureaucrats! A pox on them all. If and when I get to present my own Bill I'm gonna call it the Metric Martyr's Bill in his memory. What a crying shame for his family.' It was too.

Leaving Tony to seek solace in drink, Bob continued to seek advice from all quarters of the House. The bulk of the feedback concerned the plethora of stealth taxes that had crept in over recent years. It had been calculated that the average worker now had to work another ten days every year just to pay these extra taxes. Astonishingly, a guy now had to work from January 1st until the end of May before he started to earn anything in real terms for himself and family. That couldn't be right by any standards but what could he do to reverse the trend in his four short years as Chancellor? Not a lot maybe but he resolved to have a go. A previous Chancellor had resolved to abolish one tax for every year he was in the job. Maybe he should try and emulate him, or perhaps do even better. He would give it some serious thought. If it couldn't be done by an apolitical, non-party aligned Parliament then would it ever be done? All of a sudden Bob Meadows started to feel a great weight of responsibility on his shoulders. Shortly after ten he retired to bed. He had a lot to do tomorrow apart from starting to prepare his Budget. He had the meeting with Duncan Gibson, then depending on the outcome, he needed to speak with Reg Martin. Sometime soon all three of them would have to meet together.

Chapter 29

Duncan Gibson was bang on time for the meeting in Bob's office. He was intrigued. They'd spoken once or twice before but mostly just idle male chatter about rugby. Bob had rubbed it in about England winning the Webb Ellis Trophy, the World Cup, but much to his disappointment Duncan hadn't risen to the bait. He was more of a soccer fan if anything and wondered when his team Heart of Midlothian would ever win anything. They were the Scottish version of Middlesbrough who until recently had never won anything. Ah well.

Duncan Gibson, "Gibbo" to his closest friends, had of course been surprised when RADO picked him - just like all the other Members. He and Meadows were the only two Members with any real financial acumen if you discarded the Member for Leicestershire who just made a pile from charging high rents to illegal immigrants. However unlike Meadows who had effectively been dismissed by his former employers, Gibbo was still in full time employment as a Director of DMZ - Dalziel, Menzies and Zimmer, one of Scotland's oldest firms of Fund Managers. Established at the same address they had occupied since 1888 in Charlotte

158

Square, Edinburgh they had matured over the decades from managing funds for widows and orphans to huge Investment Trusts that were now publicly quoted companies in their own right. They managed several billions of pounds of other people's money. Following a marketing exercise into Europe promoted by Scottish Financial Enterprise in the early nineties, the DM had become DMZ when they were joined by Oscar Zimmer, a Jewish banker from Munich. Gibbo had only just joined Dalziel & Menzies and was pleased that the new face brought about a few changes. It was about time too. Those old Scottish dinosaurs were still living in Jurassic times. Zimmer brought with him a whole team of investment researchers and what was known inhouse as Team 24 – a small but welded team of investment boffins who watched the world's stock markets 24/7 as the Americans would say. Banks of computer terminals and satellite communications links replaced the old desks and telephones that were only sat at from ten until five, five days a week. Faces had changed too. Long gone were the MacDickheads and MacDuffers as nepotism was replaced by realism. The head of the Japanese section, Zeto Toshiba, had worked for the Dai Ichi Kangyo Bank in Osaka before being lured to Scotland by a high salary, free fly fishing and complimentary membership of Burntisland Golf Club. Just as well he'd never met Ron Forsyth or the All Nippon Sushi cat would soon have been out of the bag. Likewise they had specialists in North America, Europe and of course the UK. Duncan was head of the 'UK Small Companies' Section.

'Thanks for popping in Duncan. Actually, it's not the Budget lark I wanted to speak to you about. It's about raising new capital for a small company.'

Bob spent five minutes explaining to Gibbo about Reg Martin's approach to him just after the Dogger Bank had fired him. He told him everything – the Dogger Factors' involvement, how insolvency and liquidation had stared him in the face – the lot. Then he told him about the new ProAqua water filter and purifier that he had been developing that was now ready to be sold to the public. Gibbo's bright green Scottish eyes lit up like cats' eyes.

'What! And he's got it Patented? Are you sure? The full seven year Patent?'

Bob's knowledge of Patents wasn't as good as Duncans but Small Companies was his field and he had to know about these things. It was his job. 'I assume so, but I will check now you've mentioned it.'

'Yes, you must, but listen, this is really exciting, you know, what with Hamish McIver's Clean Water Act coming up soon.'

Bob played dumb. 'Oh yes, of course I hadn't realised.' He lied easily, his banking genes still lurking in the chromosomes at various locations in his own double helix.

'Wake up, Bob! This is a great investment opportunity! Does anybody else know about this? The product, I mean. Does his own bank know?'

'No, and they never will, Gibbo. Just tell me then, if Martin's Water Systems needs say, two million to put the ProAqua into full production will DMZ put up the dosh?'

'Absolutely, but it would need to have an exit route. You know. a way out to crystallise its stake into cash profits. If that can be set up then two million's a doddle. A few years down the line and the company can either be floated on the AIM or just sold outright. You know how the French are always buying anything to do with water these days.' Already Gibson was seeing two million turn into twenty in a few short years. That would do no harm to his bonus.

'So, if Martin's issues new private shares for sale to an outside investor then DMZ could be that provider.'

'No problem, in fact we would probably want to be the sole external investor if the upside was that good!'

'Splendid! Look I'll get in touch with Mr Martin and ask him how far down the line he is with his figures and projections. Shall we regroup at the end of the week?'

'Aye. Until Friday then.' He got up, they shook hands and Gibson trotted along to his own office that he shared with Linda Ross, a fellow Scot. She'd given up on Nick Grindlay who was still tomming the Welsh tart and who would soon have an even bigger family if the Defence Secretary's bazooka was still serving on the front line. Linda had soon found though that a bachelor fund manager at fifty could outperform the Footsie, the Dow Jones and the Nicki Dow on the same day if market conditions were favourable. And they usually were. They were as discreet as possible though. With one sitting in the A to L's and the other in the M to Z's it meant they couldn't play footsie all the time anyway. Linda didn't always travel all the way back to Perth at weekends. Duncan's 'wee hoos' at Cockenzie overlooking the Firth of Forth provided them with ample privacy to do whatever they wanted to do. More cock than enzie usually.

Chapter 30

The good news from "Gibbo" on the subject of investment money for the new ProAqua meant that Bob had to meet sharpish with Reg Martin. Hamish was under as much pressure from the Speaker to read his Bill in the House as he himself was to produce the Budget. First thing next morning he called Lincoln to see if he could travel up that morning. A couple of hours together should sort it. He informed the Speaker that he would be absent from the House for the whole day on 'Budget work' and took the Victoria Line to King's Cross. After purchasing a day return to Lincoln (via Grantham) he looked up at the electronic displays informing you of times and platform numbers. Damn! He had just missed a train to York that was stopping at Grantham. He would have to wait another half hour so he called Lisa Martin to tell her of the delay. She promised to pick him up at the station to save time. Bob bought a *Daily Mail* and settled down with a coffee at the café adjacent to Platform 8 that did its best to lull travellers into thinking that they were somewhere continental with their striped umbrellas, cappuccinos and ciabatta salami snacks. How different it all was now to the old days of British Rail, with big urns of luke-warm tea and sandwiches with curled up edges secreted under large glass domes that looked as if Lord Beeching had even passed them by for scrapping.

Bob turned straight away out of habit to the sports pages. His beloved Sussex were mid-table with the season about a third gone. At least football was in the summer recess period so he was spared the 'news' of suspensions, dope tests and bad behaviour of those so called stars who earned thousands a week kicking around a piece of cow's arse. In fact the balls weren't even leather anymore and were probably made from some synthetic polymer and put together in some sweat shop in a former colony on the sub-continent. Just like the Dogger Bank's new call centre. He had read somewhere else that the locally recruited staff in those centres were supplied with all the English newspapers which they were expected to read to Anglicise themselves and appear to be in the UK rather than five thousand miles further east. Goodness knows what those people must think of the Mother Country if they had read today's *Mail*. The sole front page story concerned a jockey who had been accused of deliberately dismounting his horse in order to lose the race. The story added that it wasn't the same one who had come in the Top Twenty Head of State Poll months earlier. He had been involved in a doping scam if rumours were true. This would probably give readers in Delhi the impression that the Sport of Kings in England was about as straight as the railway line up the hills to Shimla. Also on the front cover was a colour photo of a well known actress who was suing a magazine for publishing a picture of her that she considered to be unflattering. Her dress probably didn't take more than a yard of cloth to make. Little wonder that the UK textile industry was almost extinct. The reader was left with the conundrum that he or she wasn't sure whether the actress in question was complaining that the original photo depicted her wearing too much or too little.

'Bing-bong!' The public tannoy blared out a platform alteration and announced that the delayed train to Aberdeen would now leave in three minutes from Platform 1 stopping at Stevenage, Peterborough, *Grantham*, Newark, Doncaster, York, Darlington, Newcastle, Berwick, Edinburgh Waverley, Haymarket, Kirkaldy, Leuchars, Dundee, Arbroath, Montrose, Stonehaven and finally Aberdeen at seventeen hundred hours. Wow! It was a geography lesson just listening to the announcement. Bob jumped up and grabbed his paper and briefcase for the dash right across to Platform 1. He was the last person through the gate and the GNER guard who looked like a Louis Armstrong clone bawled at him –'Quicker next time Chance-cell-lor, look sharp now – all aboard!' Bob was still unused to being recognised in public and it caught him unawares as usual. He dived into the open door of Coach H which being at the end of the train was the one reserved for smokers. The train was one of the older diesel type as the line to Aberdeen was not electrified and he heard Louis Armstrong slam the door manually behind him. The new trains had electric doors. The train started to move almost immediately and he made his way towards the cleaner air of Coach G subconsciously whistling 'Hello Dolly' without realising it. He was given no less than twenty different pieces of advice on the Budget in the four minutes it took him to find a vacant seat. Reduce VAT! Increase winter fuel allowances! Put the dividends back into pension funds! Abolish inheritance tax! Reduce petrol duty! Scrap VAT on diesel! He was relieved to sit down. The train was moving quite quickly now and he could see the Arsenal football ground away on his right. The Gunners had done it again last season. He hoped his Budget would be half as successful as that Club. There was an announcement from the 'Train Manager' that the buffet car was available between coaches E and F for the sale of a variety of hot and cold snacks and beverages. The list of possible sandwich fillings was as long as your arm. The last one mentioned was a 'Thai Chicken Wrapman!' What on earth was that? Under the old British Rail it had been tea, coffee and cheese and tomato sandwiches and that was that. The Train Manager gave her name as Zoe Armstrong and she spoke with a Geordie accent that sounded as if she had been conceived somewhere on the Jarrow March. Then Bob realised that the 'man' on the end of the last sandwich filling was just a Geordie expression of speech. But even so – Thai chicken wrap? After all that bird 'flu scare in Thailand? A well dressed and genteel lady of about seventy was sat next to Bob reading the summer edition of *This England* magazine. The front cover depicted a village green with a cricket match taking place on it. In the background was a large quintessentially English church flying the flag of St.George from its spire. It was as English as it could possibly be. Only the lemonade and cucumber sandwiches were missing. If he could have seen inside the front cover he would have been informed that the scene was from Patrington in the East Riding of Yorkshire. Bob didn't know it but that village was only a couple of miles from John Didcot's egg production farm. The lady, who was from Tunbridge Wells, Kent, was totally immersed in her magazine and hadn't noticed that she was sat next to the Chancellor of the Exchequer. For that Bob was quite grateful and took out his Mail again. The journey was uneventful until the train slowed down for Peterborough. Then suddenly Disgusted, Tunbridge Wells spoke! Bob was startled – she was alive.

'Look, there it is – over there, over there!' And she pointed out a huge green dome with a tall adjacent spiky pillar alongside it. 'It's a disgrace, a disgrace! A mosque built in England. I ask you! Try getting planning permission for a new Church the size of that in green belt land. Can't you tax it or something?'

So she had known who he was after all. That was all she said during the entire journey. The train rumbled north past what was left of the old London Brick Company kilns and then past the world famous Perkins Diesels as it gathered pace. It went along the same stretch of track where the famous Mallard steam engine had set the world record steam speed of 126 mph but there was no commemorative plaque on the track. Just a little sign with an arrow pointing north that said Edinburgh 295 miles.

Bob got off at Grantham and waited only ten minutes for the onward local connection to Lincoln. Another half an hour and he was there. Lisa Martin was there to meet him with one of the firm's Citroen Berlingo vans sprayed in the firm's pale blue livery with the company's name reflected upside down in clear blue water. It was very effective even if the company was on the verge of liquidation! Didcot Eggs Ltd. wouldn't be driving French made vans, of that he was certain.

'Pleased to meet you, Mr Meadows. Jump in, it's only a ten minute drive out to the industrial estate where we are.' She wasn't sure whether he looked cool or funky in his dark suit. Not that she cared now. Her Dad had said that Bob was an 'OK bloke' and that was good enough for her.

'We really appreciate your help, Mr Meadows. Dad has cheered up no end. He was about at the end of his tether when he first spoke to your wife on the phone.'

'So Honey told me. Well, we'll work together from now on, Lisa. I got some good news yesterday but let's wait till we're all sat round the table shall we?' He caught a brief glimpse of Lincoln's magnificent Norman Cathedral before they turned out onto the western ring-road. The premises were nothing spectacular but obviously functional – single storey seventies style prefabricated sections with an apex upside down 'V' over the front entrance. No electric doors or pink stone reception desks here. This was the real world not Doggerland. Louise got up from her small desk to say hello.

'Dad won't be long – he's just been seeing one of the sales reps. Tell you what, I expect you could do with a mug

166

of tea. I'll pop the kettle on.' It was all very family. Bob felt quite at home.

Ten minutes later and all four of them were sat round what passed for the Company Boardroom table. It was actually a disused table tennis table with a big green cloth covering its entire surface. The girls had laid on some lunch for them all on the table so they could save time. There was a huge plate of fat Lincolnshire sausages bathed in fried onions, a dish of mushy peas and a big meat dish overflowing with huge straight cut chips, each as big as one of those flat shaped highlighter pens. Bob couldn't help but smile when Lisa finally brought in a big warm loaf of granary bread and a tub of the Lurpak-lookalike yellow tractor grease that Honey was trying to get him to eat. Must be a woman thing.

Reg opened the batting after he had eaten his first sausage. 'So, Bob, what news do you bring? Good I hope.'

'Better than good, Reg. Better than good.'

He told the Martins all about Duncan Gibson's almost guarantee to fund the ProAqua project. There would be a lot of work to do very quickly. He told them that Hamish McIver was under extreme pressure to bring in his Bill – they had two weeks at most. 'Have you got some figures for me yet? You know, set-up costings, unit price, distribution costs?'

'Oh yes, almost finished them.' Reg diverted temporarily from constructing a large sausage and chip butty and reached for a lever arch file on a shelf. 'Here we are then.' He put his reading glasses on and started to flick over the first few pages.

'Unit cost based on production batches of ten thousand is just over thirty-nine pounds, excluding VAT. It reduces by about a pound a unit if you add ten thousand to the batch until you get to about thirty-five pounds for fifty thousand then the exponential curve just about hits the Y axis if you know what I mean.'

Bob did know what he meant which is more than Lisa or Louise did. Bob and Reg had been at school when maths was logarithms, Euclid and algebra. Occasionally you might use a slide-rule but calculators were not even invented let alone computers.

'So, if we work on thirty-five quid max then and sell it for eighty-five quid plus VAT how much profit will fifty thousand units make? Any idea Louise?'

She held up her fingers like some sort of human abacus and started counting. 'Er about twenty-five thousand pounds – wow!'

'Lisa, what do you reckon.' The abacus reappeared.

'Wrong! That should be five hundred thousand!!'

Their father corrected them. 'Both wrong. The answer's two and a half million. Eh Bob?'

'Right, Reg. Two point five million smackeroos. That's an awful lot of Lincoln sausage!'

Lisa chirped up. 'But Dad, how do you know we'll sell them all once they've been manufactured. If it costs two million like you thought to tool up for the production and only half of them sell then we're a half a million adrift aren't we?' She was using the finger abacus again.

Bob intervened. 'Lisa, perhaps your Dad didn't fully explain but after the Clean Water Act is passed then fifty thousand units will be a drop in the ocean – excuse the pun. Another thing is the firm can't actually lose because the capital will be externally sourced on an equity basis.'

'Huh?'

'What that means is that the external financiers secure their stake by taking shares in the company, OK? But not this company. A new one that doesn't have the problems caused by the Dogger Bank. If the old one is Wound Up by a creditor then it won't affect production and profits of the ProAqua.'

Both Lisa and Louise were slowly starting to come to grips with the enormity of what Bob Meadows had told them. So was Reg who, having finished the construction of his giant butty, had now almost forgotten that he was supposed to eat it.

'But what happens then, Bob, if the new company fails?'

'It can't fail once the Act has been passed unless another firm latches on. That reminds me – Duncan Gibson asked me to check with you – is the ProAqua patented for the full seven years?'

'It certainly is. The Certificate is locked in that floor safe about ten feet behind you. The Trade Mark Certificate is with it. That's also valid for another six years at least and that can be further renewed on application. The original working prototype is also locked up. I'll show it to you before you leave.'

'Wow, Trade Marked as well! This will all add to DMZ's confidence.' Bob explained about that firm's investment in smaller companies and about how a few years down the line they opted for an 'exit route' to capture their profits. DMZ would need to take a fifty one per cent stake as they were putting up the brass but as long as Reg and the girls had meaningful personal shareholdings they were on a winner.

'Don't forget that Hamish will want a few shares for his services rendered. After all if it wasn't for his Bill you'd just be there with the also rans. Duncan will probably take his cut later from DMZ profits. I also want you to leave say twenty per cent of the shares freely available for other outside investors who think it's a winner. You'll also be taking generous salaries from the new company as well as dividends don't forget.'

Reg and the girls didn't need to know the real reason for leaving some of the shares available to outsiders just yet. In fact they might never need to know at all. It might be safer that way. Ignorance is bliss and all that.

They were all so excited and relieved that they almost forgot to discuss what to do with the old company. Bob's advice was to leave it where it was for the time being. Stuck on a sandbank! Very shortly Eric the Red and Co. would be only too willing to write the whole thing off – overdraft and all.

But they did forget to show him the ProAqua which was a snug as a bug in a rug in the safe. It didn't matter anyway because Bob knew more about rocket science than ion exchange and osmosis.

On the train back to London he passed again the point at which the Mallard had excited the whole of the engineering world and he hoped that the ProAqua would one day be recognised as an equal quantum leap in development. Had Bob Meadows been a rocket scientist he would have know that the quantum is in fact the smallest measurement known to nuclear physics and it can leap as much as it likes it is still an almost impossibly small unit of distance. He wasn't alone. It was a cliché that had been adopted by the whole of the English-speaking world.

With no Disgusted Tunbridge Wells ladies to mither him, Bob day-dreamed about the Mallard and thought back about his wisecrack in Parliament in those early days about going on holiday to the States but not bringing back any Mickey Mouse ideas. If this was America there wouldn't be a little sign saying Edinburgh 295 miles. There'd be a branch line taking visitors to Mallardland, a Mallard Motel, a Mallard Museum, a Mallard souvenir shop and a Mallard Diner where, needless to say, duck dishes would be permanently on 'today's specials' with roast mallard, barbeque'd mallard, grilled mallard, mallard Madras (if Zia Akbar was running it) and finally the ubiquitous crispy aromatic mallard (if Alice Tam was in charge). And it would all make an absolute fortune. Somebody was going wrong somewhere.

Bob got back to King's Cross and grabbed an *Evening Standard* before jumping onto the tube to Russell Square. He glanced at the headline. 'MP being probed in possible National Insurance racket.' It didn't mention any names, just the fact that somebody had leaked it out from the Commons Pay Office that two Members appeared to have the same National Insurance number.

Chapter 31

The morning had started badly for Zia when he found an envelope in his personal mail pigeon hole at the House. He knew it was an internal memo because it didn't have a stamp or a franking mark on it but did have the green portcullis logo of the House of Commons. There were several other items of mail that he could tell from the postmarks were from constituents who he was assisting with various problems but he decided to open the 'in house' one first. He sliced it open with his thumb as he walked down one of the immeasurably long corridors to the office he shared with a fellow Member. He nearly fainted when he read it and instantly gave thanks to Allah that he had opened it before getting to his desk. What if his colleague had seen it? What would he have done? Reaching his office he carefully closed the door. He was alone thank goodness. His colleague, the Member for Cornwall, Adrian Kristiansand, was not an early riser and had probably been out all night playing bandits in seedy casinos.

Zia read it again, slowly this time, and took stock.

'Dear Mr Akbar, We are sorry to trouble you in this respect but the following administrative difficulty has arisen. It may be a gremlin in our computer but we now know the reason why the payroll computer has been unable to calculate your net salary since you became a Member.'

That at least was partly right. Because he had been previously self-employed his tax affairs were by their very nature somewhat fluid and thus the Commons Pay Office had had to allocate the PAYE Emergency Code for a single person. That in itself was something of a white lie, or in his case a non-white lie, because under the Islamic Faith he was allowed up to four wives. However he had not actually declared any of them yet in fear of being declared an illegal immigrant. Would all of his wives be similarly deported? He didn't know. This had all been part of his predicament when RADO had, against all odds, picked his name out of the Staffordshire ether. What a mess! The letter continued.

'The computer has rejected your PAYE code, once again, because it has declared that you have already been paid monthly since entering the House. Further investigation has revealed that the computer has inadvertently paid Mr Kareem Khan, the Member for Leicestershire, twice over and your goodself not at all. This is because the computer has inadvertently mistaken your National Insurance number for Mr Khan's. On checking our records, however, we find that on the face of it, your numbers are identical. This is undoubtedly due to human error and the likeliest explanation is that a junior clerk in this office has mistakenly entered one number twice for different people.'

'The National Insurance number we have allocated to your name is' it was inked in by hand, 'and we would be obliged if you could advise us as soon as possible if this is correct. An identical letter has been sent to Mr Khan so it is hoped that this matter will be quickly sorted out and your back pay remitted to your account at Barclays Bank plc in Wolverhampton without delay. We thank you in anticipation of your prompt attention.' The signature of the senior Clerk in Charge was indecipherable. Weren't they always?

Zia sat at his desk, his chin in the palms of both hands, his elbows on the desk. Oh well, it had been nice while it lasted. So much for keeping his head down. On the face of it he'd had a good run, over ten years! He always knew deep down that one day his time might be up. He day-dreamed of the day he had been introduced to the "Agent" in Sylhet. The man who sold you British identity, a passport, a suitcase, Premiership programmes. Was it really any more of a con than the Dogger Bank trying to pass off its Bangalore call centre to its customers as if it were in Birmingham? But that wouldn't be his decision. Oh no. He'd be made a supreme example of illegality. He would be pilloried in the Press just like that phoney Asian businessman who'd been courted and feted at Downing Street for being the first Asian millionaire at twenty-one years of age. In his mind's eye he could see the headlines already: 'First Member of the New Order jailed for having fake nationality.' 'Random selection of MPs was Queen's error', 'Politicians never change', 'Bring back the ballot box.' Dear oh dear, why did it all have to end like this? He would almost certainly be imprisoned for the duration of this Parliament – more than three years – and then deported. His dream of the new Westminster Raj Balti restaurant would remain just that. After his deportation his case would be given a nickname like the Guildford Four or the Tamworth Two. Except that he was guilty. Fat immigration lawyers would turn his tale of woe into what they call a 'precedent' and he would probably become known thereafter as the 'Rado Reject' or something equally unflattering.

The office door opened and in strode Adrian, as happy as Zia was downcast. 'Great news, Zia! I've just had coffee with the Speaker, that's why I'm late in. He's agreed to a trial run of some fruit machines inside Westminster. Profit sharing ones for charities – you know, like I want to bring into my Bill whenever my name comes up... Zia are you listening? What's up mate?'

Zia confessed like a Catholic to a Priest. He might as well get it off his chest now. The sooner it was all over the better. Better for him and better for his family. He told Adrian about how he had obtained, or rather purchased, his bogus British Nationality from an 'agent' in Sylhet, Bangladesh. The phoney passport, utility bills, luggage complete with phoney labels – the lot! Adrian listened like a child to a nursery rhyme. He let Zia ramble on about how his father had taught him, as the eldest in a family of eight, that life after Colonial days would be difficult. The partition of the Indian sub-continent into Muslim Pakistan and largely Hindu India had brought many, many problems. Problems that not even the British could solve. After claiming the West Indies for Her Majesty, the Elizabethan ensigns had turned East and the new Jewel in the Crown had risen to add the sub-continent to the list of Gondwanalands that in future the cartographer would have to paint pink. It was not, his father had said, the fault of the British that they had inconveniently interrupted the longest of wars between conflicting religions. But sadly it was their lot to accept responsibility for the human tragedies they had caused. The Roman Empire met its Nemesis at Masada. The British would meet theirs at Masala. Specifically, chicken tikka Masala. Britain, his father had said, was fair game. He told Zia how he still considered that Britain was a decent country with decent people. Even her worst enemy, Napoleon Bonaparte, a hated Frog, had said that England was a nation of shop-keepers and allotment holders. What could be intrinsically wrong with a population that grew potatoes and onions in patches of waste ground? Zia's mind wandered back to his adolescent days in the Scouts and the picture of Baden Powell on the hut's wall. It was all very well to confess all to Adrian. Soon he would have to do it to Allah. In fact, Allah and Mr Speaker. Having accepted from Adrian that Mr Speaker was in a good mood he decided to walk the sixty yards of stone floored corridors to his office and confess all. He shook hands with Adrian Kristiansand. They liked and admired each other very much and after the initial de-briefing in that Committee Room after the 'swearing in' they had paired off to share an office in the old part of the Palace of Westminster. With the exception of Chloe Ledger they represented the first to last of the A to L's, the Akbars to the Kristiansands.

Zia tidied his desk as if he never expected to see it again, shook hands again with Adrian, and proceeded down the long corridor to the confession box. This would be partition in its truest sense. His only consolation was that he had been privileged to have been a Member of the Mother of all Parliaments, even if only for a very short time. After his sentence and subsequent imprisonment he would substitute his Seiko for a Rado so that he would never forget the short but genuine efforts he had made. After all, just as Her Majesty had requested, he had done his very, very best. That was all she had asked. He straightened himself up and knocked gently twice on the Speaker's door. 'Come in, come in!'

'Ah, Zia, I've been expecting you. One of you anyway. Please, take a seat.' And he motioned towards a battered leather sofa that looked as if every Speaker for the last two hundred years had sat on it. That's because they had.

'We guessed that one of you would come forward fairly quickly. I'm glad it's you, Zia. Coffee?'

He was genuinely taken aback. What, coffee? What, did he mean he was expected? 'Mr McLean, Sir, I do not think you understand the reason I am here to see you, Sir.' Zia's manners were always impeccable. Even a punk rocker with nose studs, facial tattoos and a haircut like a cockatoo would get at least three 'Sirs' when ordering his chicken Madras and pilau rice at one o'clock in the morning on a freezing cold Saturday night in Wolverhampton in the middle of January. At least when any foreigner learns English from a fifties style 'Janet and John' type school book they learnt proper manners. After Janet and John, Zia had progressed to Swallows and Amazons, the Secret Seven and then to Biggles books. It was no wonder that his English vocabulary was so extensive although occasionally he drove his fellow Members mad with deliberately incorrect phrases like 'up the bend' and 'round the wall'. He had introduced a new phrase in the House quite recently when the Speaker had asked him to clarify a point he had raised one day. Zia's reply that the current system drove everybody 'Harpic' that is to say right round the bend, had almost brought the house down. The speaker's gavel had taken a lot of stick that day.

'Zia, I will come straight to the point', and he reached onto his desk and produced a copy of the letter Zia had received that morning. 'Zia, this letter was not written by a clerk at the Pay Office, it was actually written by me at the behest of Sir Michael de la Nice. He'll be here in about ten minutes by the way', and he glanced up at the circular brass marine clock that was screwed onto the dark panelled wall. So that was the real reason the signature was indecipherable.

'Zia, it has been known for some considerable time that both yourself and Mr Khan, the Member for Leicestershire, had the same National Insurance numbers. Had RADO's software been a bit more on the ball then the whole thing would have come out a lot earlier but it wasn't so it didn't. RADO didn't pick it up because effectively there were a hundred and two draws. It was purely a statistical fluke that both of your numbers came out.'

At this point Zia was unsure what to say or do so he just kept listening.

'We have known now for nearly four months that one of you must have illegitimate nationality. The question was – who? After months of in depth investigation we now know.' Zia's mouth went as dry as the Deccan plateau before the monsoons arrived.

'It was Khan. Your nationality is quite in order. Khan however is now, under the terms of the last Immigration Act, an illegal resident and could be deported not just for having illegally obtained false documentation but for dealing in the organised manipulation of false work permits. The situation is still a little sketchy but we now have reason to believe from our contacts in Dacca that he somehow obtained details of your British Passport, perhaps when you were visiting relatives in Bangladesh. These details were then 'cloned' onto high quality fakes. Seems like he put one into his name as well and then took it further by assuming your National Insurance number as well. So there you go!'

Zia's brain was spinning like a kiddies top. He knew the investigators had got it completely the wrong way round.

'When all members were asked to hand in their passports recently for security checks it was all a con of course. We knew by then that either you or Khan was a charlatan. You didn't have to be Inspector Morse either to suss it out in the end which was the older and thus the genuine passport. Khan's had a BOAC baggage sticker stuck into the back cover but BOAC merged into British Airways in 1973 and as no British passports can be more than ten years old it was obviously put there as a ruse. His Passport was therefore the fake.'

Zia praised Allah that he hadn't had the spare ten quid ten years ago to buy that sticky label.

'Anyway, there's all sorts involved now. Seems like half the houses in Leicester are owned by him or his wife and they're let out to illegals paying exorbitant rents from the illegal work they do in factories and the like. Under Emergency Regulations that came into force in the last Government, Sir Michael is going to ask the Chancellor of the Exchequer to freeze all Khan's assets in the UK. The problem is we can't find him. Seems like he's gone away for the day doing some budget research. In the meantime we've leaked a little story to the Press to see if it brings Khan out of his hideyhole. We can't find him either!'

There was a knock on the door and the knocker opened it a few inches uncertain if there was anybody inside. It was Sir Michael.

'Come in, Sir Michael. I was just telling Zia you would be along in a minute. Still some coffee in the pot – milk and sugar?' He poured. 'I've just told Zia how the investigation went and updated him on the Khan situation.'

'Good. What a carry on. Look's like he's done a runner now. But the full story will probably never come out. It would be too embarrassing all round. I think we'll have to make up some story after we've contacted Khan – if we find him that is!' Sir Michael was a couple of steps ahead of both Zia and Angus McLean, both of whom looked puzzled and it showed.

'Well look, I mean we can't have a scandal in the first ever People's Parliament. Once Khan has been spoken to we'll just have to come up with some story that will satisfy the Press – you know, something like ill health and the need to live in sunnier climes. That sort of thing.'

Angus stepped in. 'So do you think that he will voluntarily contact us?'

'He might. Look, I've been thinking. Why don't we put out a story to the effect that the National Insurance number enquiry was an error at the Pay Office. We could also say that Mr Khan's departure at the same time was a pure coincidence and that his move to warmer climes was on medical advice, all Members wish him well and all that claptrap.'

Angus was appalled. 'But we can't do that, I mean it's not true...'

'My dear Angus, the last Government reduced spin and disinformation to an art form. This is a minor alteration of the truth. My guess is that Mr Khan will contact us to do a deal as soon as he hears the news. I'll work on it now. A short bulletin will go out on the six o'clock news, TV and radio. Zia, if you don't mind I have one or two other points to raise with Mr McLean.'

'Yes of course, I bid you both good morning.' He shut the door behind him and set off back to his shared office 'a free man.' He still couldn't believe his luck!

De la Nice turned to McLean. 'Did he swallow it?'

'I think so, oh yes. Like you said they were both as guilty as hell – Khan for setting up the racket and Zia for buying fake nationality. But it's like you said, Zia Akbar is just the decent sort of chap we need in the UK these days compared to most of the dross that creeps in through the Chunnel. Khan can stew – he's made his pile anyway.'

'So it's a by-election for Leicestershire then?'

'You mean a by-selection – like Chloe said in her speech.'

'Yes! And that sure was some speech wasn't it? I have to admit I was positively dreading it but what came out was startling, just startling.'

'Well, I hope we can get some more Parliamentary business concluded without undue delay. With luck Meadows will have his Budget almost ready and Hamish McIver is also about there with his Clean Water Act. By the way Sir Michael, it's slightly delicate this...but...well I was wondering if you might be kind enough to have another chat with Zia, you know maybe over lunch or something.'

'Is there a problem...I mean...are there any more slugs to come out from under the stone?'

'No, no, none to my knowledge. The thing is, speaking quite candidly here. Zia seems to have got confused with his Powells. He seems to believe that the Baden Powell who headed the Scout movement was formerly the Member for his constituency when of course you and I know full well it was Enoch Powell, the Member for Wolverhampton Southwest for so many years.'

'Good Lord, that is a tricky one! Are you sure?'

'Oh yes. Problem is he asked me recently why he couldn't find any reference to Baden Powell in Hansard. I'd recommended he do that as soon as he asked me about Powell but I thought he meant Enoch. Then he came back to me when Baden was noticeably absent.'

'Mmm. Look, tell you what, ask him to give me a call would you?' He glanced up at the ship's clock. 'Goodness, I must be getting on. I'll see to it about the broadcast on the KhanGate lark. A pound to a pinch of the proverbial that he gets in touch. Before I forget, I do like that idea of Kristiansand's about fruit machines benefiting designated charities. I don't suppose the first one in Westminster could be adopted by the East End Youth Theatre could it – by any chance?'

A wish from Sir Michael in this bizarre New Order was tantamount to a command, almost a 'Yes, Minister'.

'I don't see why not, Sir Michael.'

'Capital. Clarissa will be pleased.' Later that morning he put a little note in Zia's pigeon hole inviting him to lunch at his Club. Then he would tell him about Mr Enoch Powell.

Chapter 32

BBC Radio 2 is the world's most listened to radio station. Its most avid fans can listen to it 'twenty four seven' anywhere in the world even without a radio because it goes out live on the World Wide Web. So whether your favourite presenter is Sarah Kennedy with the dawn patrol, Terry Wogan with your cornflakes or Johnny Walker as you drive home from the office all you need is a PC and a modem.

The sun had just gone down over the Western Mediterranean and Mr and Mrs Kareem Khan were having a G & T on the balcony of their splendid apartment overlooking Agay's pleasant little harbour. The arrival of the envelope with the identical letter to Zia's in his own pigeon hole two days earlier had brought forward the departure on nofrillsairline.com to the south of France. Like Zia he hadn't known what to do for the best but with plenty of available ackers they had opted for a quick dash to the Med whilst they pondered their best way out of this mess.

Radio 2 was Mrs Khan's favourite station and she had wasted no time in setting up a PC with stereo speakers that could be directed into the main lounge or out through baronial style windows onto the large balcony. It was about a quarter to seven local time, an hour ahead of London, and they were both listening to Johnny Walker's 'Drivetime Show'. It could never be as good as Radio Hong Kong's 'Bumper to Bumper' programme hosted by the late Bob Williams but it still attracted millions of listeners as they drove home from work to their boring suburban lives. The Khans had listened to Martin Shankleman's financial report at five twenty-five – nothing out of the ordinary there – the Footsie up three points and gold up a penny a metric tonne and then Johnny moved on to the Mystery Voice competition. He played a short snippet of a celebrity's voice every day and listeners were invited to phone in and guess who the voice belonged to. Two attempts were made every day with £10 being added to the prize value each time until somebody guessed it correctly. It was sometimes infuriatingly difficult with the voice sounding somehow so tantalisingly familiar but usually incorrect. The most recent mystery voice had reached a record prize of £370 until it was won only the day before. The voice, saying 'but never mind' had been that of the late Mary Whitehouse, the campaigner for less sex and smut on TV and radio. What price a Mary Whitehouse these days? A Queen's ransom?

Today was the start of a new voice and the prize was only a miserable tenner. Johnny Walker played it for the first time – 'Order, order, we know where you are!' The Khans froze in horror at the instant recognition of Angus McLean's voice. It was Mr Speaker! The game was up.

Ten minutes later the 'Six o'clock News' announced the resignation of an MP on health grounds. It was Kareem Khan, the Member for Leicestershire. Sir Michael went 'live' to announce, with regret, Mr Khan's decision to retire early had been taken on medical advice and with the best interests of his family at heart. 'The House wished him and his wife well and their thoughts were with them.' What a road of cobras.

The BBC's political editor, Andrew Marr, gave a short comment that this would precipitate the first by-election of the New Parliament. He had forgotten Chloe's correction. In any event he was wrong. There would be two 'by-selections' but he didn't know it yet.

Kareem Khan had a short discussion with his wife. He'd been rumbled but it looked as if the Establishment wanted to paint over all the cracks. Just like the old days then really! A sort of Mutton Report but without any mutton. He would put in a call to London tomorrow admitting his guilt, off the record of course. Still, it could be worse – he could really be ill. At least most of his ill-gotten gains were accessible in his Jersey account. And he'd also had the forethought to secrete a few grand into an account with Credit Agricole SA at their Agay Branch. Life would not be too bad. There was also the rental income from the rows of terrace houses in Leicester. Or so he thought. He did wonder what would happen to Zia Akbar. Almost certainly he would have to find exile abroad somewhere – or even go back to Bangladesh. You didn't need a lot of moulah to live like a Maharajah or even a Sultan there these days. Oh no, Sahib! But of course Khan never knew about the whitewashing of Zia's position either. He would just forever wonder what had happened, or rather not happened, for the rest of his days. Mr and Mrs Khan made plans to stay in Agay for the foreseeable future. Why not? It seemed a nice agreeable, warm and wealthy spot and after a few sessions on the WH Smith's phrase books they had even made a start on the local lingo. Bon chance mes amis!

Chapter 33

'Order, order!' The Speaker's gavel came crashing down. Some sad news had filtered down to London overnight and thus far only the Speaker was privy to it. Edith Alice Coates had passed away quietly in her sleep.

'The House will rise.' It did. So did he.

'It is with the utmost regret that I rise to announce the death of one of our Members. The Member for Yorkshire North Riding died earlier today. Edith Alice, or Babs as we affectionately called her by her nickname, died earlier today in her home village of Carleton in Craven near Skipton in Yorkshire. It is not my prerogative to deliver a eulogy before her funeral but I would like to say a few words, if the House will indulge me for a minute.' He paused.

'We all accepted our responsibilities in this New Order, each and every one of us. After we had all been selected to come to Parliament we agreed to do our very best. That is all Her Majesty asked of us all. Cast your mind back to that momentous night when the whole country waited with baited breath to see which individuals would be privileged to represent their County at Westminster. It seems such a long time ago now doesn't it? Edith Alice was already a very elderly lady and she could have asked to be excused quite easily. Instead, although frail, she attended as often as she could and some of you younger ones helped her a lot with 21st century accessories.' McLean looked briefly at Chloe who looked almost in tears.

'We all remember so recently when Edith Alice celebrated her 100th birthday – and I know a few of you were pleased to have attended her party up in Yorkshire. By all accounts it was grand do – as she might have said herself. I don't think a minute's silence or anything like that was quite her style, do you?' There were a few smiles and grins around the House.

'Instead, I propose that at the next draw for Private Member's Bills only one name will be selected and that the Bill that Edith Alice was intending to introduce is automatically introduced for this House's consideration. I must admit I have a little inside knowledge of the gist of her Bill and in the circumstances I am going to formally ask the Member for Somerset, Leslie Percy, to sponsor the bill on her behalf.' McLean paused again and looked to his right into the middle of the M-Z's. All eyes were now on Leslie Percy.

'Oi would be deloited, Mr Speaker, deloited.' There was a ripple of polite applause and Percy nodded around the chamber like one of those horrible little toy dogs you used to see on the parcel shelves of Ford Sierras. Chloe's 'Uncle Wayne' used to have one. McLean resumed his authority.

'Thank you. That's settled then. Edith Alice's intended Bill will be listed for immediately after the Clean Water Bill and the Budget. Those WILL take place next week – in that order on Monday and Tuesday.' He stared sternly at McIver and Meadows as if to emphasise his point. They were not being allowed any more time. Budgets always used to be on a Tuesday and by golly nothing was going to change – not while he could do anything about it. These type of traditions must be upheld. McIver was seated directly

186

behind Meadows in the M to Z's and whispered into his ear. 'D-day then, we must meet tonight.'

'Please be seated. We will now resume normal business for today. The Head of the Civil Service, Sir Michael de la Nice, will be making the arrangements for two new Members from Leicestershire and Yorkshire North Riding.'

It was noticeable that he didn't say a few nice words about Mr Khan. In fact he didn't mention him by name at all. Hamish noticed Chloe wiping her eyes and wished he could give her a big hug but the A to L's were across the divide and all he could do was smile a little smile at his adopted second daughter. At least the divide today was purely a physical and not a political one. That at least was progress.

That evening Bob and Hamish met to tidy up a few details and Hamish was updated on the progress of the situation at Martin's Water Systems up in Lincoln. It all seemed to be going smoothly – touch wood. It would soon be time for Hamish's lunch appointment in Inverness with Ron Forsyth at the Dogger Bank. Just as predicted a brash press release from Dogger Re-insurance Ltd. had announced the first corporate solution to Chloe's Bill. The House of Lords had passed the Bill too so all that was now required was the Royal Assent. The Queen was abroad on a short official visit to the Netherlands. It was the first visit by a foreign Head of State since the passing of former Queen Juliana and she was keen to show solidarity to the little country across the North Sea that was Britain's friend at all times. Britannia never had any squabbles with the Cloggies. They had even given the Admiralty the design plans of their new troop carrier, IDS Rotterdam, for the Royal Navy to copy. Her return to England next weekend would see the first Act of the New Order become the law of the land.

Later that evening Bob Meadows, Hamish McIver and Duncan Gibson met for a curry in a rather gloomy Indian restaurant in Brick Lane near Liverpool Street. The earliest

187

established Indian restaurants in the whole of the UK were in Brick Lane. One of the waiters recognised Bob and asked him if he could make all Indian food VAT free to boost trade! The service was very slow and there seemed to be a shortage of staff. Surely they hadn't all fallen foul of the new Immigration Act? They plotted their way forward over the plan to finance the new ProAqua gizmo for Martin's and then turned their minds to Inverness. The second meeting with Forsyth would be crucial if the marlin was to not just be gaffed but landed as well. They ate well and Bob picked up the tab paying with his MasterCard. A Visa might have got nicked, particularly if it had a work permit with it.

In Truffle Street EC3 Eric the Red & Co. were beside themselves with happiness. Talk about a licence to print money! The Dogger Bank Group was light years ahead of the pack and so far advanced was their Scheme it was highly unlikely that any other bankers would be doing the Lambada over this Private Finance Initiative. One by one the other Chief Execs of the Big Banks gave up. It was like asking the driver of a veteran car to catch up with Michael Schumacher at Silverstone. By the end of the week the financial press agreed that the Dogger Bank had excelled themselves and that they should be given the chance to underwrite the scheme for the remainder of this Parliament. This was going to be a very fat marlin.

Edith Alice Coates's funeral took place on the Friday and the Speaker ordered Parliamentary business to be suspended for the day as a mark of respect and to allow those Members who wished to attend the funeral to make the journey north. About a dozen attended, including Chloe who had sent a personal wreath with a little card that read – 'Bye 4now luv until we meet again. Chloe'. Texting still ruled OK. St. Mary's Church in Carleton in Craven was packed to capacity. The entire cricket team were there in whites and blazers and the sun was shining. The clergyman asked everybody present to remember her long life and not to be sad but to celebrate a life well lived. There was also a wreath from Her Majesty with just the customary two letters written on the card – ER. It was enough. Edith Alice had one more joke to play and realising she was failing had written a little note for the vicar to read out at the end of the service.

'One of my nephews once called me a silly old cow. Maybe I was from time to time, that's not for me to say tha' knows. But just to remind him of what he said I've arranged for the funeral tea to be held at the 'Craven Heifer' hotel on the road to Grassington and I've asked the manager to make sure that he does all the washing up. Then he can read my Will. One hundred and out! My first and only century. Good luck and a long life to you all. Babs.'

They don't make ladies like her anymore – not even in Tunbridge Wells.

Chapter 34

Hamish had signed the Book of Condolence for Edith Alice then made speed towards Inverness. Ron Forsyth had called him the previous evening and arranged for a bank car to meet him at the airport. The train would have taken too long and he wanted a long working lunch. Dan Ericsson had instructed Forsyth that McIver must remain on side at all costs. He didn't care if the entire salmon farming industry ended up in the Minch and the Bank lost a million, McIver's goodwill must be maintained. No other bank in Truffle Street had an 'insider' like they did! How hasty it had been of them to fire the man who was now Chancellor of the Exchequer. With hindsight that must have been a bigger cock-up than Pearl Harbor. Not that Ericsson had even been born yet on that 'day of infamy' as Roosevelt had described it. Still, as the bank had said in its farewell letter to Meadows, probity must take precedence and there was no way the Chancellor could do them any harm. He could even be invited back onto the Board maybe once he was no longer an MP. Lots of banks had done that before after a respectable period of time had passed to make it look acceptable. Usually about a week!

They started lunch with some gravadlax and asparagus. It was Forsyth's suggestion and intended to show solidarity with the salmon industry despite the Scandinavian recipe. It had been Ericsson's idea. Say what you like about the New Yorker but when it came to PR there were few better than he. He hadn't got to the top of the Watermelon tree by going by the book.

'Hamish, I can't tell you how appreciative the bank is. You've seen all the press reports this week I take it?'

Hamish fibbed. 'To be honest I've been so busy that I ….'

'Aye, well I can tell you that you need have no further worries over the salmon farm. Just let us know when the Junko Shimada contracts have been signed and I'll mark a permanent overdraft facility on the firm's account for whatever you need.' He lied. Ericsson had already marked it up to a half a million so that the account didn't even trouble the computers, let alone any staff. With the nature of his contract any potential loss was outside his concern.

'That's great news, Ron.' He shook hands across the table as if to emphasise his gratitude. 'But actually, Ron, I think one good turn deserves another. It is however most delicate and I er...well, this has to remain absolutely confidential.' He glanced around and lowered his voice deliberately.

'My Clean Water Bill which as you know is being introduced next week, has opened up an investment opportunity for some financiers that is going to make a pile for somebody.'

'Aye?' Forsyth craned forward like he did before towards the net. He didn't know it was the net for the marlin.

'Yes, look to put it bluntly, I received a letter - quite out of the blue you understand - from a chap in Lincoln. Reg somebody or the other, I just forget now.' Hamish was enjoying the dialogue every bit as much as the salmon.

'Anyway, seems like his firm was in trouble with his bank - but, and this is the rub-he's developed a new type of

191

domestic water filter called an AquaVita or something that he says after my Bill becomes law will make squillions. Oh yes, I remember now – Martin, Reg Martin.'

'Really, how very interesting.' There were at least four v's in the word very.

'However seems like because of a major dispute with his bank, I'm sorry I've no idea which one, he will be unable to put the thing he's patented into production. Apparently his firm's on the bones of its arse and awaiting some form of adjudication from the Ombudsman. Compensation from the bank or something. You know what banks are like!' They both laughed, Forsyth nervously so and a sliver of smoked salmon fell off his fork and did a slalom down his bank tie. Hamish pretended not to notice but decided there was a joke in there somewhere to tell Bob later.

Forsyth recovered. 'So is the whole project dead in the water then – excuse the analogy!'

'No, not at all, not at all. Of course I couldn't be seen to be helping him now could I? Not with it being my Bill and his product. Probity and all that.'

'Quite. Absolutely.'

'So, I did what all Ministers used to do. I passed the buck! I sent Reg Martin's letter on to the Member for Midlothian, Duncan Gibson. Apparently before he was selected to be an MP he was involved in what you bankers call Fund Management and venture capital.'

'Gibson, did you say?' Forsyth's mind was racing.

'Yes, he was a director of one of those posh firms in Edinburgh in Charlotte Square, Dalziel Mackay or something like that.'

'You mean DMZ – Dalziel Menzies and Zimmer?'

'That's the one! You'll know a lot more than me of course.'

'You mean DMZ are backing him?'

'That's the whisper in the House. A hundred million job. But Gibson did happen to mention that twenty mill was being kept back for other outside investors. He even tried to sell me some of the shares – you know as a little thank you for the introduction. Of course I couldn't possibly.'

'No, of course not.'

'Five hundred per cent profit in four years is the expected windfall. So with twenty million pounds worth of private stakes available that's a hundred mill for somebody. I just wish I had that sort of cash to invest!'

Forsyth wasn't listening anymore. He was mentally making his next call to Eric the Red. He couldn't wait for lunch to finish and get on the phone to London before three o'clock. Ericsson was flying back home to New York for a long weekend and asked to be updated before he went. The venison casserole followed by fresh raspberries and cream was just a blur to Forsyth. By 2:30 Hamish was on his Kawasaki dive bomber back to Stornoway and Forsyth was on the phone to Lombard Street. The development reached Ericsson's ears like a lamp to a moth.

'Yeah, so this guy Reg who...yeah, Martin right? He's in trouble with his own bank but despite that Dee Emm Zee are gonna give this guy twenny mill? Jee-zuz!'

Forsyth interrupted. 'Aye, it's called an Aqua something... maybe Aquavita. And no, DMZ are investing eighty million. It's the additional twenty that's being made available for private shareholders.'

'The water of life? Vita is Latin huh right? Maybe its vita like ryevita? Shit, we have to know Ronnie.' Latin studies in Dan's 'Brooklyn High' hadn't extended much beyond 'et tu Brute' but all of a sudden he was keen to learn more.

'Listen Ronnie. Think of an excuse to call McIver over the weekend. Make up some bullshit. Just find out about the Aqua thing. You say he's gotten it Patented? Tell him you're thinking of becoming a small investor yourself. Anything! We've got to get some more information real quick OK? Do you realise we could make another little pile here? Not for the bank - for us Ronnie, us. Me and you and the rest of the guys here. Shit, is that the time? I gotta plane to catch. Listen, Ronnie, write down my Manhattan apartment number. Call me tomorrow? Bye.'

Two hours later Forsyth called Hamish at home in Stornoway. 'Hello, a pleasant flight I trust?' Giving Forsyth the answers he wanted was like giving candy to a baby. Twelve hours after that the baby was cooing in Manhattan. It would take a week or more to raise the twenty million between all the Directors of the subsidiary companies of the Dogger Bank. All they had to do then was to make sure that they received preferential treatment in the application process.

Hamish called Bob Meadows later that evening. 'Looks like the marlin's on the line. But don't forget to do your little bit for the cause in your Budget speech on Tuesday will you?'

'I won't! See you Monday then – looking forward to your Bill. Goodnight.'

Chapter 35

'Order, order! Mr McIver, the Member for the Western Isles if you please.'

The great day had arrived for Hamish. He stood and waited for the noise to reduce to zero and cleared his throat. Six months ago he was a salmon farmer with an impossible overdraft and facing bankruptcy. Now here he was in the Mother of Parliaments introducing a Bill that the whole nation thought was the most environmentally decent thing since sliced bread when in fact he was doing it to save his own skin, shaft a bank and its board of directors and help some nice people in Lincolnshire avenge the same bank that had tried to shaft him. One day it might make a good book but who in their right frame of mind would believe it?

'Mr Speaker, fellow selected Members, ladies and gentlemen.' Across the divide Chloe Ledger was beaming at him with a smile as bright as a million candles. He had copied her opening words when she had introduced her Bill but added the word 'selected.' He would get an extra hug and a shortbread for that. No doubt it would be noted in Hansard.

Fifteen minutes later and Hamish had finished. There was polite applause all round. There were no surprises as the Bill had been well discussed since that interview under Big Ben with Andrew Marr. The introduction of domestic water purifiers and filters was to be compulsory in all new houses built after January 1st next and retrospectively all existing domestic residences within two years. But the Bill didn't quite get the smooth ride that Chloe's Bill had done. Several questions were raised from the floor. What about those areas where local authorities deliberately added fluorides to the water to help fight children's tooth decay? Wouldn't filters take them back out again? What about poor people? Would they be able to get a grant to fit such a filter? Unperturbed, Hamish rose again.

'Mr Speaker, these are all valid points that will be looked into and discussed in the fullness of time. I'm sure all Members would agree that it is the spirit of the Bill that is important.'

'Hear, hears' were heard from all quarters and the Bill went to the vote. The result was ninety-nine in favour and none against. They were still two Members short pending the two by-selections. The draw for those two seats was to be made next Saturday. In Leicestershire and North Yorkshire millions of people started hunting for their National Insurance numbers again. There had never been so much interest in Parliamentary affairs. The Second Elizabethan Era was well under way.

RADO was dusted off and its software given the electronic equivalent of a spring-clean – a defragmentation of its hard drive.

The Draw was also prepared for the next Private Member's Bill – the one to accompany the late Edith Alice's intended Bill that Leslie Percy would introduce as her proxy. Her Majesty thought it would be rather nice for the two draws to be shown live on TV and she thought that lunchtime on a Sunday just before the start of the British Grand Prix might be quite nice. People would be in a holiday mood already.

Chapter 36

Later that evening Bob, Hamish and Duncan Gibson met at the same curry house near Liverpool Street and were greeted by the same waiter as before. They had a lot to discuss and as soon as the food was ordered they went straight into conference. Bob said his bit first.

'Right then, we have to work fast now. That's the Bill well on the way to becoming law. Reg Martin needs the money very soon to commence production of the ProAqua.' He glanced at Duncan.

'No problem there. I've already run it past my partners. It can't really lose. The money's available whenever Martin's needs it. Two million.'

Bob butted in. 'They don't need it. Another company needs it.' The other two looked puzzled. 'Look, until we know what gives with Dogger Bank, Martin's Water Systems is still vulnerable. It could still go to the wall. So the money will go into a new company altogether called ProAqua Ltd. – the same name as the patented product. OK? I've already told Reg what to do. He may even have done it already. That is what DMZ's investment will go into with some spare shares for family, you Hamish and well...you know...well I wouldn't mind a few myself! What about you, Duncan?'

'Well, it's just a bit too close to the bone...you know. No, I'll take my reward from when DMZ sell out. I'm quite happy.'

Bob resumed. 'Right, Hamish, you have to put a bit more bait on the line now. Tell Forsyth tomorrow morning that you've heard that Reg Martin is trying to pull a fast one on his Bank and that he's set up a new Limited Company that banks elsewhere. That's all you have to say for now. I bet you a pound to pinch that they'll start to panic. The first thing is that they'll almost certainly back off on the existing company once they find out they are the bankers! I'd love to be a fly on the wall! After tomorrow's Budget they'll be champing at the bit to get a slice of the action, just like they were after Chloe's Bill. Thanks to you Hamish.'

'Me?'

'Yes, you. Cast your mind back to that awful day – it seems an eternity ago – when you e-mailed me from Stornoway. Remember?'

'How could I forget. My world was about to end. But what are you on about?'

'Remember I told you to write down all that malarkey about Junko Shimada and the phoney sushi deals?'

'Yes but you instigated that, not me and...'

'You didn't quite catch what I said. You said Junk? Junk as in Junk Bonds. Remember now?'

'Vaguely, yes, but I don't really know why I said it...it just came out like a cliché. Where it came from I don't know. Honestly.'

'Duncan knows what a Junk Bond is, I'll wager.'

'Aye, they were big in the Eighties. A yankee inspired idea. A Texan bank called Texel something ...er...well anyway the Bonds were composed of the stock of companies that had gone tits up and could either recover and make a spectacular profit or become just junk – hence the nickname of the Bonds.' Hamish was out of this conversation now but Bob picked up where Duncan left off.

'Well done, almost. Texel is a kind of sheep you dipstick – excuse the pun! But you weren't far off. The bank was called Drexel Burnham Lambert Inc. of Dallas and they made a bloody fortune. Loads of people copied them but they were the first into the game and got rich. But that's not going to happen to the Bonds that the Dogger guys will be buying. Believe me they will be real junk!'

Hamish stopped him. 'So what are you going to do tomorrow then?'

'It's better that you don't know yet, just to protect yourselves. While we're all here is there anything else that you two would like me to stick in the Budget – short of abolishing income tax? Now, who wants a chunk of this naan bread?'

They were all back at the Russell Hotel before eleven. Bob burned the oil well past midnight as he put the finishing touches to his speech. Angus McLean had politely asked him how long he thought it might last. Twenty minutes? Half an hour? He had thought Bob was pulling his leg when he said two hours. He wasn't. That night he dreamed of salmon trapped in water filters and going big game fishing on the Dogger Bank. Isn't the human subconscious a strange but powerful computer and predictor? It was no coincidence that the former British Tunny Club had its Headquarters in Scarborough not far from the Dogger Bank. The Sir Thomas Liptons of this world had between the wars landed the fattest blue fin tunas ever seen near that bank. In fact what they would eventually catch on the Dogger Bank would make their tunny mere sprats in comparison.

Chapter 37

'Order, order! Order I say. The Chancellor of the Exchequer, Mr Meadows.'

The gavel wasn't needed. The House, indeed the entire nation, was hushed. This was the first Budget from an apolitical Chancellor and a former Board Member of a Big Five Bank. It was either going to be boring or something else. Meadows rose to his feet, the file in his hands was ominously heavy. It didn't bode well for a short speech. Already Members were reaching for their packets of Polos. Zia had often wondered how considerate it was of an English confectionery company to name a sweet after his country's national sport.

'Mr Speaker, fellow selected Members and Ladies and Gentlemen.' Without realising it Chloe had set a pattern of Parliamentary etiquette that would last another thousand years.

All over the nation millions of ordinary people were glued to their TV sets. It was almost like a live footy match of national import – nearly an FA Cup Final. Lisa Martin had brought a little twelve inch set to the office and it was parked on the table roughly where the yellow tractor grease had been some weeks earlier. Bob had called her the day before and told her to make sure that all three of them watched it. It was the same story in Truffle Street except at the Head Office of the Dogger Bank the entire Board was looking at the same type of huge plasma screen TV that Ron Forsyth had up in Inverness. Once again the guy with the corner shop and the overdraft was paying for it. Hamish had made the call to Inverness first thing that morning and by 6 am Eastern Daylight Time even Ericsson had been informed that there would be something in the Chancellor's speech of major interest. Was it to do with the Motor Insurance Bill or the Clean Water Bill? Or even both? All twelve Board Members were sitting watching the big screen while secretaries brought in little trays of nibbles, teas and coffees. Ericsson had asked to be kept informed continuously on a permanently open trans-Atlantic phone line and his PA had called him as soon as the Chancellor stood up.

'Mr Speaker, it is my pleasure to present the first Budget of this Parliament. I can only apologise for the several months' delay in its being brought to the House. The reasons for this are many and complex and I will not bore the House with all the intricacies of the research and preparation. Suffice it to say that a non-political Budget is a very difficult kettle of fish to a party political one.' He didn't mention marlins although he thought of one particularly fat one.

'I hope this Budget will put an end to the constant bickering that seemed to be inevitable when party politics was involved. I ask the House to bear with me while I go through the long list of mostly corporate taxation details.'

He trundled on as fast as he could about rates of Corporation Tax – full rate, starting rate, small companies rate, marginal relief limits, marginal relief fractions, small companies distributed profits minimum rates – until everybody thought he could not possibly find anything else to do with the subject, and then suddenly he said, 'However,

I intend to reduce Corporation Tax to zero, repeat zero, for the first five years of a company's legal entity, that is to say since Incorporation, not necessarily the first five years of trading.'

He paused whilst the most financially aware of Members took stock but the majority took the opportunity to take another Polo. Not so some of the financial journalists up in the public galleries whose pens seemed to be dancing across notebooks like Home Counties North couples in a 'Come Dancing' final. People watching at home on TV could see a white ticker tape move across the bottom of the screen like it was the latest score coming in from a big Cup Tie somewhere. The message read 'Chancellor effectively abolishes tax for new companies' and it was repeated every twenty seconds until the next headline.

'Moving on now to more relevant issues to ordinary people…I want now to consider Capital Gains Tax…the effective annual exemption stays the same at £9,200 per annum but I want to end the nonsense of what stockbrokers call Bed & Breakfasting. This has nothing to do with the tourist industry in general or Blackpool in particular', said Meadows as he smiled at the Member for Lancashire who he knew had a slimy little guesthouse not far from the Tower. 'No, I refer to the ridiculous practice whereby shareholders sell them one day and buy them back the next so that they have made a profit in a particular tax year. All this does is make even more money for stockbrokers who are usually owned by banks these days. As from next April shareholders will be deemed to have effected this exercise and also any CGT allowance not used in any one year can be carried forward to the next year. Later I will mention certain classes of companies whose shares will always be free of CGT.'

And so he went on from National Insurance contributions and then to Inheritance Tax. 'On the vexed subject of Inheritance Tax I want to remove forever the effect of the increase in property prices that has brought with it unnecessary taxation implications. The average house price here in the South of England is now over three hundred thousand pounds which means that even modest families are having to pay IHT at a time when sadness is usually the order of the day. That will end at midnight tonight. From then private domestic residences will not be taken into consideration. This should remove a million families a year from this grossly unfair and heinous tax.' There was widespread applause from all over the House. Another white ticker tape trickled across millions of screens.

Over at the Dogger Bank the directors were fiddling with papers and calculators. 'I don't know how old Bob is going to pay for all this! He's cracking up! I make it he's about eight billion down already. Where on earth is it all going to come from?' piped up one of them as the eggy bit of a custard tart fell onto his tie. At least it wasn't a slaloming salmon.

'I want now to move on to matters relating to pensions. What a mess, Mr Speaker, that preceding Governments have made!' More applause. 'The first thing I want to do immediately is to restore the dividend income that was robbed from all Pension Funds by my predecessor. As from next April that practice will not only cease but the dividend income that has been lost for this Fiscal Year will be restored. Quite simply it just wasn't fair. It is not incumbent upon a Chancellor of the Exchequer to pretend that he's Dick Turpin. Don't forget what happened to him!' The Dogger Director with the eggy tie added another nine billions to the deficit as he currently perceived it.

'And so to the subject of direct income tax. Mr Speaker, I believe it was the late Lord Clyde who once famously said that it was the prerogative of every person in the land to arrange his financial affairs so as to minimise his liability to Her Majesty's Exchequer. I believe that that is as true a maxim today as when his Lordship said so over a hundred years ago. However, there is I believe, a difference between tax avoidance and tax evasion. The latter is illegal but sadly the former has led to a growth industry of so called tax accountants and Trust experts who charge exorbitant fees whilst maintaining themselves in the fullest corporate splendour surrounded by yucca plants, marble reception desks and black-suited members of the Corps of Commissionaires.' Laughter all around the House.

'So, I intend from next April to simplify direct taxation. All personal allowances will be abolished – including those applying to the blind and the disabled.' The House was stunned. Not only had Dick Turpin come back from the dead to haunt them but Black Bess was trampling them into the dirt.

'However as from next April there will only be one fixed rate of income tax – ten per cent! This will simplify the job of the Inland Revenue to the extent where only one fifth of current staff levels will be required after four more years. I calculate that the amount of tax actually collected will be about the same but the Treasury will save hundreds of millions in salaries alone. It will also, Mr Speaker, lead hopefully to less overall tax evasion. The dreaded tax returns will thus be a much simpler matter for everybody in future. If you earn money you pay tax on it at ten per cent – full stop.' Adrian Kristiansand was smiling more than anybody else in the House as he mentally hummed to himself – TIC, TAC, TEN – TIC, TAC, TEN.

'Mr Speaker, I now wish to turn my attention to the two Private Member's Bills already passed by this House. Firstly, in the matter of the mandatory Motor Insurance Bill, er sorry Act, I did appreciate my honourable friend for Essex's comment about extra Insurance Premium Tax for the Treasury. However, once again, in the interests of minimising evasion I have, after considerable thought, decided to zero rate all future motor insurance premiums from IPT.' Down at St. Mary's Axe the guys from Dogger Re-insurance Ltd. were ecstatic. This would do them no harm at all – more business.

'In a similar manner, Mr Speaker, I wish to enter into the spirit of the Clean Water Act, er Bill, by assisting industry in this great crusade. I am sure you will appreciate that as the Bill only obtained its first reading yesterday I have had insufficient time to consider detailed proposals. However, I can inform the House that in the coming months I will be looking at ways of assisting manufacturing companies that come to the fore with the possibility of Treasury Grants, tax breaks over and above those already announced and, in a radical new departure, I am looking at the introduction of special Water Bonds whereby ordinary members of the public can buy into regulated investment products that will concentrate solely on this new and exciting industry. As with the old TESSAs, PEPs and ISAs there will of course have to be carefully safeguarded limits to prevent the already rich and avaricious from getting even fatter. Those limits will however be fairly generous and I am currently looking at an annual limit of ten thousand pounds. It is hoped that these Bonds will be up and running by the time Parliament re-sits after the summer recess. As this is a niche industry in a niche market which, we trust, will be backed up by law and compulsion, the anticipated profits will be astronomical. That is why these Bonds must be regulated to the utmost degree and the specialist manufacturers properly licensed.'

Up in Lincoln the atmosphere was euphoric. In Truffle Street, at the Dogger Bank, there were mixed reactions. Forsyth's spy had been right but now they had a major problem. Their furious research that morning had revealed that Martin's Water Systems Ltd. was one of their customers and that their Peterborough Office wasn't far off winding them up until Reg Martin had informed them that a formal complaint was now being sent to the Ombudsman for mis-selling. The Ombudsman could order the Bank to compensate Martin's up to a hundred grand and then on top of that the Financial Services Authority could fine them five times that. And now the Chancellor of the Exchequer was talking about extra assistance to them and firms like them. Ericcson's PA was talking non-stop to her boss. This was bad news. Jee – zuz! There were decisions to be made quickly. He booked the overnight 'red-eye' on American Airlines to arrive back in London the following morning. He hung up on his PA before the Chancellor had sat down. That was a mistake.

'To continue the aquatic theme, Mr Speaker, in order to aid start-up companies in the water purification industry and to encourage the population and even investment banks to invest in them, all dividends declared by such companies will be tax free for ten years. In a similar manner disposal of all company shares in this category will be treated as free of Capital Gains Tax from midnight tonight.

'Moving on, I have looked long and hard at the way that fuel tax is levied in the whole country.' Dai Williams came out of his daydream and looked straight at Meadows.

'My predecessor seemed to regard fuel, or rather the taxation of fuel, as some sort of high calorie snack that he could nibble at whenever the coffers were low. If the former Government hadn't wasted so much public money on things like expensive helicopters that can't fly in cloud and tanks that can't drive in sand then he wouldn't have needed to rob blind the guy driving to work because there wasn't a bus.' Williams was beaming.

'However, this is not a problem that can be solved overnight but what I can do is freeze VAT and duty on all petrol, derv and diesel for the next twelve months while we see how the price of basic crude pans out over the next year after the Iraq debacle. Yes, it is true the oil companies do make huge profits but the amount they spend on new exploration is mind boggling. I am also going to look into ways of levying the duty on fuel at different rates in different parts of the United Kingdom. People in Wales, Scotland and Northern Ireland very often have to drive much greater distances just to go to work or to shop. I will study this very closely.' He meant what he said.

'Mr Speaker, I have received much advice from fellow Members from Scotland on the effects of a strong pound on exports of Scotch Whisky.' Archie Murdoch came out of his daydream. 'I have decided therefore to reduce the duty on Scotch by fifty pence a bottle as from midnight tonight to help domestic sales.' The police and driving organisations would have his guts for garters over that one but no one was prepared for what was coming next.

'On the subject of spirits I have also decided to assist the nation to celebrate the two hundredth anniversary of Trafalgar. Throughout the whole of my Chancellorship all Navy Rum will be free of all excise duties. Wouldn't Uncle Albert have been pleased?' The Chancellor's reference to one of the nation's favourite TV characters from 'Only Fools and Horses' brought laughter then silence from the House as everybody remembered the actor, the late Buster Merryweather, who had been Captain Birdseye, Nelson, Drake and Jellicoe all rolled into one. England would now indeed be 'Totland' – at least for a few years.

'And finally, Mr Speaker, I am sure that the more fiscally aware amongst us will be wondering how the twenty billion pound hole in my arithmetic is going to be filled.' Bob Meadows told them inside thirty seconds then wrapped up his speech.

'Those Mr Speaker, are the salient points of my Budget. I commend it to the House.'

He sat down. He thought he had pleased everybody who was on the train that day going to Lincoln. Damn – he had forgotten to tax the mosque 'but never mind' as Mary Whitehouse might have said.

The television producers had run out of ticker tape. Forget Dick Turpin. Robin Hood was alive and well and all his Merry Men rejoiced across the length and breadth of the land.

An hour later and it was Bob's turn to be interviewed by Andrew Marr under Big Ben. Honey was with him. Denied the customary photo-call outside No.11 Downing Street with the bright red dispatch box, she had agreed to be with him for the short and expectedly pleasant interview. She looked absolutely fabulous – Patsy without the Bollinger. She held his hand as Marr waved the mike around like Johnny Cobra in Marrakesh. When it was over even the BBC's political editor finally realised that party politics was finished for good and that the House of Commons finally belonged to the Common Man. At Aintree racecourse a dozen trumpets play 'Fanfare for a Common Man' before the Grand National but it was 1992 since Party Politics had actually won it. That was a long, long time ago. It wouldn't race again. Never.

Chapter 38

The Dogger Bank Bentley Mulsanne Turbo, painted of course in the bank's corporate colours, had picked Ericsson up from Heathrow. A friendly jetstream had brought him back to Ingerland almost an hour earlier than anticipated and he was in Lombard Street by eight thirty. He had not slept on the plane and was not in a good mood. Eric the Red Eyes.

'Where the hell is the rest of the Board? I'll have to start introducing new working rules soon if these guys don't measure up.'

His secretary calmed him down with coffee and his favourite bagels. 'I'm sure they won't be long, Sir, probably delays on the Circle Line as usual.' She lied, hoping it would satisfy him. There had been a big celebration bender down at St. Mary's Axe last night and she knew that the Bank's entire Board had been drinking until the early hours. While the cat's away the mice will play. Goodness knows what time they would all start to trickle in. She had all their mobile numbers and would sent out some text messages telling them that the boss was already back and waiting.

Ericsson passed the next hour watching 'Budget Highlights' that his PA had thoughtfully recorded from

BBC2 the previous night. He was munching and sipping coffee until he reached the last thirty seconds of Meadow's speech. Then he spilt his coffee and hit the roof. 'Jee-zuz! What? A windfall tax on "Big Bank" profits!' He hit the rewind button and listened to it again.

'The deficit between revenue and expenditure, Mr Speaker, is never precisely quantifiable. I estimate the figure for this coming fiscal year to be about eighteen billion pounds, maybe slightly more. There is only one way where I can pinpoint that sort of money being made anywhere in the country apart from the oil industry and for reasons already explained I want to leave oil companies alone as they brave new frontiers of exploration. No, there is only one source of huge profiteering and that of course is the Big Banks. Many of you will recall how in the late Seventies one of my predecessors levied a "one-off windfall tax" on their profits. Their unexpected treasure trove resulted largely from very high interest rates pertaining at that time. However interest rates are now exactly one third of what they were then and yet, even in real terms, the banks are making three times as much. I am sure that Members will join me in attempting to assist the banks to redistribute their swag.' Laughter and applause all around the House.

'I therefore, Mr Speaker, with effect from the end of this year, intend to introduce a top rate of Corporation Tax of seventy-five per cent which will apply to the banking sector only for the remainder of this four-year Parliament. It will be the prerogative of my successor to either maintain the rate, alter it or abolish it.'

Ericsson threw the last bagel on the plate across his office narrowly missing his PA who had just walked in to top up his coffee. He was slumped across his desk, head in hands, and looked like a man who had just lost most of his future bonus from his contract. She felt almost sorry for him. Well almost. Within another hour all of Ericsson's 'lootenants' had arrived and he convened a War Cabinet in the Board Room. He started to get his act together and asked for another senior staff member to join them. The bank's Company Secretary revealed his research to the Board. He had been quick off the mark. Since the leaks from Hamish via Forsyth in Inverness he had been a busy man and it showed.

'Gentlemen, these are the facts as known to me at this point in time. One. Martin's Water Systems Ltd. is under pressure from creditors and the Inland Revenue. At the close of business last night their overdraft stood at fifty-three thousand. Creditors will probably be about another thirty if the previous pattern of trading has been maintained. There have been four County Court Judgements against it, all for sums in excess of £750 which means they can petition to have it Wound Up. Two. I checked the Register of Companies in England and Wales to see if ProAqua had been Registered as a Limited Company. It had not. However, just to be absolutely certain I then checked the Scottish Registry and there it was – ProAqua Ltd. which was incorporated less than seven days ago. Its Directors are listed as R.Martin, L.M.Martin and L.A.Martin all of the same address in Lincoln. The Company Secretary's name was some Scottish name Mac something. It didn't seem relevant and was probably the same name as a hundred other companies on the list. However, its Registered Office is, get this, in Charlotte Square, Edinburgh. But the most interesting discovery is the capital structure of ProAqua – a hundred million one pound shares all issued but currently nil paid.' There was a low whistle around the Board Room.

'Three. In addition, Gentlemen, purely as a precaution, I checked the Patents and Trade Mark Registries in Newport, Wales. The ProAqua is both a Patent and a Trade Mark for the next six years minimum. Does anybody have any questions?' There were none. Ericsson was impressed and on behalf of the Board thanked him for his efforts and then asked for the meeting to continue in his absence. The

Company Secretary, Berkley, left the room. He was worth every penny of his two hundred grand a year salary. There were times when Directors had to close ranks and this was one of them. Eric the Red took the bridge and headed for Greenland. He had made copious notes and started to give the orders.

'I want Peterborough Regional Office to write to Martin today. Offer him a hundred grand and then we write to the Ombudsman saying the matter has been settled amicably.'

'Gentlemen, you can see how fast Martin has been working. I can smell a rat. A big fat water rat.' Nobody laughed. 'It's almost like he knew about this Clean Water Act coming up but who cares a shit – as long as we can get a slice of the action! We have a very short time indeed to raise twenty million privately and get the applications up to Dee Emm Zee in Edinburg. We have to beat that deadline crap and hell after September it's just ten grand a head for a Water Bond. No Siree, we are gonna have all that twenty mill allocation. I want a confidential memo to all Directors of all the Group's subsidiaries putting them in the picture OK? Anybody who squeals will be fired. I will personally put up five mill that leaves fifteen for you guys and the others. We regroup seven days from today. OK you guys – outta here!'

That was how they did it in New Amsterdam and that was how he would do it here. In a few hours time when the sun had risen over the Western Atlantic he would put in a call to his 'offshore bank' in Nassau, Bahamas and make the necessary arrangements to wire five million sterling to London for conversion into a banker's draft, or a cashier's check as he called it. For the first time since stepping on the plane at JFK he felt at ease with the world. He decided to take the rest of the day off and catch up on some sleep.

Somebody should have told him that Peter Stuyvesant hadn't become the first Mayor of New Amsterdam by being a smoking gun.

Chapter 39

It was a hot, sunny day and typical of mid-July at its best. It seemed like half the population of Central England had gathered at Silverstone in Northamptonshire for the British Grand Prix. A few years before some optimistic organisers had rearranged the event for Easter Sunday and it had been a disaster. A front coming in from the Atlantic brought with it continuous rain for four days prior to the race, turning the green fields to be used as car parks into absolute quagmires and that mistake would never be repeated. No, July it always used to be and July it will always be. They should have remembered what Bob Dylan said in the 60's – 'you don't need a weatherman to know which way the wind blows.'

Opposite the main VIP stand the organisers had erected a huge temporary TV screen a bit like those at the New Wembley but not as sophisticated or permanent. Everybody wanted to watch the RADO Draw for the two Parliamentary seats that had become available and there was the added bonus of the Draw for the next Private Member's Bill. Who would it be this time? After the two Draws the screen would show live those sections of the course that could not be seen from the grandstand.

It was almost 1:30 pm, the scheduled start for the Draws and down on the grid the drivers were giving their gleaming Ferraris and Hondas a final checkover. The bimbos and groupies were starting to thin out as the mechanics and Team Managers took over and made their final tactical decisions. How much fuel to carry? One stop or two? What sort of tyres to use? Would it rain? Where was Bob Dylan when you needed him?

At 1:30 exactly the screen flickered into life to a ripple of polite applause from the vast audience and across the whole of the UK millions were watching ITV as the cameras reverted from the action on the grid to the big screen. There he was again, Sir Michael de la Nice, wearing what looked to be the same suit as last time. Viewers couldn't see the whole set this time but it looked like the same desk and the same bust of Churchill by the master sculptor Albert Toft was still visible. Despite his naval State funeral, code-named by himself as 'Operation Hope Not' he had actually been buried in the village of Bladon only twenty miles to the south of Silverstone. Geographically they were about as far from the sea you could get in the United Kingdom. What would the great man have thought of all this?

Sir Michael said a few words. Nothing as historical as his previous speech but poignant nonetheless. He was as polite as always.

'Good afternoon, Ladies and Gentlemen. It seems a long time ago since the start of the New Parliament doesn't it? And yet a lot has happened, much for the good I believe. Since that momentous night when over a hundred people good and true were selected to be Members there has been a refreshing change to the whole of the governmental system. New ideas and new ways of conducting the nation's affairs. The Realm is still protected of course and the Civil Service, freed from party political influences, can perhaps advise more circumspectly than before. Today we will welcome two new Members to the House.'

He said a few genuinely kind words about Edith Alice Coates and then told a lie about how sorry he was that the Member for Leicestershire had to retire early on health grounds.

'So, to proceed, the format will be as before except of course that only two National Insurance numbers will flash up – one for Yorkshire North Riding and one for Leicestershire. Assuming there are no gremlins in the system like last time there will then be a short break of about a minute and then the County whose current member is to introduce the next Private Member's Bill will illuminate. And just to add a sparkle to the proceedings we have asked the TV race commentator to do a voiceover as the three affected seats become known. Good afternoon to you all.' The picture faded then the former electronic scoreboard came into view with the one hundred and two squares.

The commentator took over and tried his best to emulate his predecessor Murray Walker who was actually there in person up in the VIP stand. The Leicestershire square started to flash red, then amber as before all those months ago. 'Go! Go! Go!' he shouted and a million viewers in a million households shouted with him. Ten seconds later and there it was in green, Chloe's favourite colour, and the new member for Leicestershire had been selected. RADO moved across the screen and down almost to the bottom. Only the square for Yorkshire West Riding was beneath it. 'Go! Go! Go!' he screamed again and the millions screamed with him. RADO had selected the new Member for Yorkshire North Riding. It was so much fun. Maybe the whole of the next Parliamentary Draw should be done at Silverstone?

The commentator was trying to sound still excited for the next bit. 'So, the RADO's moving on fast, foot hard down now, up the gears, seventh, eighth, fifteen thousand revs, braking, into the chicane...and the flag's in sight...he's nearly done it...and here it is its...its...Lincolnshire Lindsay! Repeat, Lincolnshire Lindsay is the winner of the Private

Member's Race sponsored by Pizza Shed.' The last bit had been Sir Michael's idea. Why not? The viewing figure was huge and the fifty thousand pound fee would go a long way towards the East End Youth Theatre. To Chicken Shed from Pizza Shed – sounds about right. The viewer was left with two flashing National Insurance numbers in the two counties and the whole of the Lincolnshire Lindsay square glowing dayglow orange. What would have happened if the new Bill draw had been one of the other two seats? Nobody questioned it – at least not yet.

Up in the little market town of Louth, Lincolnshire the Member of Parliament was mowing the lawn. Grand Prix Racing was not to his liking at all. Far too noisy! In any event he already knew both results. His own and the actual race. The German cobbler would win again. Not for nothing was the English shoe industry centred in Northamptonshire.

Chapter 40

By the time the race was over two more people in the nation knew they had been selected to serve their country. In a little village about fifteen miles from Leicester a twenty-two-year-old stable girl called Sally-Anne Smith had a smile as wide as the nearby M1 motorway. She was one smart lady was Sally-Anne. She had worked at the stables of the Quorn Hunt since she was sixteen and was horse mad. The threatened 'Hunting with Dogs Bill' by the previous class conscious Government had almost cost her and hundreds like her their livelihoods as the muddled thinkers of mediocrity had almost got their Bill passed. Only Her Majesty's intervention to dismiss the House of Commons had stopped it getting onto the Statute Book. Sally-Anne had often wondered if it was one of the Queen's reasons for acting just when she did. After all members of her family often rode to hounds and the Prince of Wales himself had even ridden with the Quorn. She had rather hoped that one of his dashing sons had come with him but no such luck. Never mind, one day she would move in higher circles she had thought. And now she was an MP! She had once been a minor celebrity when as Queen of the Hunt she had visited

HMS *Quorn*, a Royal Navy minesweeper of the Hunt Class. A dozen officers and ratings had chatted her up that day, all without success. There weren't many riding opportunities in Plymouth, Portsmouth or Rosyth so a sailor's wife she would not make. Life in London wouldn't be too bad for the next three and a bit years. Maybe she could help out during the week down at Chelsea Barracks where they kept the horses for the Life Guards and the Blues and Royals. She was so excited.

Not quite so excited was the new Member for Yorkshire North who was a farmer called Harry Jewitt. He kept sheep mostly – Texels not Drexels – on his farm between Settle and Skipton. At seventy he was deeply sceptical about all Governments of whatever political complexion. The foot and mouth outbreak in 2001 had almost wiped him out and he was resentful of most higher authorities. If the recent Mutton Report on the death of a civil servant had been a whitewash then what was the point in a having a Beef, Pork and Lamb Report on the foot and mouth lark. 'Nay, they're alt same in London that lot!' It took his two sons John and Peter several days to persuade him that he had to attend Parliament or face jail. He was under eighty and didn't have the option like Edith Alice. 'Just think of the extra brass, Dad', Peter had said to him. So he did and he went. All he had to find now was the muck to go with it. During those terrible days of 2001 he had been told the joke about an American film company making a movie about the outbreak. It was called 'Sheepless in Settle' but Harry had never understood the joke. He always slept well and he'd never even heard of a spot called Seattle.

The town of Louth is famous for only two things. Firstly, and extraordinarily appropriate, it actually lies on the Greenwich Meridian of zero degrees west and zero degrees east. You could say it was where east meets west except the ethnic population of Louth was almost exponentially zero. Louth seemed to be zero everything until a few decades ago it elected, under the old archaic system, a Member of Parliament who ended up in the House of Lords. He also ended up in jail for perverting the course of justice which proves that it was possible to be detained at Her Majesty's pleasure despite attending Parliament as well as refusing to attend it. There was a moral in there somewhere.

After he had finished mowing the lawn he put away his mower and went inside for tea. At sixty-one Peter Ambridge had been sanguine about his selection. He was a widower and lived alone. He belonged to the local horticultural society and growing fuschias was his main hobby. The landlord of his local pub had noticed him only once or twice popping in for a pint or two of best bitter and by and large he kept himself to himself. His neighbours thought that he'd been in London most of his working life. They were right he had – at the Home Office mostly as a junior to middle ranking civil servant. In the House he usually sat next to or near Zia Akbar on the back row of the A to L's. He hadn't said very much and preferred an early night and a good book to an evening of drink at the Russell Hotel. The Lioness of Clackmannanshire had once had her beady eyes on him as her next conquest, but when he showed little interest in becoming a sexually devoured wildebest she went back to the Serengeti for yet another Peer. She was beginning to run out of those under sixty years of age and had started looking at Commoners. The old tart!

After tea Ambridge called Angus McLean at his home just outside Aberdeen on the road to Inverurie.

'Hello, Peter. How are you? Yes I did indeed see the draw at Silverstone. Congratulations!'

'Thank you. I'm not a big sports fan as you might recall but it was quite exciting wasn't it?'

'Which bit? RADO or the race?' They both laughed. Ambridge hadn't even had his TV switched on.

'Have you any ideas on your Private Member's Bill, Peter? Sorry to ask you so soon but well you know old Leslie Percy

220

isn't the sharpest tool in the box and he could be a few weeks getting his act together – excuse the pun!'

'No problem, Angus. My Bill is already drafted in its entirety. Tell you what, if there's time in the House's diary I'll do it next week. In fact what about on the Friday, the last day before the recess?'

Ambridge's alacrity had taken even Angus by surprise. A most pleasant surprise! 'Done! It's a deal as far as I'm concerned. I'll call Sir Michael at his home this evening to tell him the good news.' He needn't have bothered. He already knew. He knew a lot more too. McLean was so pleased at the progress made so quickly he clean forgot to ask Ambridge what his Bill was about. Not that he would have told him. Only three people in the whole Queendom knew about this and that was the way it was going to stay.

Chapter 41

The House was packed to capacity for the last session before the summer recess. Nobody else in the House bar Peter Ambridge had any idea of what his Bill entailed. It was a mystery. He was such a quiet man and nobody had an inkling of his ideas or opinions on anything. Lincolnshire was perceived by the man on the Clapham omnibus as perhaps the most boring county in England, if not the UK. Nothing ever happened there. Zero everything. Just like Louth.

'Order, order! Mr Ambridge, the Member for Lincolnshire Lindsay.'

He looked half asleep and Zia gave him a friendly poke in the ribs with his tube of Polos to stir him. Peter stood up. He still looked and sounded like a superannuated civil servant. That was because he still, secretly, was one.

'Mr Speaker, fellow selected Members, Ladies and Gentlemen.' Chloe beamed again across the divide.

'I do recall some years ago after another Budget Speech from a previous Chancellor, that the acting Speaker, a Yorkshireman if I remember correctly, was asked a rather complicated fiscal question by a Member of the Opposition questioning the Chancellor's knowledge of the Poll Tax in Scotland.'

Bob Meadows visibly groaned and a TV camera caught him mouthing an 'expletive deleted' comment. Surely Ambridge wasn't going to introduce a Private Member's Budget – not after all that hard work he'd put in? Bloody tosser. He needn't have worried.

'The Speaker's reply, Mr Speaker, was that it was not his job to interpret the Act of Union of 1707. Nor was it. Nor is it still.' The House was hushed. What on earth was this?

'My Bill today, Mr Speaker, will I hope, become the New Act of Union. On that momentous night early this year millions of people saw Sir Michael address the Nation. He spoke of the Queen's hope and belief that this would represent a new dawn, a new beginning for the whole country. A new Jerusalem. The Act of Union between England and Scotland was the Entente Cordiale of its day. Only then did Hadrian's Wall, figuratively speaking, really come down. Except that unlike the Berlin Wall which was pulled down on that momentous day in 1989, Hadrian's Wall, though crumbling, has been allowed by certain sections of politicians to remain standing and to be used for their own ends whenever it suited them.'

'As you look at the House today you see the whole Kingdom represented by just over a hundred Members, thirty-three of them Scottish, six Irish and twelve Welsh. The remainder are English – like me.

'Mr Speaker, you yourself are a Scot and proud of it, I'll bid?'

The Speaker nodded 'Aye' and was slightly flustered by this unexpected turn of events.

'Indeed Mr Speaker, your home city of Aberdeen, the Granite City, even renamed its longest street Union Street to mark the Act did it not?'

'Aye, it did so.' He didn't like the way this was going at all. This wasn't going to be about whisky duty that's for sure. He looked reassuringly at his trusty gavel feeling fairly sure that he was going to need it soon.

'The point I am trying to make, Mr Speaker, is that the Act of Union 1707 was perhaps the greatest Act of Parliament ever passed by this House. And yet in recent years successive Governments have sought to undermine its orthodoxy. Just look at the new Welsh Assembly. What is it for? So a few hundred people who speak a totally indecipherable language can meet for coffee? And as for the new Scottish Parliament in Edinburgh – well to be honest Mr Speaker, words almost fail me. It's even worse than the Dome fiasco!' There were several 'Hear, Hears' from both sides of the divide. 'I read only the other day that over one hundred million pounds had been spent just to keep contractors on site while discussions were held on the reasons for the delays. Do you realise that it's now cost over four hundred million pounds and they are still looking for another twenty-five thousand for the desk top refrigerators for the mini-bars. Is that profligacy or politics, Mr Speaker? Both probably. Either way it is a disgrace. A disgrace that must be ended, right now, today, by this House.'

Ambridge reminded the House of how the United Kingdom after 1707 had spread its knowledge and influence all over the world and how tiny Scotland had played a huge part in that process. He told them how Scottish regiments had fought alongside English at the Somme in the First World War and in Burma in the Second World War. Could either have done it alone? It was Scottish engineers who had practically built the Indian railways and Scottish universities that produced the doctors who practised in every corner of the Empire.

'And you are going to let a bunch of mealy mouthed weasels in that Scottish Dome decide the future of Scotland? I don't think so! Scotland is adequately represented here at Westminster. If anything it's the English who should complain!' Much laughter.

'No, Mr Speaker, the responsibility belongs to all of us in this House to ensure that the Kingdom stays intact. We must effectively outlaw the Scottish Parliament before it is even finished. Can you imagine what they will be like up there once they start? You can see what they think and hope will happen – that Scotland will become an independent country like Eire, within the European Union. They foresee millions of Euros swilling in from Brussels to keep their ideals intact and prop up their tiny minds and fiefdoms. If that happens I can guarantee the House one thing – Scotland will become of similar value and consequence to the EU as Andorra. It will decline to become nothing more than a flag on the conference table and the Royal Scots and Black Watch mere toy soldiers for the Tattoo tourists. Do you want that to happen? The same will apply to the Welsh Guards at Cardiff Castle. Don't forget too quickly those Guards at Rorke's Drift in South Africa and Bluff Cove in the Falkland Islands. Nor so recently the Irish Guards in Iraq. Her Majesty said that your country needs you! Whether you are Scottish, Welsh, Irish or English you will do well to remember that when the Bill goes to the vote. It is for all of you to decide which country your Queen asked you to do your best for. That is all she asked of us.

'The New Act of Union, Mr Speaker, will bring an immediate end to the Scottish Parliament. It will be sold off and the taxpayer reimbursed at least some of his losses. It might make an excellent national Library for Scotland or perhaps a place of learning where today's young Scots can learn of the huge part their small country played in the establishment of the biggest Empire the world had ever seen. In fact anything, truly, would be better for Scotland than the current intention.

'Mr Speaker, I am sure that many Members will wish to input to the debate today. For the time being I therefore rest my case. Perhaps you will allow me to sum up before the House puts my Bill to the vote?'

'Indeed, Mr Ambridge, indeed.'

Poor Angus McLean. He was having kittens. Talk about a turn up for the Statute Book. He had been furiously doing some arithmetic on the back of a big envelope. He'd wrongly assumed all the Scots were present. Then it dawned on him that Gibson and Ross were off 'sick' and where the hell was Laura MacDonald? Not another Peer surely. It wouldn't be Wigan Pier that's for sure. It would be somebody with money. He was praying that the vote, when it came, would not be a dead heat. He would have to use his casting vote. Oh my God. Now he realised how that acting Speaker had felt all those years ago. It wasn't his job to interpret the Act of Union either. Was it?

A score of Members were waving their order papers in the air, all wanting to speak. Were they English or Scottish or what? With his system of A to L and M to Z they were all over the place. Suddenly his brilliant idea had turned sour. The Bill's proposer, Ambridge, was sitting next to an Asian who was sitting next to a Scotsman, who was sitting next to a Welsh woman opposite an English Chancellor who was sitting next to five Scotsmen, all of whose names began with Mac. It was the Mississippi and Missouri of Parliament. All those Ms again! Whose bright idea was all that?

For the first time that Parliament the House sat until midnight when the Speaker ordered a break like a Judge ordering a jury to a hotel for the night. Three coaches arrived to take them all back to the Russell Hotel and then the Speaker realised that tomorrow was a Saturday. For the first time since Argentina had invaded the Falklands in 1982, Parliament was going to sit on a Saturday. It would be tea time the next day before the future of the whole Kingdom had been decided.

Chapter 42

The news of the top rate of Corporation Tax for the banking sector had hit Dan Ericsson like a bazooka. Gone were the huge profit-related bonuses so cleverly incorporated into his 'compensation package' by his lawyers in Manhattan. It was just a pity he couldn't blame the lawyers and bring a lawsuit for negligence against them. But nobody could have predicted what Bob Meadows had done. Too late now to cancel his forced resignation and bring him back into the fold. Far too late. It wasn't as though the drought would be temporary either. There were still three full years of this Parliament to run – in fact the time span exceeded his current contract but even if he extended it there would be no guarantee that Meadow's successor would revert back to the norm. Far from it! The public's reaction had been almost euphoric and the general praise for 'Robin Hood Meadows' had almost no bounds. He was feted wherever he went throughout the whole country. The share prices of all the big banks had taken a big knock in the days immediately following the Budget but many investors used this as a buying opportunity; not least the Truffle Street Directors exercising their share options to buy.

Eric's immediate problem lay in the fact that his wife had exchanged contracts to buy a six million dollar 'condo' at the exclusive resort of Massapequa Bay, Nassau County, on Long Island and she'd paid out a million dollars as a deposit from their joint account at the Watermelon Bank believing incorrectly, that Eric would reimburse it from the offshore account in the Bahamas. He'd omitted to tell her that he'd almost emptied that account to fund the investment in ProAqua. In less than thirty days he would have to find another five million to complete the purchase of the condo. Until recently he had figured that he would take out a three year short term loan repaid from his anticipated London bonuses but now, following 'Bob's Budget' as the press had dubbed it, he couldn't do that because those bonuses looked like sand running thru' fingers. Hellfire! There was no other option. He would have to remortgage their fancy Upper East Side brownstone apartment in Manhattan. It was the only way he could raise the five million bucks that quickly. Reluctantly he e-mailed his attorneys in New York to make the necessary arrangements and to get the best deal he could. He clean forgot to tell his wife.

That was three weeks ago and she flipped when legal papers arrived for her to sign remortgaging the property. The mortgage company also wanted a charge over the new condo as extra security. She called him straight away.

'Look, Hun, I'm sorry OK? I genuinely forgot. Hun, it will all work out just fine and dandy.'

Then he told her about the 'insider deal' with ProAqua and how five million sterling was gonna become twenty-five within five years and she calmed down.

'So in greenbacks, Hun, that's about forty million depending on the rate of exchange at the time. We'll be able to pay off the mortgage eight times over. You can bet on that!'

She was almost wetting herself with anticipation. The extra thirty plus million in five years time meant they could retire quite comfortably and spend the hot New York summers hosting parties out on the cooler Island. Eric had been quite a catch after all despite her Daddy's initial reservations about the Viking dude with the big ideas!

Eric was in his office counting through the big cheques received in from all the Group's Directors following his personal and confidential missive. No less than forty-two directors had gotten into this little deal and 'applications' and cheques arrived from subsidiary companies all over the world – from Dogger Merchant Bank, Dogger Asia-Pacific in Singapore, Bank Al-Saudi Al-Dogger in Jeddah, Dogger Europe SA in Paris, Dogger Nederlanden in Rotterdam, Dogger Australasia in Melbourne to name but a few. Noticeably absent were the guys from Dogger Re-Insurance but maybe they were content to make their own pile far sooner from Chloe's Motor Insurance Bill. Those guys were incredibly lucky. Their bonuses were measured from Dogger Re-Insurance gross pre tax profits not like his from Dogger Group's net profits after tax. If only his lawyers had been that smart but wasn't twenty twenty hindsight a wonderful thing.

Eric added up all the cheques on his pocket calculator. Exactly nineteen point five million sterling. There was still room for another investor. He noticed that Ron Forsyth wasn't among them and he was genuinely sorry. After all if it wasn't for his inside information none of them would be in this enviable position. Should he call him? Maybe best not to. His demotion to the Highlands and Islands Division had probably left him short of ready cash and he didn't want to embarrass the guy. He would reward him later with a seat on the Board before the next Annual General Meeting. Little old Ronnie deserved that at least and it would boost his retirement pension contributions no end. Yes, that's what he would do but he would keep it as a surprise for the time being.

Eric flicked his desktop PC to go online and check Wall Street share prices. He had always done well on his Watermelon Bank stock options that were held by Nominees that even his wife didn't know about. It was standard procedure at Watermelon to protect the senior staff. A few years before two Vice Presidents had been divorced by their Jewish American Princess wives and their bank stock had been taken into account as assets. Since then it had been the rule for such stock to be held by 'Nominees' just in case. At the last count he held forty-four thousand shares at today's price of seventeen dollars and eighty-five cents each. Plenty! He would issue sell orders and buy sterling. Shame about poor old Ronnie but there was no point in letting a half a million pounds worth of investment going to waste. He sent his New York broker an e-mail and closed down his PC. It would take a few days for the dough to come through and then to make up the personal Dogger staff investments in ProAqua to the available twenty million. He filed all the other cheques into his personal office safe where they could wait for a while. The Bank's Company Secretary would forward the cheques to Dee M Zee's offices in 'Edinburg' some time the following week. Eric also filed a diary note in connection with Ron Forsyth's promotion and appointment to the Board for passing on to the Secretary for inclusion in the Agenda at the next Board Meeting. He felt real good. Yessiree real good! His cash flow problems were only very temporary. So he thought.

Chapter 43

Reg Martin was starting to feel like a cat with all the cream. An official letter from the Regional Office of the Dogger Bank had offered him a hundred thousand pounds in compensation in lieu of a possible award from the Ombudsman. He accepted at once knowing that this sum was the maximum within the Ombudsman's remit anyway. At a stroke this cleared the overdraft and paid all the creditors leaving a few thousand in the kitty for working capital. The Agreement with Dogger Factors was 'in the bin' by mutual consent but it didn't matter in the slightest. His natural reaction would have been to change banks at this point but Bob had persuaded him not to. It was imperative that the Dogger Bank hierarchy didn't get suspicious.

Martin's Water Systems was back in the black and within a few short weeks the first tranche of the genuine two million input from DMZ would be available. The company had negotiated to purchase an adjacent industrial unit so as to allow increased production of the ProAqua filters up to a rate of two thousand units a day. However once the implications of Hamish's Clean Water Act started to really bite then even this rate would be totally inadequate. Reg decided that sooner or later he and Bob, and probably Duncan Gibson too, would have to have a real brain storming meeting to point the way forward. Given the desperation of the situation a year ago though by comparison it was a great problem to have.

The House was back in session for the Autumn term and once again all the Members were busy arranging their own Private Member's Bills for when 'Baby Rado' picked their name out of the hat. The New Act of Union was now law. Her Majesty had taken the greatest of pleasures in signing it. A top notch firm of real estate agents in Edinburgh had been given the task of selling off or leasing the 'Scottish Dome' and it wasn't long before a media consortium had come forward with firm proposals. The Chairman of the consortium had also approached Duncan Gibson for venture capital via the offices of Dalziel, Menzies & Zimmer. They were having a field day. It just went to show what having a helping hand in the House could do for a firm. It was ever thus!

It was the arrival at DMZ's Edinburgh offices of a letter, and an awful lot of money, from the Company Secretary of the Dogger Bank that prompted Duncan to call Bob Meadows as a matter of urgency.

'Morning, Bob. Guess what's arrived at my Charlotte Square desk?'

'Morning, Duncan. How about a lot of wonga?! Let's see – say twenty million?'

'Right on! But as you know we haven't actually issued a formal Prospectus yet, let alone invited subscriptions. What the hell do I do with all the cheques?'

'Whose cheques are they? Not all Ericsson's surely?'

'No. They range from five million down to fifty thousand and are offered in the names of over forty applicants. Ericsson's is the biggest as we expected – hang on a sec I'll just have a shufty through them all.'

'Is Forsyth's name there?'

'Can't see it. No – definitely not. Does it matter?'

Bob played dumb. Duncan didn't need to know everything. Not yet anyway. 'No, it's OK. Are any of the other names familiar to you apart from Ericsson's.'

'Oh yes! There's Berkely, Dogger's Company Secretary with two hundred grand. Smith, the Chief Exec of Dogger Merchant Bank, he's dabbled a quarter of a million. Hang on a mo...oh yes, here's another big one – eight hundred grand from Nick Chin drawn on a Singapore Bank. He's the MD of Dogger Asia Pacific. I remember him well do you? He only just escaped investigation after that big scam in Singapore when Her Majesty lost a pile of loot when a dealer went ga-ga gambling on the Nickei Dow. Remember?'

'Yeah, do I! What a nightmare that was at the time. If it wasn't for some Cloggie Bank that baled us out Lord knows what would have happened. Anybody else of note?'

'Just a whole string of names. Tell you what, I'll do an immediate search at Companies House in Cardiff and get back to you. It will only take an hour – I'll do it online. OK?'

'Thank's Duncan, catch you later.'

Bob used his own mobile to call Hamish McIver. Like Reg Martin, Hamish was a new man. Ericsson's misplaced generosity had resulted in his firm's overdraft limit being totally academic. Under Bob's guidance he'd siphoned off a hundred thousand and set up a new firm '21st Century Sushi Ltd.' that banked with another bank. Forsyth hadn't even noticed as Ericsson had set the limit on the computer to such a high figure. Even when the salmon mousse hit the fan it wouldn't matter a jot. Dogger Bank could exercise their Debenture over the old company if they wanted to. There wasn't a fat lot left of the old firm's assets, fixed or floating. Good luck to them. The family home in Stornoway was also safe and Forsyth had had to privately concede that the Guarantees were invalid. Shona McIver was blissfully happy. If RADO hadn't picked Hamish's name out then they would never have met Bob Meadows and personal and financial disaster would have befallen the whole family. She arranged with Hamish that Bob and Honey be invited to Stornoway for the next Hogmanay as their personal guests.

'Hi, Hamish. It's Bob. Not back in London this week?'

'Hi, Bob. No not yet. You won't believe this. This morning I was just getting ready for Shona to drive me to the airport when our new sales manager called me urgently. It was a potentially huge prospective order from a store in Japan!!'

'Pull the other one it's got bells on...'

'I'm serious. Apparently with our new name that has the word *sushi* in it they found us via an internet search engine. The old name of McIver's Fisheries just never got picked up. I suppose it was obvious to them but not to us. Anyway I'm flying out to the new Kansai International Airport first class on All Nippon Airways next week, all at their expense. Can you believe that?'

'Right now I'll believe anything, Hamish. But listen just remember to steer clear of those geisha bars.' They both laughed. 'Listen before I forget, it's important. Did you have that little chat I suggested with Ron Forsyth – you know, the one good turn deserves another larky?'

'You mean about keeping his money in the Post Office?'

'Yeah, that conversation.'

'Yep. No problems there. He wanted to know why of course. I just said that all would be revealed in due course.'

'Good man. Let's have another curry before you hop off east OK?'

'You bet, aye! Cheers for now then.'

An hour later and Duncan called back. 'Bob, you won't believe this. Every single applicant for the shares in ProAqua is a Director of either Dogger Bank or one of its wholly owned subsidiaries. It's amazing isn't it?'

'Not really Hamish. But there again you've never worked for a bank have you?!'

'So what the hell do I do now with twenty million pounds and applications for twenty million shares that don't exist?'

'Well on the face of it it looks like fraud doesn't it – insider dealing and all that. At the very least all the applicants should be orally examined by a higher authority. I think you should place the cheques into an imprest account with your firm's bank and report the matter without delay to the Head of the Treasury which regulates banks. Don't you? Just to cover your own arse you understand.'

'Damned right. Who's that then?'

'Me!'

When the formal acknowledgements from DMZ failed to arrive in Truffle Street within ten days Eric the Red started to get a bit squiffy. He ordered Berkely to investigate but his ever so polite enquiry by e-mail then fax then telephone and finally by recorded delivery first class mail still went unanswered. Ericsson was finally forced into sending a round robin memo to all his Directors explaining that his 'tip' had been made in good faith and that he was sure share certificates would arrive shortly. Privately he was having nightmares.

Another week went by and then he received an overseas call from Nick Chin in Singapore reminding him that 'if this was some kind of scam, cookie boy, then his Triad friends might have to assist in the recovery of the money from the person who had given the advice.' Within seconds Eric the Red metamorphosed into Eric the Brown.

To make matters even worse, his wife was talking about him coming back home for a spot of leave and to see the new pad on the Island that so far he had only seen e-mailed digital pictures of. That was all paid for but the Manhattan apartment was now mortgaged and he had monthly loans to meet. Jezuzz, things had better look good soon. Just when were those ProAqua Ltd. stock certificates gonna arrive? They didn't ever arrive but the next morning's mail brought even worse news.

Chapter 44

D.Ericsson Esq.
Chief Executive
Dogger Bank plc
Lombard Street
London EC3

Dear Sir

It is with the utmost regret that as the Minister with ultimate responsibility for Her Majesty's Treasury I feel it necessary to write in these terms.

My Department has received a Formal Complaint from a well respected and long established firm of Fund Managers in the City of Edinburgh. Their credentials are impeccable. The gist of their complaint is as follows:

1. They have received an unsolicited Application from yourself for 5m (five million) shares in a recently incorporated limited company Registered in Scotland in the name of ProAqua Ltd., a firm for which they have provided initial setting up advice and a Registered Office.

2. That Application was in writing and accompanied by a banker's draft drawn on your Head Office in the sum of £5m (five million GBP) and payable to their firm – DMZ.

3. As no formal Prospectus has yet been issued for the purchase of these shares DMZ are concerned that there has been a leak of information prior to the actual Prospectus being published.

4. Having instigated the fullest enquiry the Directors of DMZ are confident that no personnel at their firm are responsible and the only source of 'insider information' must have been via your Bank which we know to be bankers to a sister company – Martin's Water Systems Ltd. of Lincoln.

5. The Complainants are concerned that their unblemished reputation for integrity over almost two hundred years of trading remains intact.

I have considered the matter fully in recent days. As your predecessor explained so succinctly when I was selected as an MP and appointed Chancellor of the Exchequer, I must act at all times with 'total probity' and it was for that reason that the Board of the Bank decided that I should have to 'resign' for the duration of my tenure in Office.

My duties now are evidently quite clear. I am duty bound to ask the Serious Crimes Squad to instigate a full and searching Enquiry, the results of which will have to be published in the general interest of the public – not to mention the Bank's shareholders. It is not of course my prerogative to speculate on the possible outcome of such an official Enquiry but from where I am sitting at the moment I have to say that it does look very bad from your perspective. It can be no coincidence that, in addition to yourself, no less than forty of your fellow Directors in the Dogger Group (not to mention the Company Secretary) were co-Applicants.

Strictly in confidence between ourselves I do not wish there to be an Enquiry which might expose certain people to possible criminal allegations and charges. I do not consider it necessarily in the greater public's interest for there to be an Enquiry which would at the end of the day have to be funded by the taxpayer.

I am therefore suggesting, privately you understand, that the whole matter be treated as a 'gross misunderstanding' and that the 'Applications' were inadvertently made by the Bank on behalf of its Private Clients not wishing to miss out on the exciting new Water Bonds that will very shortly be available following my Budget. Anticipating your acquiescence to this proposal I am thus writing today to the Directors of Dalziel, Menzies & Zimmer suggesting that they retain ten thousand pounds per Applicant for such a Bond (when they are issued). The balances of the twenty million will, I am sorry to inform you, have to be frozen indefinitely. Perhaps the Bank might ask DMZ to treat the other nineteen and a half million or so as Charity Contributions. I recall from my time at the Bank that such donations were not uncommon but of course of a very much smaller quantum than the one I am proposing.

I am enclosing a partly completed Form 286b (Resignation of a Company Officer) for your signature and onward submission to Companies House in Cardiff. Also enclosed are forty-two identical blank forms for your co-Directors. I am sure I do not have to spell out their purpose or significance.

Yours sincerely,

R.E. Meadows

Bob was sorely tempted to tell Ericsson that the word 'Lombard' was in fact nothing to do with Italy but rather an acronym for *Loads Of Money But A Right Dickhead.* However he thought better of it and stuck to officialdom.

For 'Dan' Ericsson this was the end of the road. His options were nil. He signed the 286b unhestitatingly but with regret. He would cite 'family reasons back in the States' as the reason for his sudden resignation and departure. The Board would have to agree to it as they were all in the same longboat. At least he wasn't going to get a Viking's funeral. Not even Nick Chin's burning arrow could reach across the Atlantic. Could it? He compiled a heart-searching letter to his wife apologising for the huge family loss and telling her that things just hadn't worked out as planned and that he would be returning home to New York within days. His father-in-law would be full of 'I told you so's.' Viking schmuck!

Chapter 45

Three years passed and the first Parliament of the New Order was coming to a close. What an exciting time it had been. No less than eighty-five Private Member's Bills were passed into law and the Statute Book. It was 'People Power' at its absolute best.

Angus McLean had come up with the idea that there should be a Grand Ball in London to mark the end of Parliament and he had broached the subject with Sir Michael who, in turn, presented it to Her Majesty as his own idea. Some things never change! Particularly British Crown servants.

'What an absolutely splendid idea Sir Michael. Just splendid. In fact, let's take the idea a little further shall we...excuse the pun...let's have it in Edinburgh...yes at the marvellous new Scottish Exhibition Centre...you know, where the old defunct Scottish Parliament was going to be. I hear the developers have done a marvellous job and as I haven't yet visited there it will provide a great opportunity. Make the necessary arrangements will you? Shall we say after the Tattoo in August ...yes...early September when I will be at Balmoral anyway.'

The great day arrived. It was not unlike a State Banquet for a foreign Head of State but much less rigid. Her Majesty had issued formal invitations to all Members of the House who, with the sole exception of one member, had done their very, very best just as she had asked. She wanted everybody to feel comfortable and the invitation had said Black Tie & Cocktail Dresses. She didn't want all the ladies dressed like Cinderella. There would only be one lady wearing a diamond tiara and she instructed her chief dressmaker to create a gown that epitomised the unity of the whole Kingdom.

The seating plan had been a huge undertaking for the Speaker who had also agreed to act as an impromptu Master of Ceremonies. The Queen had invited all Members plus up to three guests each and an additional handful of others including Sir Michael and Lady de la Nice. All the names had to be submitted seven days earlier to give Mr McLean ample time to get the balance of personalities right. There was the Top Table for Her Majesty and her Consort and he decided to place the de la Nices to her right and the Home Secretary, Mr Usher and his wife, to her left. He would not put a foot wrong he was sure. Yet another story to tell his grandson one day. There were of course one or two people who would have to be 'buried' as far away as possible from the Top Table, in particular the heavier drinkers who had a propensity to quaff and slurp profusely especially if the booze was free. Angus particularly had in mind Archie Murdoch and Dai Williams on this point and also decided to separate them by at least two sprigs of tables if room allowed. He was only bringing one personal guest himself and decided to place the two of them amongst those he knew could at least maintain social decorum when it was needed. Sally-Anne Smith was bringing her sister and the Master of the Quorn Hunt (an ex-Guards officer) and his wife and he decided to seat himself and his guest alongside them. He also didn't want all the Celts conglomerated into clans either so consideration had to be given there too. It proved to be an even bigger job than arranging the Members in the House almost four years ago. Two Members had already sent their apologies in advance – one Scottish and one English.

It was exactly seven o'clock and Angus McLean tapped a silver spoon onto a wine glass to request silence. Nothing happened, very few people had heard it, such was the general hum of conversation and excitement. Unflustered he reached into the pocket of his dinner jacket for his trusty gavel and banged thrice onto the table top.

'Order, order, order! Please be upstanding to receive Her Majesty.'

Everyone rose in silence. Suddenly high up in a Minstrels' Gallery a dozen pipers of the Black Watch snarled into a tartan fanfare that a century earlier would have had every native in the Pink World cringing in fear of imminent attack. The Act of Union once again meant exactly that.

Her Majesty and her Consort were escorted amid synchronised clapping to their two reserved seats at the Top Table. But what was this? Where was the Duke of Edinburgh or even the Prince of Wales? In fact they had both gone down with a cold virus and Her Majesty had detailed her grandson to accompany her. The man who would be King one day. He was thrilled. So was Sally-Anne Smith who was suddenly so glad she had brought her sister and not the layabout boyfriend she had so recently dumped. Would she get the chance to meet him later she wondered?

Angus had asked Daz Davies to say Grace and he strode smartly over to the slightly raised dias and a microphone. His late father had been a typical God-fearing Welsh chapel goer and a lay preacher to boot. Daz's mother had helped him pick out a nice Grace that she thought his father might have approved of. He rattled it off with total aplomb and in his father's memory sang the last three lines in Welsh. Amen. His mother had travelled all the way up from Wales to be there. It was such a fitting end to his four years' service. Next week he would be starting his new job as Chief Fundraiser for a nationally renowned charity. Without him knowing it Sir Michael had put a good word in for him at Angus's request. Even in the New Order it was still *who you know not what you know* in this world and Daz didn't know anybody.

Chloe had brought her Mum and two virtual strangers – a Mr & Mrs Fred Barrett from Skipton, Yorkshire. In fact they were the late Edith Alice's former neighbours and Chloe had only met them at the funeral. Chloe was sure that had she been alive then 'Babs' would surely have invited them and another trip into town for another posh frock would have been on the cards. Chloe was wearing green again of course in the form of a modestly cut knee length dress. So dark was the shade of green that at first glance it looked like Black Watch tartan. This would be her last appearance in public as a Member of Parliament. In a few weeks she would start her new job as a presenter on TV's 'Watchdog' consumer affairs programme. Her mother had suggested to her that she changed her name by Deed Poll from Ledger to Lager to emulate Alice Beer but sensibly Chloe had relegated that idea to the same status as the 'topless' photo opportunity four years ago. Her mother would always be an 'Essex Girl' – what a good job her father had come from Kent. Secretly, Chloe had decided to go back into politics and had already been selected as a prospective candidate for the next round of elections to the European Parliament. No need to guess which Party – everyone knew what her favourite colour was.

Tony Marconi was accompanied by his wife, and two teenage daughters. He would dearly have liked to have invited the late Steve Thoburn who would have made a great MP himself as a 'Man of the People.' But RADO was totally random and Tony had had to deputise for him in the role of law maker. One thing was for sure – all the fruit on his market stall next week would be priced up in pounds and ounces. There was no 'post Parliament' career waiting for him and at six o'clock next Monday morning it would be business as usual on Edmonton Green. He had done his bit.

Alice Tam looked just stunning in a blue traditional Chinese cheong sam. Her long shiny black hair was done up in a bun which made her look at least four inches taller than her modest five feet two. She was with her English fiancé, an accountant, and her parents. Mr Tam had initially smarted when she had announced their engagement. Weren't there any nice Chinese boys to marry? He had calmed down after learning that he was in line for a Partnership in a big firm in Bristol. At least the 'gweilo' would be in the money. Alice's Bill to regulate the employment of foreign workers and control the gangmasters who used to earn a fortune from illegal immigrants had been amongst the most respected of the Private Member's Bills. As she had promised, it earned money for the Exchequer too. All gangmasters were now registered with the Department of Employment and were personally responsible and liable for paying the income tax for their guest workers - all at a straight ten per cent now following Bob's Budget. Tax evasion had fallen dramatically across the whole country following the simplification of taxation. Tonight would also be Alice's last time in the public eye. She had done her very best too.

Leslie Percy from Somerset was in fine form and as sponsor of Babs' Bill was in line for a commendation from the Sports Council. He had travelled to Edinburgh alone and was secretly hoping that given enough G & T's down her neck he might just have a last crack at the Lioness. Laura MacDonald had been very friendly towards him recently and had smiled and waved whenever she saw him. Either she was up for it or teasing him! He had been trying to spot her all night - where was she? He was hoping that she hadn't brought a Peer along for dessert. Even so, he wouldn't mind being the petit fours.

Mr and Mrs Nick Grindlay were seated with their personal guests – the Chief Executive of Independent Television and his wife, no less. Was he aspiring to a new career in the media? Nick was an intelligent chap and the nation's defences had been in safe hands for the last four years – with the help of the Bwana as well of course. His Defence of the Realm Act had introduced minimum numbers of fighter squadrons and front line infantry divisions that the country should possess. He had become a hero overnight in all four countries of the kingdom. He left matters naval to Her Majesty and Ray Grant.

Towards the end of the dinner Daz Davies returned thanks. They were his last words as an MP. Well almost his last words. The Speaker rose to announce the Loyal Toast but just as he was about to do so a hidden hand signal from a person unseen caused an almighty chorus of silver trumpets to erupt from the gallery. It was just like the Grand National again – 'Fanfare for the Common Man.' Angus McLean completely lost his bearings. All the wind had gone from his sails. This wasn't in the brochure. As the last silver note disappeared into infinity the conductor of the trumpeters clad in a scarlet tunic wheeled around one hundred and eighty degrees and barked out:

'Ladies and Gentlemen – pray silence for the Queen!' This was new ground. Her Majesty rose slowly to a standing position, pushing her reading glasses up her Royal nose as she did so.

'I almost said My Lords, Ladies and Gentlemen!' Much laughter.

'Of course, there aren't any Lords here tonight. Ladies and Gentlemen, I trust Mr Speaker will pardon my interruption to his well laid plans but I could not allow this evening to pass without saying a few words.' She coughed quietly to clear her throat.

'Four years ago, this country of ours embarked on a new voyage of discovery. It was claimed by many at the time that by dismissing career politicians from the House of Commons I was in some way gambling with the nation's future. I didn't believe that to be the case then and I don't believe it now.

'When you were elected, I beg your pardon, selected, I asked you all to do your very, very best and I told you that the best Civil Service in the world was there to help you.' She glanced sideways at Sir Michael who stifled a modest nod and smile.

'That momentous night when the computer picked all your names out from the millions of citizens of this land will forever be remembered as a defining moment in the history of this nation. A moment when the shackles of sleaze and corruption were shaken off and at last the future of the country could be decided by ordinary people leading ordinary lives. Very shortly most of you will return to those lives having done your duty for four years. Some of you will use the experience gained to change your lives and move forward in a different direction. Whichever is the case I want to thank you all for your service – not service to me, but to your country.

'There will be no loyal toast, therefore, this evening. The toast is by me to you. But first I have a very special announcement to make. It gives me enormous pleasure to tell you that your Speaker, Mr Angus McLean and the Member for Clackmannanshire, Mrs Laura MacDonald, were married at Leith Registry Office this morning and I therefore would ask all of you to stand and...' Her Majesty didn't finish the sentence. Everybody present stood up cheering and clapping, even Leslie Percy.

'Nice one, Jock' shouted Daz for the second time in four years. An 'English' Member had sent his apologies. It just wasn't his cup of Darjeeling. He was busy anyway.

Chapter 46

'Desert Island Discs' is one of the nation's favourite radio programmes. A single guest is invited to pretend that he or she is stranded on a desert island like a latter day Robinson Crusoe. Asked to choose eight tunes that they would like to have with them on this mythical paradise where rescue is uncertain and long hours of solitude a certainty, the choice of music has been staggering. A former Prime Minister dubbed a Grey Man had started his selection with 'The Happening' by the Supremes, recalling that he listened to it a lot in an African hospital ward following a motor accident. Another former PM had picked 'Jerusalem Tomorrow' by Emmy-Lou Harris. Bizarre or what? The listener often suspected that the programme afforded the guest in question the opportunity to be a bit of a poser and to pretend to be a fan of highbrow classical music when in reality the nearest they probably got to it in real life was listening to the all female band called Bond who played violins whilst looking like they were dressed for a night out clubbing. They, not Britten, represented the new Britannia.

Almost four years had passed since that fateful night of high drama at Wembley when the Queen had announced her intention to dissolve the Mother of Parliaments. It would soon be time for RADO to produce another 'hundred men and women, good and true.' BBC producers had decided that it would be fitting to have a Member of Parliament as the guest this week. Thus all the Member's names had gone into yet another draw – Desert Rado in this case. The tabloids were having fun again speculating as to who might pick what tunes if their name came up. Leslie Percy would pick 'The Green Green Grass of Home' by Tom Jones. Mari Jones would pick 'Those were the Days' by Mary Hopkin. Peter Ambridge would pick the theme tune from the Archers. Linda Ross would pick 'Leaving on a jet plane' by Peter, Paul and Mary. And so it went on. But who would the MP be? The Member selected was sent a letter by Sue Lawley the programme's presenter and it was all very hush hush.

The programme was going out on the Sunday morning following the dissolution of Parliament by the Queen the previous Friday but was recorded the previous evening on the Saturday. Thus whoever had been picked to go on the programme could not attend the Ball in Edinburgh. It hadn't mattered one jot to the person concerned.

The familiar music of the programme wafted over the airwaves with seagulls squawking as listeners try to pretend that it is they who are marooned on the Desert Island.

'Good morning, and welcome to this very special edition of the programme. My guest today is, sorry was, the Member of Parliament for his county for the last four years. Zia Akbar, welcome.'

'Thank you. It's a pleasure.'

'Let's play your first tune shall we?' Twenty million fascinated listeners leant towards their radios from Cornwall to Cromarty.

'When I first came to this country I was very much a stranger in a foreign land – alone. So my first choice is "Stranger on the Shore" by Ackers Bilk please.' Three minutes later and the sweetest piece of music ever written for a clarinet drifted to a close.

'I think you meant Acker Bilk, Zia, not Ackers.'

'Oh no. Mr Bilk was said to have derived his pension from forty years of royalties from that tune. Ackers Bilk is far more accurate.'

Sue Lawley didn't quite know what to say. Unlike Enoch Powell she didn't speak Urdu or Hindi let alone Latin or Ancient Greek. Zia had learnt a lot about Mr Powell from Sir Michael. Anybody who had studied the sub-continent that much couldn't have been that bad a chap. He wished he could have taken him to lunch to find out more about him.

'How do you think you would cope on your island Zia? Would you hope to be rescued soon or would you let God decide your fate?'

'God will decide everybody's fate ultimately, Sue. But yes, I would do my best to attract attention from any passing ships. I would build a fire at night as high up as possible hoping it would be spotted.'

'Let's have your second tune, Zia, please.'

'OK. But I think I've given listeners a clue already.'

'Really? How?'

'My second tune is "All Along the Watchtower" by the late Jimi Hendrix.' Bob Dylan had written that too but there wouldn't be any weather forecasts on his desert island.

'And tune number three, Zia.'

'It's from the same album as "Stranger on the Shore" actually and to be quite honest I hadn't heard it before. It's called 'Petite Fleur' by Monty Sunshine.'

Unlike Her Majesty Zia spoke no French. Nor did millions of children listening to the programme despite billions spent on education. Most of them thought that the Entente Cordiale was some kind of fruit drink in the vogue of Sunny Delight.

Zia picked four more tunes with a reason behind each one. The one item of luxury that he was allowed on his island was a CD player and the one book was Hansard covering the last four years. Half an hour later and the programme was coming to a close.

'And your final choice, Zia?'

'The Seekers singing "The Carnival is Over" please.' The full, soft tones of the delightful Australian girl Judith Durham lulled the listening nation to the programme's end for surely the show was truly over.

'Zia Akbar, thank you for being my guest today and jolly good luck with your new restaurant The Westminster Raj when it opens next week.'

'Thank you, Sue. The pleasure was all mine.' It was too. The seagulls squawked again.

A week later the head of BBC Radio announced record listening figures for the show that day and said that he hoped that it would be possible to repeat the exercise in the New Parliament. Privately he was dismayed that Zia had not chosen even a single Asian or Bollywood ballad. He was in trouble now trying to justify spending millions of licence payer's money on ethnic radio shows. Maybe it was a sign of the times. And maybe Cool Britannia had finally arrived.

Chapter 47

Whitehall
London

The first Parliament of the New Order was over. Contrary to their doubts and disparaging comments almost four years earlier, the Press were giving rave revues of the first four years.

The *Daily Express* had added a second figurehead to its front cover to accompany its legendary crusader. It was obviously a Queen but at a glance it could have resembled either Elizabeth the First or Elizabeth the Second, so cleverly had it been drawn. It was like one of those holograms on a credit card. Look at it from one angle it depicts Elizabeth the First, from another angle and it looks like Elizabeth the Second.

The *Sun*, to its credit, had a full twenty page colour supplement in which it reprinted the hundred and two caricatures and cartoons of four years earlier alongside photographs of the real people who had actually represented their constituencies. It was awesome and at the same time quite humorous. Thus, Daz Davies was alongside the Welsh miner with the lamp and pickaxe. Leslie Percy alongside the drunken cider apple grower. And so on. Only one photograph depicted sadness – that of Edith Alice Coates, the late Member for Yorkshire North. The paper had tastefully printed a neat black border around the photo of her taken at her 100th birthday party with the letters R.I.P. and the year of her death in Roman numerals. By 'eck, she would have been chuffed! There were also aerial photographs taken from a helicopter of over one hundred green school playing fields from all over the UK. These represented the playing fields saved from the builders' bulldozers so far since her Bill became law. The paper had printed it as a double page pullout in full colour (mostly green) and it looked like a mosaic. Tucked into the top right hand corner was the birthday photo again – this time without the black border. By the end of the week a million school children had stuck it to their bedroom walls in every corner of the kingdom. Edith Alice had never had children of her own but this was her legacy to a million children she had never known.

The broadsheet pro-Establishment papers were, if anything, even more full of praise. *The Times* leader stated that 'this radical experiment in political sociology must be repeated for at least one more Parliament' and even the *Telegraph* said that 'as long as the House of Lords was untampered with and the Judiciary was protected ad nauseam, then the system should, ceteris paribus, continue pro bono publico ad infinitum.' When Zia Akbar read that last bit he wondered if Old Enoch had written it himself. Chloe didn't understand it, bless her. Badly Drawn Boy's pop songs hadn't been that user friendly to so many conjugations and declensions.

Sir Michael and Angus McLean were having afternoon tea together. Parliament had been dissolved and RADO was already being prepared up at the DSS in Newcastle upon Tyne for the second big draw scheduled for a month's time.

The database was updated to include all the new eighteen year olds and delete all the deaths since the last Draw. Studio producers had revamped the set for next time and Florence Nightingale, Nelson and Co. were being replaced to show some of the achievements of the previous Parliamentarians. Edith Alice's green mosaic had been reproduced in stunning watercolours by an up and coming young artist as a mural and it filled a large portion of the backdrop. There were photographs of new sports centres, day centres and social clubs – all paid for from the proceeds of fruit machines following Adrian Kristiansand's New Gaming Act. Students from the East End Youth Theatre were tasked to put the finishing touches to the set in the days before the Draw. There was only one token pretension to anything military thus far and that was a ship's crest depicting a lion rampant on a rock protruding from the sea. That rock was Britain being protected. Only the 'unicornus' was missing. The ship's crest was Albion's.

'The second time around should be a lot easier this time, Angus.'

'Let's hope so. Those little glitches when RADO stopped working for a few moments will have to be ironed out. We don't want anybody smelling any rats if RADO hesitates at precisely the same Counties do we?'

'You bet. That certainly was a close one. I was practically having kittens. The whole shebang could have gone 'tango utopia' at that point. That was a brilliant idea of yours to bring in the extra seats in Lincolnshire. Ten out of ten old chap!'

'It was the only way we could insert those vital people into the House without any rats being smelled. Of course Her Majesty went along with it to boost the English seats a tad.'

'But, of course that didn't matter in the end anyway since the New Act of Union was passed almost unanimously. Do you know, it even feels like a United Kingdom again to me.

Does it to you?'

'Yes, but maybe we should ask an Ulsterman!'

McLean continued. 'Of course we had to have a little bit of luck, didn't we? You know, with Bob Meadows being available as a Chancellor and all that.'

'What? Oh that. Well that couldn't be left to chance either. That's why the extra seat in Sussex was created. You know, Sussex East and Sussex West. At one point we thought we might have to *do a Thomas Hardy* and re-introduce Wessex! In any event we slipped him in there nicely.'

'Good God! And he agreed?'

'No way. He was entirely in the dark. Met him at a Lodge once, in the Queen's Chambers underneath the old Baltic Exchange if I remember, years ago. A good egg. Far too good to work for a dozy bank. Sharp as a knife. And he's sorted out the whole banking system now from what I've heard.'

'Was Her Majesty privy to the extra Members and the reasons why?'

'Oh no. Good Lord no. Ignorance is bliss in this case.'

'Like Good Queen Bliss?'

'Yes! I like that, very good. But it was of course her idea to have a true People's Democracy but in practice we had to tamper with it a little – to make sure that it actually worked. We could have been in real trouble if a Woodentop had wanted to become Chancellor. The two top jobs had to effectively be pre-selected.'

Angus was puzzled. 'Two? The Chancellor and who else?'

'The Speaker of course. More tea?'

Epilogue

Buckingham Palace
London

Her Majesty was over the Royal moon. Four years since making the historic announcement at the New Wembley Stadium her decision had borne fruit beyond her wildest dreams. The kingdom did indeed seem United again for the first time in a generation. The nation seemed at peace with itself. There would always be problems of course, that's life, but already she was looking forward to the next RADO draw and the next intake of a hundred and one Members. How patriotic it was of Angus McLean to agree to stay on 'unselected' as it were as Speaker for another four years. Her English, Welsh and Irish subjects actually seemed to enjoy having a stern Highlander banging his gavel from time to time to keep them in order. He had become like a prep school headmaster - firm but fair, with his rounded vowels and reverberated r's echoing round the House like a friendly Doberman. Maybe he would quieten down a bit now he was a married man.

Mentally she reviewed the changes and progress that had taken place in the First Parliament of the New Order. The Realm was safe and secure. The Bwana was her own Black Prince, the ultimate defender of her faith. But not just her faith. In the New Britannia all faiths and creeds were equal from Atheists to Zoroastrians. That reminded her. It was her turn to send the Aga Khan a racehorse for Christmas this year.

The Royal Navy, her Navy, was being expanded, just as under her illustrious namesake. Ray Grant, the Member for Renfrewshire, had introduced the Shipbuilding Act as his own Private Member's Bill. It ensured two things. Firstly it gave massive tax breaks to UK shipowners who had vessels built in UK yards crewed by British staff. The six Members from the Six Counties had jointly sponsored the Bill, keen to try and preserve the famous Belfast yard that had built the Titanic. At least they had all agreed on something. They had also arranged, covertly, for the BBC to film three Ulster youths performing their skateboarding skills so brilliantly in that shipyard under the watchful eye of Samson and Goliath – the two monstrous yellow cranes that dominated the skyline – and which twenty million viewers subliminally watched before the six o'clock news almost daily. It had been the biggest cost free advertisement for any company anywhere in the world! Secondly, it committed present and all future UK Governments to maintain a Navy of no less than one hundred fighting ships. This became law and would guarantee shipyards work for ever. Grant had produced compelling evidence to the House that over the centuries the nation's wealth was in perfect correlation to the amount of money it spent on its Navy and now that would ever be thus.

The Black Watch was safe – her Mother would be pleased up there, smiling down from the firmament. Sterling was strong – at least for the time being and until it came round to considering going into the dreaded Euro. Still, at least thanks to Mr Marconi's Metric Martyr's Bill all fruit and vegetables were now priced and sold in sensible pounds and ounces. Everyone knew there were four Cox's Orange Pippins to a pound. Nobody knew how many to a kilo. Common sense prevailed. Manufacturing industry was on the up, particularly in the water purification industry. Millions of youngsters could look forward to learning active sports on their schools' own fields. Globally, Perfidius Albion was back in business, and HMS *Albion*, the newly commissioned Commando assault ship, was already teaching Johnny Foreigner that Pax Britannica ruled OK. Greenwich Mean Time was, once again, the world's universal clock. The Second Elizabethan Era had not just dawned. It was blooming. Nightly, she prayed to Almighty God that her grandson, the one who had learnt Swahili in his gap year, would one day present the kingdom with a daughter who, at the end of this century, would become the Third Elizabeth to steer the nation to glory and salvation. She was so pleased she had sneakily arranged for him to be introduced to Sally-Anne Smith at the Ball in Edinburgh so recently. She was a fine well bred girl with all the right credentials and rode so well she looked as if she could command the Blues and Royals herself. At least the Private Member's Bill she introduced would make it illegal to kill foxes with guns or with poison. Now they would have to be hunted! A bell rang to stir Her Majesty from her thoughts. It was her equerry, fittingly the same one who four years earlier had summoned Sir Michael to that all important meeting.

'Sir Michael, Ma'am.' They took tea and buns as they always did.

'So all in all, Sir Michael, can we say that the experiment has been a success? Even a qualified one?'

'Absolutely, Ma'am. And if I may say so, Ma'am, your idea to do away with the office of Prime Minister was capital, absolutely capital. Of course there was never an official announcement to that effect as you know, Ma'am. Hardly anybody seems to have noticed that we haven't had one for four years, Ma'am.'

'Quite, Sir Michael. But of course the hundred men and women good and true couldn't have managed without you and the Civil Service. You're being too modest. If I didn't need you in your current position a peerage would be more than deserved.'

'I am your humble servant, Ma'am and I...' He didn't finish.

'I've been thinking, Sir Michael, that perhaps it is an appropriate time to invite the President and his First Lady across again, only this time it would be different wouldn't it?'

'Different Ma'am?'

'Well yes, altogether quite different. They would be my guests for a start not the nonexistent Prime Minister's. The President wouldn't have to be dragged off to some awful backwater constituency just to prop up local party support. And another thing it would save a lot of money on unnecessary added security costs.'

'Indeed it would Ma'am but without all the associated political razzamattaz how would you entertain them exactly?'

'I've already given it some thought, Sir Michael, particularly in view of heightened security concerns. I heard only this morning by letter from the family of the late Baron Macdougall of Jura who passed away so sadly recently. His son Lindsay, the sixteenth Baronet, has offered us the use of the whole island for a month. I do so miss popping into Craighouse in the summer when we used to take Britannia to the Islands. Damned politicians!'

'Ma'am, security on Jura should be a doddle – it's so difficult just to get to.'

'My thoughts exactly. And you know what Texans are like! Huntin' shootin' and fishin' crazy. Yes, Jura will be ideal. I will write to the President today with a formal invitation. As soon as we receive a reply in the affirmative I'll ask the Bwana to take personal charge of all security arrangements.

'Now, Sir Michael, digressing – what's all this about a huge bank scandal only narrowly being averted during the last Parliament?'

'So I understand Ma'am.'

'And which Bank is it whose Directors all had to resign after some internal wranglings – was it that Bank, you know – the one that lost One a lot of One's money when one of its Far Eastern rogue traders played Crown and Anchor on the Tokyo Stock Exchange a few years ago. Was it that same Bank?' Her Majesty chuckled at her own little joke.

'Indeed, Ma'am – Dogger Asia-Pacific, all part of the same Group Ma'am. Apparently Ma'am there was indeed a huge scandal about to erupt. All the bank's directors tried using insider information to make huge personal financial gains. Mr Meadows was going to confiscate it all to the Treasury but in the end Ma'am they all did the honourable thing – resigned and donated twenty million pounds to charity.'

'I see. So who exactly is running the Bank now, Sir Michael? Is my money safe?'

'I would certainly think so now, Ma'am. A shrewd Scotsman, a Mr Forsyth I believe, is the new Chief Executive and Mr Meadows has a non-Executive Directorship, one of several I believe following his successful Chancellorship.'

'Excellent, excellent. There is some justice in the world then.' She threw a fig biscuit to the nearest corgi.

Like her illustrious forbear at Tilbury, she had indeed read the mind of the nation.

Other titles by this Author

The random selection of MPs by a new computer nick-named "RADO" has thrilled the nation. It is going to be repeated for a second Parliament. Against a backdrop of economic recession and dodgy bankers the Queen invites the President of the United States for a State Visit. With his second term in office coming to an end he is easily persuaded to use RADO back home and dissolve the Senate. In the UK the nation's mind concentrates on fund-raising for the forthcoming London Olympics. In a 'credit crunch' can the country afford to emulate the success of Beijing? Are there more deserving cases than a three week jamboree for a few hundred athletes? Her Majesty thinks there might be. Is she right?

Australia watched from afar as the Mother Country ditched its career politicians amid a sea of sleaze and corruption. They were replaced by ordinary citizens selected at random by a new computer knick-named RADO. Within a few short years Uncle Sam followed suit. With a rising tide of indiscretions and scandals rocking Canberra, public opinion from Perth to Parramatta demanded similar change. The new system was working well in the UK and the US. Why shouldn't it work in the "Lucky Country" too? The Governor General, Sir John Macleod, flew discretely to London for a secret audience with Her Majesty. Australia would never be the same again. Not ever.